Ex
Libris

Lowell R. Kantner

A World of Profit

Louis Auchincloss

A World of Profit

"Divinity, adieu!
These metaphysics of magicians,
And necromantic books are heavenly;
Lines, circles, letters, and characters;
Ay, these are those that Faustus most desires.
O, what a world of profit and delight,
Of power, of honour, and omnipotence,
Is promised to the studious artizan!
All things that move between the quiet poles
Shall be at my command."

Doctor Faustus

Houghton Mifflin Company, Boston

1968

FOR

Jack Pierrepont,

MY FRIEND IN YALE, IN THE NAVY

AND IN THE LONG WALL STREET

AFTERMATH

Part I

1

A HOUSE WITH white columns and a lawn descending to the water is always handsome, always aristocratic. Shallcross Manor, behind its six pillars facing Flushing Bay, was actually a rather nondescript dwelling, having been originally, in 1800, a mere wooden rectangle to which boxlike wings had been added throughout the century. But that row of thick, fluted supports, if almost ludicrously large for the small pediment, still gave dignity to the two and one half stories of irregularly placed, green-shuttered windows that peeked out from between them to blend with the swept, clipped turf which, between a boatyard and a small sailing club, ran down to the dirty waters of the bay. A hundred yards out a swimming raft with a diving board, painted the same fresh white as the manor house, represented the family's claim to the remnants of their ancestral marine dominion.

This portion of the Borough of Queens, in 1960, although long urbanized, was still saved from the heartlessness of the uniform housing that stretched like a graveyard to the east, by its dedication to transport. From the west of the manor, across the bay, came the muffled but never interrupted roar of traffic along the Grand Central Parkway. On the retinas of thousands upon thousands of motorists' eyes the image of those six columns must have been at least transiently stamped, while to other thousands of daily commuters, seeing it to the right in the morning and to the left in the evening, it may have become confused with other symbols of early Federal distinction: the Lee Mansion overlooking Arlington, Jefferson's rotunda in Charlottesville, even the White House. And when it would have disappeared, at least in memory, it might be vaguely missed, then remembered again, or perhaps falsely identified with columns seen as a child, an old church in New England, a schoolhouse, a postcard of the Parthenon, something proud, something departed. It might even have been seen by passengers as they left by plane from La Guardia to the Northwest and have given them, thundering aloft over it with a prayer for safety as they clutched for altitude, a strange second of reassurance and peace.

In the summer haze of a late afternoon the spires of the Whitestone Bridge sparkled, gray against a gray sky. Traffic was moving homeward, not with the beaten haste of August, but in the easier, happier flow of late June, the time of prizes, of graduations, of finished tasks and pleasurable nostalgia. Seated on the edge of the raft off Shallcross Manor, a man in red bathing trunks watched a young woman swimming slowly about before him.

"It isn't cold once you're used to it," she called to him.

"It's not only the cold," he said, peering doubtfully into the dark water. "I distinctly felt something slimy against my foot."

"A shark, no doubt. But the water's too dirty for him to see you."

"Why do old families like yours always go in for uncomfortable things?"

"Noblesse oblige."

It was obvious that he was not an athlete. His skin was pale and smooth, and he was panting from the exertion of swimming a hundred yards. But there was nothing that would have kept him from being one had he chosen. His body, if tending to the short and thick, was well knit, the only threat of weight being in the stomach, where a slight rounding betrayed the sedentary life of the urban man in his late thirties. In other ways he seemed almost boyish. His thick blond curled hair descended on his eggish forehead in a crisp triangle; on either side of his aquiline nose and over the puffy skin of his cheekbones his yellow-green eyes peered intently at the young woman.

His stare made Sophie Shallcross uneasy. She suspected that he preferred girls who were catlike and fashionable, and she liked to think of herself more as a puppy dog. The concept, anyway, seemed to excuse the loose, rather aimless blond hair and the epicenism of her strong browned arms. Sophie's gray eyes had a serenity that was quickly shadowed by distrust. Her out-of-style black bathing suit covered so much of her figure that it almost looked as if she were ashamed of her own appeal. She had a hopeful suspicion that if she starved herself she would turn into a beautiful Pre-Raphaelite. But she knew she would never starve herself.

"Everyone agrees with you about the water," she admitted. "Mummie and Daddy haven't swum off the place since I can remember. But I love it."

"You love everything about Shallcross Manor, don't you?"

"Everything." She pulled herself up the meager two-step ladder and sat down, shaking out her wet and ragged hair.

"Did you always love it?"

"Always. At least, as far back as I can remember. I was the youngest, you see, and alone a good deal of the time. That teaches a child about a house. Daddy was busy with law and politics. Oh, he tried to be a family man, the poor darling, but it was always in a Sunday rotogravure kind of way, 'the great man at home.' And Mummie, well, she and I have never quite touched. She doesn't feel the way I feel. For example, she did over the living room once, when Daddy was abroad. She took out the *papier maché* tables and the ottoman and the Hudson River paintings, and got Dorothy Draper to do it all over in a ghastly green and white. Ugh! I wouldn't go in it. I screamed and screamed! Then Daddy came home and made her put it all back the way it was."

But her listener was more interested in the family than in its décor. "You say you were alone. But surely you had your sister to play with. And Martin."

"No, Martin went off to boarding school and then Columbia, and Elly was always too girly-girly, giggling about boys and lipstick. I hated her, and that made me feel even more wicked. So I had a kind of love affair instead with the house. I adored being alone in the library with the portrait of my great-great-grandfather Shallcross in Mandarin robes and reading Swinburne and Christina Rossetti. And I used to write stories, too, long romances about people in the past. Always in Shallcross Manor."

"Didn't you have to go to school?"

"Of course. I went to Miss Chapin's. The car took me in and out every day. But Mummie and Daddy could never send me to boarding school. They tried, but they couldn't. And when it came to college, I went to Barnard so I could live at home."

"I wonder if an old house was a healthy preoccupation for a child."

She couldn't help laughing at his judicial expression. "Why, you silly, of course it wasn't. It was the worst thing in the world! And do you know something else? Shallcross Manor isn't even a *good* house. It never gets in any of those great homes of America books. It's simply a survival. A Victorian mish-mash stuck onto the plainest Greek revival front." She paused, seeing that he was bored again. "But I shouldn't be talking this way to a realtor. I have a sense of bulldozers behind that green gaze of yours. Martin probably brought you down here to bid on the place."

He had no comment to this, either. "Your brother doesn't care about the place?"

"Oh, Martin doesn't care about anything but money. Most of his friends simply drifted into the Stock Exchange, but Martin wanted to be a broker from the day he was weaned."

"You don't think much of Martin."

"But I adore him!" she exclaimed, shocked by such misconstruction. "Martin has been the most ideal older brother any girl ever had! From the beginning he always watched over me at parties and never shooed me away when his friends came to visit. It's just that I want a bigger life for him. And now, at last, he's going to be married, and Alverta is the very girl I would have picked for him. Oh, you'll see, it will make all the difference! Martin will grow. He'll end up like Daddy."

"You mean a judge?"

"Heavens, no, he's not even a lawyer. And, anyway, Daddy was only on the bench a year. Al Smith appointed him to the Court of Appeals in Albany to fill out the time of some man who died. No, I mean that Martin may become a thinker like Daddy. A philosopher."

Thinking and philosophy, however, were evidently of no more interest to her companion than interior decoration. "Al Smith? But he was a Democrat. Why should he have appointed your father?"

"Because Daddy's a Democrat. Lifelong. He worshiped Al Smith." She shook her head to fluff out her drying hair. "Oh, I know. You're like my friends at the sanatorium. Or, the 'retreat' as Mummie insists that I call it. They think if you're old New York, you must be a Republican."

"That isn't so?"

"For old rich, maybe. But Daddy was old poor. When he was a boy, Shallcross Manor had degenerated to a kind of seedy boarding house. And he went to Columbia, not even Harvard or Yale. He had to work his way through. Mummie's family, who had originally been poor Scotch immigrants, nothing *like* the Shallcrosses, quite looked down their noses when he first came calling. But that's New York."

"And later they looked up?"

"Well, that's New York, too."

Her companion was gazing again at the facade of the old house. "Did you know I've been here before? Years ago. At a birthday party of Martin's. We were classmates at Columbia."

"Really?"

"Yes. And I remember you. You couldn't have been more than twelve or thirteen at the time."

"I must have been awful!"

"Let us say you were enthusiastic. You told me about the presidents. You were full of statistics of their domestic lives."

"Fancy your remembering! Poor you."

"I remember your older sister, too, the one who's now Mrs. Kay. What a beauty!"

"Ah, everyone remembers Elly. That's my tragedy!"

He seemed to think that for the moment they had disposed of her family. "What do you do?" he inquired. "Besides living in Shallcross Manor?"

"Oh, I don't *do* anything. I'm still getting used to being home again. I've come back, you see, at thirty-two. Like an old maid Rip Van Winkle."

"I wouldn't call you old," he said, as gravely as if she hadn't been joking. "I wouldn't give you a day over twenty-nine."

Sophie felt more complimented than if he had said "twenty," as he might have had he meant to flatter, and she appreciated, too, with only a tickle of her old habit of apprehension, the frank inspection that he made of her.

"Why were you in a sanatorium?" he demanded. "Did you have some kind of nervous breakdown?"

Of course, she had seen it coming. Had she not, indeed, invited it? Now it lay before them on the raft like a gasping marine creature that had leaped up, in a freak effort, from the dirty deep. Her companion evidently regarded her illness as he regarded her body, as something present before them, something as discussable as the temperature of the water or her father's political affiliations. Was it reading too much into it — was it be-

ing too much Dr. Damon's ex-patient — to find a sexual conno-
tation in his equating the two? Men did not have nervous
breakdowns, not *real* men. Wasn't it a female function?

"Yes," she said at last with a sigh, "it was what you might call
a breakdown. Or at least a long depression."

"What depressed you?"

Oh, now, come, he could do better than that! But wasn't it,
on the other hand, what she wanted? Didn't she, all of a sudden,
brazenly, shamelessly, want to tell him? "All I can really explain is how it started. I mean the bad part. The really bad
part. I'd always had small depressions. What Mummie used to
call 'dumps.' But not a big one like three years ago."

"Can you tell me about it?"

Ah, that was better. He seemed very young, very boyish again
and pleasantly curious, not just above it all, the business male.
She looked over the bay at the thickening traffic on the Parkway.

"It happened at the end of my first year away from home.
Daddy had rented an apartment for Martin and me on East
Eightieth Street. Poor Martin! I'm sure his taking me in was a
condition of Daddy's paying the rent. Anyway, I had a job as a
doctor's receptionist. Oh, I was so proud of myself! Employed,
and independent! You will say: high time, at twenty-eight, and
so it was, but I had always suffered from the most terrible home-
sickness. I couldn't even go away for a weekend! So you can see
when I finally jumped out of the nest, even if it was only into
my brother's, it was a red-letter day."

"And you weren't homesick?"

"Not at all! That was what was so wonderful. I had a whole
year, the most marvelous year of my life. I didn't know that a
girl could be so happy. Martin was perfect. He knew that what
I needed was a group, and he plunged me right into the middle
of his. It was the most congenial group you can imagine, some
fifteen or twenty young people, half of them married, half not,
young lawyers and doctors, and bachelor girls like myself with

jobs which we were obviously going to discard as soon as we married. For marriage, of course, was the point. Those who were married were happily married; those who were single planned to be. But there was no hurry, do you see? It was a lovely, full interlude for just plain living. I don't think any of us even had affairs. Maybe I was naïve—I always have been—but I don't think so."

"People aren't always having affairs."

"No, they're not, are they?" she agreed enthusiastically, thinking how odd it was that he should have struck just the right note. "Anyway, the group was interested in all kinds of nice things: operas, concerts and movies, too, good movies, usually Italian ones. I don't remember that we ever took a very active part in politics or civil rights, but we were always on the side of the angels, never reds or McCarthyites. And we did imaginative things, too. We had weekly picnics, in fall and spring, in unusual places: under the George Washington Bridge, at the Narrows, in Prospect Park. The girls would bring the supper, and the boys the wine. Oh, it was a *dear* group, really, not very intellectual, but earnest. And I *was* so happy."

"Until?"

"Until." She glanced at him quickly, suddenly afraid that he might be impatient. But he wasn't. "Well, there was this boy. I shouldn't say boy. He was well over thirty. I liked him very much, yes, really very much. He was so funny, and gay and considerate and always *listened* if he asked you a question. And he liked me. I knew he was supposed to be gun-shy with girls—he was the one member of the group who had been divorced—very bitterly—and I didn't want to put him off. I was careful, *so* careful. I really was! But one night at a picnic in the Ramble we had some kind of *rosé* that went to my head—I really shouldn't ever drink at all—and I squeezed his hand and told him not to worry, that everything was going to be all right. And it wasn't. It wasn't at all! He looked at me — just for a moment;

before he ducked back behind the mask of his party smile — as if he were terribly disappointed in me. As if I'd let him down by being just another girl looking for a husband. Oh, he didn't *say* anything; he didn't have to. And in another minute he was his old self again. But the difference!" She did not even try to conceal now that her eyes were full of tears. "Oh, how could there be such ugliness in the very core of happiness?" she exclaimed, thinking of all the wasted years. "It was then that I began to have my horrible moments. I'd be with a man in a restaurant or a nightclub, and he'd go off for a moment, to telephone or the washroom, and suddenly I'd know, absolutely *know,* that he was never coming back! And even when he did, I'd still know that he wasn't!"

"And so you went to the sanatorium?"

"And so I went to the sanatorium," she responded, disappointed by the flatness of his question. "And so I was cured. And so I lived happily ever after."

In the silence she remembered what her brother had always told her. What right did one have to be disappointed in other people's reactions to one's problems? What business did one have to bore them with one's bleeding heart?

Yet he wasn't bored. "Do you know something?" he demanded. "You and I appear to be in the same boat. Starting our lives over again. Except you have the advantage. You're younger."

"But Martin tells me you're on your way to the top!" she protested, astonished by his comparison. "He says you're a 'go-getter,' and in Martin's vocabulary, I can assure you, that's the highest kind of praise!"

"Just because I've had a bit of luck with a scrap of land here and there," he replied with a deprecatory shrug. "You wouldn't even notice if I hadn't started from the bottom. Anyway, business isn't everything."

"It isn't?"

"Oh, no, there's a man's personal life," he replied soberly.

"Believe me, that's very important. And what's mine been? My parents died when I was a kid. I had no close relatives except an uncle, here in Queens, a small-time realtor. And what did he want of me, for all his lavish affection, for God's sake? Well, he hadn't a son, you see, and he wanted one. I had to marry his daughter, my own cousin, to get into the business!" He became excited now, emphasizing his words by slapping the raft. "You may say I didn't have to, that it's a free country and all that stuff. But it's not, Miss Shallcross! Uncle Bobbie took me into his shop. I *had* to marry Hulda!"

"But I gather you didn't have to stay married to her."

"What do you mean by that?"

"Martin told me you and she were separated."

"Oh. Yes." He stuck his feet in the water and wiggled them. "She went home to her old man. Flounced out. She has one bitch of a temper, if you'll excuse the term."

"Do you have children?"

"No, thank God, no children. Is there any reason two people should stay together if there are no children?"

"No reason. So long as neither of them cares."

"Well, I can't help it if Hulda cares! The point is I've gone beyond Hulda."

"Beyond her?"

"Yes. Intellectually, socially, any way you want to put it. I started managing tenements for her old man, but now I'm in bigger deals. Veterans' housing. Contracting. Inevitably, I mix with a better class of people. I gave her her chance to move ahead with me, but she wouldn't take it. I offered her elocution lessons, and do you know what she did? Threw a plate at me!"

"Well, I don't blame her! Why shouldn't she talk the way she wants?"

He reproached her with a look of weariness. "May I say something candidly, Miss Shallcross?"

"Please call me Sophie."

"Sophie. May I say that that last remark is typical of your whole class? You're brought up to be loyal and respectful to parents and spouses. To stand by them in times of adversity. But what's hard about that? Your parents and spouses are charming, cultivated people whom it should be a pleasure to stand by. They're assets, socially speaking. But in my walk of life a man's got to shed his antecedents if he wants to get ahead. Suppose Hulda were having tea right now with your parents." He pointed across the water to the table on the lawn under the white portico where a little group was seated. "You can bet your last buck your mother would be staring at her as if she were some kind of freak. And your mother'd be right, too! For Hulda would be talking in her best British movie accent and putting on her God-awful lady act. Crooking her little finger, and switching her ass!"

Sophie wrinkled her nose. "I'm glad you think your own tone is so cultivated."

"Martin says it doesn't matter with a man. Some of the parties he's taken me to, the talk's really rough."

"Obviously you've been moving in the highest society."

But nothing daunted him. He moved on, relentlessly, from fact to fact. "Those people only laugh at me. They *sneer* at Hulda."

"Poor Hulda!"

"Poor Hulda, indeed!" He seemed to be angry again. "She wouldn't learn, I tell you. She thinks she knows it all. Well, she's had her chance!"

But Sophie found that she, too, was becoming irritated. "Do you never regret turning your back on the past, Mr. Livingston?"

"Call me Jay."

"Jay."

"You mean, am I sorry that I changed my name? Yes, but only because I picked such a damn fool one. 'Jay Livingston' sounds like a society character in a musical comedy. I picked it when I was young and foolish, and I got a hell of a razzing for it at Columbia. But that got my back up, and I stuck to it. Now I'm stuck *with* it."

"I didn't mean just the name. I meant the whole Jewish tradition."

He laughed, but without the least resentment. "Do you know what the worst kind of anti-Semite is, Sophie? It's the man who says: 'I don't mind a Jew who's proud of being a Jew. It's these name-changers and nose-scrapers I object to.' And why does he object? Because he's afraid of a world where he wouldn't be able to tell a Jew from a Gentile. What would happen to his sacred prejudices?"

Sophie was disturbed at the imputation of bias. She had always laughed at her mother's warning look when any topic remotely suggestive of a religious or racial issue was raised in "mixed" company. Mrs. Shallcross was convinced that Jews and Catholics were embarrassed at being Jews and Catholics. But now under the level stare of this young man's candidly mocking eyes, she wondered if she were as free a soul as she aspired to be. "I suggest you may be lumping too many people under one label," she retorted. "If I criticize you for changing your name for social advancement I'm not necessarily the biased one."

"But supposing I never cared about the name or the religion!" he cried. "Supposing I loathed and detested the whole business of being a Jew! Why shouldn't I shed it? And why shouldn't I shed it for social advantage? Am I obliged to be a Jew simply because anti-Semitism exists?"

"I suppose in a way I think you are," she admitted. "Otherwise it seems like abandoning the fort under fire."

"Which is only bad if you care about the fort. But, you see, I don't. That's my philosophy, Sophie. I don't think it makes a smitch of difference what you're born. Jew, Arab, Negro, Eskimo. I don't believe that you can inherit any duty of loyalty. What you want to be in this world is what counts. And a man, a real man, can be anything he really wants. So what difference does a name make?"

Sophie was ashamed to catch herself reflecting, even for a second, that she was a true Livingston, a descendant of Chancellor Robert.

"I've grown up in such a different atmosphere," she said ruefully. "I suppose I care too much about the past. My friends call this place the 'cherry orchard.' "

"Well, at least your family have a past to live in."

"Oh, it's not *them,*" she corrected him. "It's just me. Daddy has always been very much a man of the moment, and Mummie at least thinks she is, and Martin — well, you know Martin — and my sister, Elly, goes to all the most fashionable parties and sees the most up-to-date people. No, it's me. I hug the past. *My* past. The bits of it I feel sure of. Right here. I suppose you'll say it's because I'm afraid of the future."

"You know something, Sophie? You and I might be the perfect combination. The perfect partnership. The past and the future!"

She smiled at the utterness of his predictability. "You mean you being the past?" she teased him. "With your mid-Victorian ideas of business tactics? And I the future? With my sympathy for the underdog and my dislike of class distinctions?"

"That Victorian past may not be as dead as you think."

"As I think? Or as you hope?"

Sophie turned now to watch her mother's plump figure detach itself from the group around the tea table and move down the lawn toward the water's edge. Soon she would hear her call to her. The figure moved slowly, and Sophie could see that the gentle wind was rippling that serene crown of undisciplined gray hair. Hilary Knowles, half a head taller than Mrs. Shallcross, in gray with a scarlet tie, had followed her and was now climbing into the rowboat. Her mother had raised her hands to her lips.

"Sophia! Sophia, my dear! It's getting cold. I've asked Hilary to row you and Mr. Livingston in."

Sophie had a sudden, giddy wish that her new friend would shout back something rude, even obscene, and she closed her eyes for a minute. When she opened them, Jay had transferred his attention to the tall back of Hilary Knowles, now slowly approaching them in the tiny boat.

"What sort of a guy is Knowles?" he asked. "I haven't seen him since school. Is he as bright as Martin says?"

"Oh, yes. And a first-class critic." She watched Hilary's oars rise quickly and slowly drop back to the water. "And a wonderful friend. He's almost a member of our family."

"Is he married?"

"Not now."

"Is he a beau or more like a brother?"

"Really, Jay, you're impossible."

"Now, anyway, I know who the guy was who didn't respond to the *vin rosé!*"

As she turned to stare at him in dismay and anger, he simply flung up his hands and laughed. It was a loud, infectious laugh, different from his others, and it was so imbued with gaiety that it was impossible to resent it. For a long second on that raft Sophie had to face the totally unexpected fact that he had charm, a charm that could suddenly paralyze even her very real exasperation. Then she rose and dove into the water. The cold shock was glorious, and she let herself slide down into redemption. When her hands hit the slime at the bottom, she felt the usual little spurt of panic and struggled quickly upward. Breaking the surface, she breathed deeply and was glad, after all, to be alive. She turned her head and watched Jay descend awkwardly into the little boat that Hilary held against the raft. But she was disappointed to note that despite the awkwardness of his clamber, he sat so jauntily in the stern under the hulk of Hilary that he might have been a cocky little despot rowed by a giant slave.

2

HILARY KNOWLES was a large, handsome man who had never wished to be either large or handsome. The gray streak in his wavy brown hair, the large soft eyes, the big nose pushed a bit to one side, the full, thick lips, the rounded, cleft chin, the hunched-in shoulders all seemed to protest, if not quite the promise of strength, at least the threat of ruthlessness. Hilary strove to emphasize in his tailored suits, in his bright, almost gaudy display of jewels in his cuff links, in his tie pin, in his watch chain, the gentleman cultivated to near decadence, as if in fear that otherwise someone might expect Tarzan to come swinging through the trees. He laughed continually, a pleasant, bubbly laugh, always throwing his head back.

"I was watching you and Jay together," he called to Sophie as he rowed up abreast of her swimming figure. "I was wondering what he could be telling you to make you seem so rapt." He turned to his passenger. "Were you telling her of your exploits in Queens housing, Jay? Sophie was like Desdemona listening to the feats of Othello. She loved him for the dangers he had passed, and he loved her that she did pity them."

"We didn't realize that we had Honest Iago's eye upon us, did we, Jay?" Sophie cried. But she didn't wait for an answer, plunged her face into the water and reached the beach in a few hard strokes. Her mother stepped gingerly down the narrow beach to throw a robe over her shoulders.

"You know how prone you are to colds, Sophie. You

shouldn't really swim in the bay at all, let alone as early as June. I'm sorry, Mr. Livingston! I hope my girl hasn't frozen you to death. I tell her that other people may not share her enthusiasm for suicide, but she won't listen."

With age some of the cavernous austerity of Mrs. Shallcross' Scotch Presbyterian forebears had begun to plow itself into the soft pink blandness of her countenance. Her nose was taking on a note of the ponderous, her lips thinning to a line, the skin beneath her eyes turning to olive-black. One might have expected her pronouncements to be couched in the hard tones of a confirmed wisdom. But in Mrs. Shallcross principle had remained stuck behind fatuity. Sophie hurried across the lawn to escape her reproaches and join the more neutral company of her father and brother.

The Judge was clenching his pipe in his teeth as he did when he was irritated. He must have been expounding one of his theories about the Supreme Court when interrupted by his wife's departure for the water's edge. Hilary Knowles and Jay Livingston, walking on either side of Mrs. Shallcross, rejoined the little group, and he resumed.

"As I was trying to explain, the Court's chief characteristic is to be behind the times. The Dred Scott decision brought on civil war, and the judges in the depression damn near killed the New Deal. Now God knows I was no New Dealer — I've always been a Jeffersonian Democrat — but it was surely an unconstitutional impertinence for a bunch of old men to tell the nation it couldn't try a few social experiments when a third of its breadwinners were out of work. And today, when our states are desperately trying to cope with an unprecedented wave of crime, sure enough, our consistent Court trots out every worn-out liberal formula of the nineteen thirties to turn police detection into a parlor game!"

Eben Shallcross was a magnificent old man. He looked like a judge in a movie. He was dressed in the immaculate white into which he always changed at home in summer, the same white of his thick long hair. He was lean, gaunt, brown-skinned, wrinkled, with a smooth aquiline nose and cold blue eyes that he kept blinking. He entirely expected the attention that he invariably got.

"Then you disapproved the school desegregation decision, sir?" Hilary asked, with the boldness of a household intimate. "You would leave that question to the tender mercies of the Southern states?"

"I disapproved the decision as a *decision*," Judge Shallcross retorted testily. "Which doesn't for a minute mean that I approve of segregation. You know that, Hilary. I believe that legislatures should legislate. If the Southern schools were to be desegregated, Congress had ample power to accomplish it."

"But Congress hadn't acted!"

"That's no concern of the Court. However, I will admit that there at least the issue was substantive. It was not like the ordinary civil rights case that the Court delights in: whether an old woman has to agree to bear arms, whether a school child has to say a prayer, whether a bus can pick up a Catholic child, whether a dope peddler's privacy has been invaded. Show me one case where a man's freedom has been at stake. Except, of course, during the war, when the army flung thousands of American citizens of Japanese ancestry into concentration camps. And what did the Court do? Chicken out! I tell you the whole thing's a parlor game, pure and simple!"

Sophie jumped up to get herself a glass of iced tea. She hated this mood of her father's. Her brother Martin was at the bar table on the porch, pouring himself whiskey.

"Will the old man never get over not having been appointed to the Court?" he asked her. "It's more and more embarrassingly obvious."

Martin was the realist of the family, a thin, slight, clerkish-looking man with over-pressed dark clothes. But his eyes gave him a distinction that the rest of him lacked. They dissented. They were a light, faintly yellowish brown, and they imparted to his air of stillness, his general attitude of caution, of polite restraint, a standoffishness, a distrust, a refusal to be taken in that was almost surly. For all his good manners people did not overlook this in Martin.

"Can't you get him on another topic?" she whispered. "Al Smith? The New Deal? Anything. I don't want your friend Livingston to be laughing at him."

"Oh, how did you and Livingston get on?"

"Well enough."

"Did you like him?"

"I did and I didn't. Now, don't tell me he's got a big future. I don't *care*. I simply hope that Shallcross Manor isn't in it."

"That's up to Father."

"Oh, Martin, he's not going to sell it, is he?" she cried. "He wouldn't do that to me!"

"Nobody's going to do anything that's not in your best interests, sweet."

"That's what I'm afraid of!"

Martin left her at this to return to the group, and she stood alone on the porch, pretending to be pouring iced tea, trying to get hold of herself. For suddenly the whole horizon, as far north as La Guardia, seemed to have darkened, as if she had put on a pair of sunglasses. It was one of those moments again, one of those terrible moments that had put her under Doctor Damon's care, and she had to be able to throw it off. He had analyzed the groundlessness of her early fears: that her father would die, that they would lose the family place, that nobody would love her. And now they were not groundless. But that was just the point that Damon always made! It didn't *matter* what happened, or whether it was likely to happen or not likely. It was only the terror that was waste.

"I quite agree with you, Judge," Jay Livingston was saying.

"In our society a strong man is always free. We overdo this business of liberty for the flabby and the weak. Like that child you were speaking of who's afraid to leave the schoolroom when it's time for prayers. Why must the other kids be kept from praying because he's embarrassed not to?"

"I see we have a rugged individualist in our midst," the Judge commented drily.

"Caveat emptor, sir!"

"Indeed. And I wonder what *your* emptors say, Mr. Livingston."

Sophie looked over at her brother who was already on his feet.

"I think if we're going to get back to town, you'd better get dressed, Jay," Martin said to his friend, and the latter rose to follow him into the house.

"Livingston," the Judge muttered scornfully under his breath. "A cousin of mine, no doubt."

"Hilary, are you going back with them?" Sophie called from the porch. "Take me for a stroll first."

"Sophie, you're soaking, my child. Go up and change."

"Oh, Mother, I'm perfectly dry."

She took Hilary's arm, and they sauntered back down to the water. It was the time of year in which she had always been happiest and unhappiest at Shallcross Manor.

"Oh, Hilary, don't you wish we were young again?"

"You are young, silly."

"Me? I'm older than any of you. In moods anyway. A year with Doctor Damon is five in any ordinary life."

He tucked her arm against his side reassuringly. It was the Shallcross policy to keep Sophie away from the subject of her breakdown, and the friends adhered. "What a marvelous old ham actor your father is!" he exclaimed. "He can take any side of any question. But when he saw Jay Livingston in his camp, he was wise enough to strike his tents and move on."

"Poor Mr. Livingston!"

"Did you know he was at college with Martin and me? He was always pushing in where he wasn't wanted."

"Well, he wasn't pushing in anywhere today that I didn't want him. I thought he was rather a dear."

"Sophie! Will you never plug that leak in your milk bottle of human kindness? The guy's after Shallcross Manor!"

"Daddy'll never sell it! Don't talk about it!" She was suddenly furious at Hilary, furious at all of them. "Anyway, it's not wicked to *buy* old places. It's only wicked to sell them. It's perfectly natural for Jay Livingston to be interested. That's his business." Her anger increased as she felt the impertinent, pushing tears. The old white house with its brave new paint, the rolling lawn, Hilary and his aggravating, pointless, never-ending kindness, herself and her nostalgia, what was the *use* of them? What were words under the hum of traffic, going and coming? "I haven't so many friends that I can afford to reject new ones because they happen to have changed their names. What good have the friends I've had done me? Can you tell me that, Hilary? Can you tell me the answer to that!"

Hilary was almost nurselike in his instant, soft-spoken solicitude. "Very little, I'm sure, Sophie, if I'm any test. Don't get excited about it. I shouldn't have said that about Jay Livingston."

"Oh, you all treat me as if I was a nut!" she exclaimed in disgust, and breaking away from him, she ran back up the lawn to the house.

3

THE JUDGE LOVED to point out that the Shallcrosses were so old a family that they had been twice impoverished and twice enriched during their two and a half centuries in New York. The Honorable John, seventh son of Baron Shallcross of Claran-on-Clyde, had had the good fortune to marry a sister of Lady Cornbury and to accompany his wife's brother-in-law across the ocean when the latter was appointed Governor of the Province of New York in 1702. He and his family had managed to avoid implication in the subsequent Cornbury disgrace and had stayed on to administer the large land grant that they had obtained in Long Island. But the next two generations had proved improvident and by the Revolution the land was all gone, and the last male heir, Peter Shallcross, had taken to a maritime life.

He prospered. He became a ship captain, a ship owner, president of the Shallcross-Aspinwall line and one of the richest merchants in Manhattan. He built a square Greek revival house on Fifth Avenue just north of Washington Square, and another, for summers, on Flushing Bay. He married one daughter to a Van Rensselaer, another to a Jay, and a third to a niece of the diarist Mayor Philip Hone who described him as a "prince of our renaissance."

His death in 1840 started a second reversal of the family fortunes. The division of the fortune among seven daughters and a son was one factor; another was that that son was a gambler and alcoholic. When Eben Shallcross was born in 1888, the family property had shrunk to Shallcross Manor, now a boardinghouse run by his grandmother, and a scant ten acres rented out for a sheep pasture. So total had been the deterioration that Eben's family were no longer considered even decayed gentility. They had fallen to a state where most of their Van Rensselaer and Jay cousins across the East River were no longer aware of their existence.

In some ways this state of affairs made life easier for Eben. He did not have to pass his youth trying to cover his shabbiness from rich friends. He did not have to worry about inviting boys from Groton or St. Paul's to visit him in the summer. He did not have to rent a tailcoat to go to debutante parties in Manhattan. He could grow up in Queens, like any other boy in his neighborhood, and work his way through Columbia College and Law School, aided by the one old-maid Jay cousin who had not forgotten this high twig of her family tree. And when he went to work for Elmer MacManus, the negligence lawyer, he was able to develop talents in the courtroom which, had he gone to Harvard Law and thence to Wall Street, would most probably have atrophied under the stress of a busy corporate practice.

But he never lost sight of the glories of the past. Eben was infernally proud. If he had been spared the humiliation of aspiring to a social group to which he was qualified by birth but not by pocketbook, it did not follow that he was unaware of that group or of his qualifications to enter it. He knew that he would never do so — even if in later years he should fill that empty purse — but he knew with equal sureness that he would never settle for anything *less,* and hence, from an early age, he avoided intimacies that he would always be too much of a gentleman to sever. By college time he was self-sufficient: a cool, appraising, well-mannered youth, widely read, witty, attractive, sardonic, surprisingly hilarious when moved to laughter, afraid of nothing, respectful of little, yet throwing out some kind of unspecified challenge. "Wouldn't he be a wonderful ally —

friend — lover?" people would ask themselves, according to their need. For people were always trying to break in. But that was the other side of Eben Shallcross. They never succeeded.

At thirty he was still alone in the world. His parents were dead, and Shallcross Manor, renovated and rented, had become a financial asset. He was well known as a trial lawyer and a partner now of Elmer MacManus. He lived in a handsome bachelor's apartment in Washington Square, not far from the site of Peter Shallcross' mansion, and entertained many prominent Democratic politicians. When he met Marian Chalmers at a tea party given by the old Jay cousin who had not forgotten him, he decided that it was high time that he married. She was passingly pretty, only moderately gushing, had apparently read some portion of the books that she talked about and appeared to have a good temper. Eben's first impression was tolerably exact. Where he made his mistake was where cool young men who arrange their own marriages are apt to make mistakes. He thought that he had been careful not to overestimate either her intellectual curiosity or the degree to which he had impressed her. In fact, he had overestimated both. Marian was not only totally uninquisitive; she was totally indifferent to his brilliance. She simply wanted to get married.

The Chalmerses had known no such reversals as the Shallcrosses. If their position was not grand, their rise had been steady. In 1800 they had been simple Scottish weavers on the looms in Dunfermline; by the middle of the century Chalmers Brothers, on Barclay Street, were established textile importers. The Chalmerses never achieved wealth, but they achieved a massive, brownstone respectability that was almost as good. They were numerous; they were plain; they were happy in the least decorous and least comfortable conformity. Above their high stoops, within their black walnut, Presbyterian interiors, they seemed "older" New York than many more lively families who descended from Revolutionary patriots. Marian's parents were not in the least dazzled by a young political lawyer who seemed to have neither relatives nor a church and who was partner of a prominent Catholic layman, but if he could support Marian, he could certainly have her.

She had her virtues. She agreed to live in Shallcross Manor; she bore him three children; she was not extravagant. As the children grew older, she transferred to them all of her limited human interest. She became so soft and gray and comfortable, so full of blameless aphorisms and homely religiosity that she might have been standing on the stage of the Waldorf ballroom as a "mother of the year." But though she asked many questions, she heard few answers; though she laughed at imagined illnesses, she cosseted her own; though she talked of God, she dreaded extinction. She sought refuge from panic behind a wall of set habits and attitudes. The truth for Marian was always in the well-remembered sayings of her long dead parents, never in the present witticisms of her brilliant husband.

Eben found her irritating, but not importantly so. His home was made up, complete, like a brown paper package waiting on the front hall table to be mailed. He could turn all his energies to his career, and that was what he wanted, wasn't it? Of course, there were doubts; nothing was ever *that* clear. He tried to be a good father. He tried not to be put off by the "little lady" airs of Elly, by the priggishness of Martin. He had periods of romanticizing his love for the baby, Sophie, born when he was past forty, of thinking of her as the old man's darling, the prop of his later years. He even saw that it might be a duty to make up to the child for the fact that Marian, for all her perfunctory efforts to conceal it, so obviously preferred her older daughter, but when Sophie was on his knee, when she responded, as she vociferously did, to his stories and jokes, it used to strike him uncomfortably that the picture conjured up was a bit too much that of Little Dorrit and the old debtor of the Marshalsea. He must have been constantly disappointing the child by returning from Dickens to Flushing Bay. And to his career.

But what was that career to be? From 1910 to 1922 Eben the lawyer was either in court or writing briefs. He accepted every kind of case, negligence, larceny, murder, stockholders' actions; he argued at trials, he argued appeals. He became much respected and not a little feared by his fellows at the bar. He was icy, succinct, alert, merciless and brilliantly clear. His only flaw as an advocate was that he found it impossible to be sentimental, even when sentiment, as in some negligence or criminal cases, was urgently required. Sarcasm at such moments was always apt to seep through the would-be honey of his tone. But when it came to synthesizing facts or laws, to making sense out of a jumble of incidents or rules to a bewildered jury or to an exasperated appellate court, he was without peer. Speaking always briefly, always simply, always without notes, he made even his opponents grateful for his elucidating analyses.

Yet Eben was not satisfied to be only an advocate, even a great one. His cases, and their preparation, were only a part of the vast reading program in which he was constantly engaged, a program that included philosophy, history, even fiction and poetry, and that had for its aim no less a goal than the preparation of Eben Shallcross for some undefined but still major role in designing an ark for civilization in the floods threatened by the twentieth century. When Eben, preparing a witness, leaned back in his chair and tapped his knee with his ivory paper cutter, his blue eyes seeming to be trying to tear some consistency out of the jumbled words spilling out before him, he was relating the speaker in his mind to questions of evidence, of ultimate truth, of justice, of the existence of justice, or even to less relevant issues suggested by an early-morning perusal of the volumes selected for that week's bedside reading: *Antigone*, Montaigne, *Adventures of Ideas*.

When Al Smith, whom he admired as devotedly as only a detached intellectual can admire a man who is all heart and action, appointed him to the Court of Appeals to fill out a brief vacancy, Eben enjoyed the unique satisfaction of exercising power over his fellow men without losing his status as an intellectual. What other public position could offer this peculiar joy of the bench, this gobbled and retained cake? From now on Eben knew perfectly what he wanted in life: no less a thing than a seat on the United States Supreme Court. Here was a chance to play the greatest intellectual power game of the century, the interpretation and enlargement of the American dream itself!

Nor was fulfillment so very unlikely. Al Smith might well become president, and Al Smith might well appoint him. The seed of suggestion burst into the weed of conviction, and Eben came to regard the great depression as a scourge justly visited upon a people which had preferred Hoover to Smith in 1928. But his bitterness against the anti-Catholic faction to which he attributed the Smith defeat was as nothing to his wrath against Franklin Roosevelt for the "treachery" of 1932. Some of his more stinging remarks were quoted to the new president, and appointment to the least New Deal office, let alone the Supreme Bench, became an impossibility during the dozen years that ended only with the massive cerebral hemorrhage in Warm Springs. And by that time Eben had been too long out of politics and too heavily identified with litigation against the government ever to be considered again.

Careers, of course, are always half coincidences. Eben knew that he might have ranked with Cardozo had the cards fallen differently. As it was, and as he passed into his fifties, the biting manner that had once been a mere useful tool of his advocacy began to seep out of its compartment to contaminate his whole personality. The judicial philosophy that he devised and expounded in two popular volumes was created less by deduction from a lifetime's study than by his need to depreciate the Court on which he was never to sit. As a "Jeffersonian" liberal, he became the champion of the school that would have denied the Court's power to strike down legislation in any field where Congress or the states had been given power to legislate. If Eben

Shallcross was not to be allowed to pose as the champion of liberty, no other judge should have that privilege!

Old age, coming as an impertinence to a man who had still so much to accomplish, who was indeed only a failure according to his own lights, found him nonetheless in the best of health and mind. He had been spared the slow corrosion of spirit that is the fate of those millions of elderly who allow themselves to slip into the slothful habit of automatic whining at things present. Eben's dissent from the world in which he lived was, on the contrary, an actively brandished axe. His invectives, his satires, his sneers had a positively rejuvenating effect upon his mentality. He reached for his newspaper in the morning, not with a tired anticipation of further stress to his spleen, but with the vibrant enthusiasm of a Cassandra who is quite satisfied to be an audience of one to the accuracy of her own predictions. His home and family had begun already to merge with the deprecated world of printers' headlines in the frightening detachment of his septuagenarian vision. Eben did not thank his stars, like many of his contemporaries, that he might not live to see Armageddon. He hoped to survive it and count the dead.

4

SOPHIE STOOD by the north window of her father's office on the top floor of the New York Central Building, looking up the double ribbon of Park Avenue to a blue and smoking Bronx, and waited for the family conference to begin. She always felt plain and awkward in the presence of her sister Elly. Elly's plucked eyebrows, her golden blond hair, the way she allowed her sables to fall about her elbows bottled up Sophie's spirits as effectively as they unbottled her mother's. Marian Shallcross could hardly keep her hands from touching her older daughter. She sat by her now at the glass-topped table in the center of the big white chamber, fairly trembling with solicitude. Martin took papers out of his briefcase and put them back.

The Judge began: "You are all aware that title to Shallcross Manor is in me and me alone. However, I have always taken the position that moral title is in the family. That is why I have called you together to give Martin's proposition a fair hearing. Martin, the floor is yours."

Martin did not look up from his papers. "What it all boils down to, Dad, is that Jay Livingston is ready to put up four hundred thousand, all cash, for Shallcross Manor. Considering the state of the house and the neighborhood, and the cost of our upkeep, I think it's the best offer we can expect. I've pretty well canvassed the other prospects."

"What will he do with the place?" Elly demanded.

"He will turn it into a veterans' housing development."

"And the Manor, of course, will be pulled down. Or could it be converted?"

"Into a high-rise apartment? Use your bean, Elly."

Sophie rubbed the palms of her hands together to try to keep them dry. She felt as if all the moisture in her body were going into her hands. Yet should not the ancient predictability of the crisis help now to make it more endurable? The offices of Mac-Manus & Shallcross were at least a fitting spot for the death of the past. Sophie had always secretly suspected that, like most men's things, it must be a cruel firm. Hadn't she seen the splendid offices of the senior partners and the one-windowed cubicles for the middle-aging hacks who served them? Hadn't she always hated its atmosphere: silent, servile, sullen? Everyone knew the firm would not survive the two old men who ran it, but this did not make them love the two old men. The slaves who were burnt up with Sardanapalus, after all, had not been expected to be happy about it. And Sophie felt herself another slave.

"Elly's question was perfectly proper," Eben Shallcross was saying testily. "You may not care about historical landmarks, Martin, but Shallcross Manor happens to be one."

"It has not been so designated."

"I'm not speaking of political designations. I'm speaking of historic facts. You don't give a rap for history or for family. All you care about is making a fast buck. I don't say that is positively wrong, but I do insist that you recognize that other people may have other values. How much do you estimate that your friend Livingston — if I must call him by that name — stands to make out of this deal?"

"It's hard to say. All these things are gambles. He might lose his shirt."

"Ah, but he won't." The Judge rose now and walked over to take a stand by the book cabinet, the court lawyer again. "And, if I may venture to contradict you, Martin, these things aren't gambles at all. Let me instruct the ladies, as simply as possible, how they are done. Mr. Livingston, once in possession of our ancestral acres, will borrow what he needs from Uncle Sam to erect his oval of six 'high-rise' apartment houses. He will then rent out his apartments to veterans at a price that will cover taxes, interest and amortization, plus a tidy extra for the 'risk-taking' landlord. Not to mention his killing on the stores in the center of the oval. At the end of the leasehold, with everything paid off, Mr. Livingston should come into full title to a project for which he hasn't put up a single penny, not even the initial four hundred grand which he pays to me. *That,* of course, is carved out of the housing loan by the use of cheap building materials. When Martin says it's impossible to estimate his profit, he means it's impossible to say whether it will be ten millions or twenty!"

"Father, you always exaggerate!"

"All right, we'll settle for five. What is your cut, my boy?"

"Ten percent. I'm not trying to hide anything."

"Ten percent! Why not a hundred? Why not do the project yourself? Why give it all to a little kike like Livingston?"

"Because the 'little kike' as you call him — and I wish some of your political friends could hear you — has the necessary know-how in contracting."

Sophie had almost to admire her father, even when she most deplored him. As an actor, he was sublime. She tried to lose some of her pain in the anesthetic of his performance. He might have been, as he pointed a scornful finger at the son who was only trying to enrich him, the grizzled old lawyer for the defense in the climax of a film dramatization of some historic miscarriage of justice.

"Meaning you don't understand the technicalities of paper-thin walls and cheap plumbing?" he exclaimed now. "Meaning that your private school aesthetic sensibility might wince at the prospect of rearing six pink boxes to mar the remnants of the landscape? True, Martin! We who only wish to profit from the bulldozer without driving it ourselves must be content with the mouse's share. That's the tale of America. The better sort are too good for the dirty work. They have to be creative. They have to be lawyers, doctors, brokers, bankers. They must leave the essential task of reducing our homeland to a rubble of unplanned housing horrors to the new Livingston. Livingston! Why doesn't he take *our* name? Jay Shallcross, the Attila of 1960!"

"I don't see what other people make out of it has to do with us," Martin grumbled. "It's still the best deal you can get for the place. I should think you'd be glad that some part of the profit will go to a Shallcross."

"Maybe I should be, Martin." And Sophie knew now that her father was preparing one of those rapid volte-faces that used to bewilder her as a child. "Maybe we should all be glad that you've made your adjustment to our unspeakable century. Maybe we should even follow your suit."

Here he walked over to Sophie, and put his arm about her shoulders, turning her so they were both looking out at the city. "Shallcross Manor is an anachronism, my dear Sophie. You and I, who love it, have to face that bitter fact. The neighborhood is deteriorating. Sneak thieves abound. Young savages copulate on our lawn at night. Look down at that proud double line of great apartment houses moving north up Park Avenue like the Wall of China! That's how the modern elect are meant to live. In glass or concrete towers, with guarded entrances, high over streets where the scum of Puerto Rico eddies dangerously at night!"

Marian Shallcross now spoke for the first time. "You needn't put it all on that high plane," she reproved her husband. "Poor Martin has taken a lot of abuse for caring about the money. What about you? Aren't you anxious to stop invading your capital? Didn't you tell me the other night that you had no younger man capable of taking over your firm? Martin at least is being straight about *his* motives!"

"The things you remember, Marian!" the Judge exclaimed.

"I hear more than you think, and it's lucky I do. If we're going to sell Shallcross Manor, let's be frank about our motives. I don't mind saying that I shall be delighted to be rid of the housekeeping and relax in a nice, manageable apartment."

"In Elly's building," the Judge added slyly.

"What do you mean, in Elly's building?"

"Are you going to deny, Marian, that you've already looked at the vacant apartment directly below Elly's? So long as we're going into real motives?"

Sophie detached herself from her father's arm. She wished he would leave her mother out of it. After all, her mother had not been born a Shallcross; there was no reason that *she* should pine to live on Flushing Bay.

"I suggest it's high time we all faced the fundamental issue," Elly intervened. "And that is what Shallcross Manor really means to each of us. Isn't it a symbol of pride?"

"Whose pride?"

"Yours, Daddy! Your insistence that Eben Shallcross never belonged to any person or any group. Your Byronic superiority in living behind crumbling white columns on Flushing Bay! We could never be like anyone else. Don't you see it's symbolic? I suggest it's time we joined the twentieth century!"

Sophie now discovered that she was trembling all over with anger. Not indignation, or even resentment, but a sudden hot, stinging rage. She had felt nothing like it since the sanatorium. She might forgive the others their motives, but how could she pardon Elly? Elly who was rich, who had no housekeeping problems?

"Each of us has a different twentieth century!" she burst out. "I don't see why mine, Elly, on Flushing Bay, has to be any less real than yours at some charity ball!"

"Of course, it's just as real, dear," Elly said quickly, shocked, as they all were, by her sister's tone. "But it's less . . . less, shall we say, characteristic?"

"Would I be more characteristic if I hired a press agent to get my name in the papers?"

Eben Shallcross looked up. "Does Elly do that?"

"Of course she does! She likes to read all those blurby praises of her beauty and graciousness!"

"Really, Daddy, this discussion is becoming ridiculous. I'm afraid Sophie has lived too far out from society to know what things are commonly done today."

"Girls, girls," the Judge interrupted, walking back to his desk to face them all again. "Let us cease this wrangling. It is sufficiently clear to me that Elly has a press agent."

"I was simply trying to explain, Daddy . . ."

"I don't even want you to try, my dear. That you, born a Shallcross and married to a millionaire, should feel obliged to adopt the tactics of the commonest social climber, while your brother, educated as a gentleman, should go into partnership with an unscrupulous contractor, seems to me the epitaph of an era. In Russia it took a revolution to destroy the aristocracy. Here, just hand us the rope!"

"I think we came here to discuss the disposition of Shallcross Manor and not to be insulted," Elly pointed out angrily. "And I believe that four of us, for one reason or another, have indicated approval of Martin's proposal. You, Sophie, of course, are against it?"

"Oh, what do you care about me, any of you?" Sophie burst out passionately. "You've all decided to do the deed. How can I stop you?"

She hurried across the room, through their embarrassed silence, and rushed out past her father's secretary to the waiting room. She only hoped that she could get to the lobby before the cascade of her tears should betray her. But who was this talking to her, taking her arm, impeding her?

"Leave me be!" she almost screamed.

"Sophie! What is it?"

For a moment she stared in simple astonishment at those peering green eyes.

"Mr. Livingston!" she cried. Then, in a second, she saw her last chance. "You won't really tear our house down, will you? Couldn't you save it? Couldn't you use it as a clubhouse or a marina or *something*? Oh, please!"

He blinked at her for a second. "I guess that might be possible."

"Would you let me help you? Would you let me work on the project? I've had a course in industrial design. I'd do it for you free. Oh, so happily! *Please* say you'll give me a chance!"

"Why, honey, of course. ₁Suppose we go downstairs and discuss it over a sandwich? I guess your old man isn't ready for me yet."

To Sophie's bewildered gaze he might have been a shiny-eyed, golden-haired cherub blowing his horn in a fleecy-clouded blue sky above scenes of wars and damnations. She suddenly threw her arms around his neck.

"Oh, hold me, Jay, hold me. Hold me for a minute, please!"

And before the scandalized receptionist he put his arms about her waist and held her.

Then they went down to the cafeteria even though the receptionist protested that her father had told him to wait. Jay simply waved a hand to her as he went out and said they would be right back. At their table Sophie found that she was still shaking with excitement and feeling very unlike herself as she moved the cutlery about to illustrate the different uses to which the old house might be put.

"Why don't *you* live in it?" he suggested, winking. "We might turn it into a museum and put you in a hoop dress to show people around."

"Now you're laughing at me!"

"Honest, I'm not."

"Live in that big house all alone?"

"Would it make things better if I lived there with you?"

Sophie flushed hotly. "I'm afraid I'm no good at that kind of badinage, Mr. Livingston."

"It's not badinage. Didn't I tell you that day on the raft that we'd make a great couple?"

"Is this a proposal or a proposition?"

"Whichever you want!"

"Well, considering you're married, I must assume it's the latter. Or at the least a very crude joke." And suddenly her heart was throbbing with anger again, as it had been against Elly in her father's office. She simply could not sustain such soaring followed by such drops. "I'm sorry. I had thought we were going to be serious. Forgive me for intruding myself and my silly ideas."

She was too upset to know quite what she was doing as she jumped to her feet, but not so upset as to be unaware that the tears that had started to her eyes were her own recognition of her own asininity. Surely, she was as conspicuous in that body-thronged cafeteria as if she were wearing the very hoop skirt in which his imagination had so appropriately clad her! She was almost relieved when he grabbed her hand and pulled her back down to the bench.

"Don't be a goat. Do you think I'm some kind of stage villain demanding your chaste jewel as the price of Shallcross Manor? I wanted us to be friends, that was all."

Sophie looked doubtfully at those sober, staring eyes. Was he really indignant or was he laughing at her? "I thought this should be strictly a business matter."

"I don't do things that way. The Shallcross way. All business or all pleasure, never mixed. So well bred, isn't it? Except, of course, it's fake. A polite way of telling meatballs like me that you'll do business with them but not be friends."

"How sensitive you are!" she exclaimed in sheer astonishment. "I don't want to tell you that at *all*. I should like very much to be your friend!"

"Well, that's better." His irritation subsided as rapidly as her own. "We might work out a plan for Shallcross Manor. Why not? We can talk it over, anyway. We can go out for dinner. Or the theater. You like the theater, don't you?" Some of his enthusiasm reappeared as he gazed at her. But he was ready, she felt sure, to be angry all over again if she said the least wrong thing. "Maybe our friendship will develop into something. Maybe it won't. Who knows? Who cares, even? We take our chances."

Sophie felt a small, involuntary shudder of titillation at the frankness of his suggestion. Could she imagine doing such things — things which she had never done — lovelessly, with *him?*

"All I'm saying is that you never know the future," he said, when she still said nothing.

"No, that's true, isn't it?" she replied, as if suddenly awakening again. "Who would have ever believed, for example, that *you'd* be the savior of Shallcross Manor? Oh, Jay, you're so much nicer than my family! And what a funny day it's been!"

She felt it was even funnier, after their sandwich, when they went back and found the others fretting with indignation at the enforced wait. And the climax of it all came when her father rose to his feet, like a sovereign conferring a coveted honor, and announced his reluctant consent to the proposed sale. Jay, far from bowing his head, not only had the audacity to wink at the old man but actually tucked his arm around Sophie's waist and replied that the purchaser had just acquired a partner!

5

JAY'S FATHER, Jesse Levermore, who was fifty when Jay was
born, had been a distant cousin of the Schoenbergs, a Jewish
banking family which had emigrated from Hamburg to New
York in the 1840s and obtained considerable wealth in the ensu-
ing decades. This relationship had dominated Jesse's life. A
social rebel and an atheist, a bad painter and a constant talker,
he had never ceased to butt his head in helpless rage against the
bland wall of contempt and affection that the Schoenbergs presented to him. They had staked him to an atelier in Paris, to the
editorship of an art magazine and to a drawing school, and, after
all of these, when he had stubbornly reduced himself a third
time to destitution, they had granted him a small pension on
condition that he marry his pregnant model, who, for all her
seeming Bohemianism, had turned out to be the daughter of a
Bronx rabbi. So Jesse, in the end, was able to curse his rich
relations for making him a middle-class conformist as well as an
economic slave.

Jay was apt to think of his mother, who had died early and
agonizingly of breast cancer, as seated at her dressing table in
their small apartment on Riverside Drive. She had been a
rather lugubriously pretty woman, with big strong features and
lank blond hair, who had seemed able to spend an unbelievable
number of hours patting ointments and unguents into her skin
with long, dexterous fingers. She was agreeable, but lazy and *dis-
traite;* she would have liked to be taken into the Schoenberg

milieu, but not enough to work to overcome their prejudice that she was "common." She had to make do, poor tepid creature, with the mirror, with matinées, with the talky friendships of women who had no more in common than the apartment building in which they desperately coexisted. Who else was there? Her husband's bad temper and general misanthropy had cut her off from such young friends as she once had had. She died as she had lived, with that surprising indifference to boredom and nonfulfillment that must be nature's anodyne to the pain of living pointlessly amid the towers of Manhattan.

Jay was fifteen at the time. An only child, he had been able to do pretty much what he wanted, for his father, whether from motives of vanity or simply to keep him out of the studio, had given him an allowance that enabled him to outspend all but the wealthiest boys in his class at public school. He made himself the leader of a small, mobile gang that covered the city on afternoons and weekends, experts in subway routes, parks and zoos, but at the time of his mother's death the boys were already restive under his leadership, tending, with new discoveries in themselves, to be less adventuresome, to want to spend more of their time whistling in movie houses or stealing in the side doors of burlesque shows. Jay, in his turn, was beginning to find them tiresome. If he proposed now to explore the marshes of Great South Bay on a Saturday or to slip past the pier gates of the Hudson to watch the ocean liners docking, he had to do so alone or with tamer companions. So when he learned that the great Mrs. Peter Schoenberg, whom his father was always mocking but whom he knew his mother had secretly admired, manifested concern with his lonely plight and asked him to spend a summer with her family in Connecticut, he nagged old Jesse until he was allowed to go.

The big place in Stamford fixed in Jay's mind for a long time to come his conception not only of how the rich lived, but of how they ought to. The house was a long, rambling Norman manor with high eaves and narrow windows, filled with dark, carved Renaissance furniture and precious objects that gleamed in the dusk. In the daytime the family lived outside, gathered about the ever-clear, sapphire pool, or playing tennis on the red, raked dirt court, or passionate croquet on the most level of green lawns fringed by a leafy wood. At night there was always a dinner party; the gloomy interior was lit up, and the peerless Monets and Manets of Mr. Schoenberg's collection glowed under beams from concealed bulbs in the ceiling. Yet the atmosphere was never formal. Florence Schoenberg saw to that. She was a beautiful woman, with a long, gentle, melancholy face, blue-gray hair and blue eyes, eyes, indeed, as sapphire as her swimming pool. She was highly civic and intellectual, yet as gentle as her face implied, and inexhaustibly kind. To the constant disgust of her robust and very Schoenberg sons and daughters — direct, unsubtle, vigorous children, some years older than Jay — she collected lame ducks, and on her house parties there was always a young man or woman to fiddle, to play the horn, to dance, to sing, to do something beautiful, who with just the *least* bit of encouragement, perhaps the least bit of a loan, was going to do it more beautifully than anyone could imagine.

Yet she was no fool. She understood some of the problems of this prematurely and precariously independent young cousin, this brash, impertinent, undersized and over-active adolescent with the impossible clothes, whom the rest of her family deplored on sight. She proposed to send Jay to boarding school in the fall, and she went to work herself to teach him to play tennis and to introduce him to music. They listened to records and read Shakespeare aloud in the evening, sometimes joined by the other children who grudgingly accepted Jay, once they had recognized that their gentle but ineluctably determined mother was taking him on as a permanent project.

How Jay always remembered that low, musical voice!

"These things must become necessities to you, Jay, as they are to me. Handel, Bach, Mozart, Shakespeare and Keats. They are not harmful dopes. If they're taken away, you can live on the memory. People say that art has taken the place of religion in my family. Our orthodox friends are particularly critical. Yet I gladly confess it. Peter has joined the Ethical Culture Society, but I am nothing. Nothing but Bach and Shakespeare. If that's a romantic heresy, then I am romantically heretical."

Jay's brief suspicion, his fear of being patronized, were gone, or at least gone where she was concerned. He had large wet handfuls of hostility left for her critical family and snooty servants. But Cousin Florence! He swept aside the atheism that had been his father's only contribution to his instruction and built her a shrine in the troubled forum of his boyhood jealousies. He became her page, her knight-errant, garbing his aggressiveness toward others in the officiousness of his service to her. Cousin Florence was not fooled.

"Remember, dear boy," she warned him. "Sir Walter Raleigh flung his own cloak over the puddle before Queen Bess. He didn't tear off someone else's."

But Jay rather fancied the situation where he would have only to worship, obey and love a single other human being. By promoting that human being to godship, he could solve all questions of personal humiliation, and toward the rest of mankind he was still able to preserve the enameled defiance of his cheeky smile. "Sure, I'll play," he made his suspicious, mocking green eyes say, "but don't think I'm not on to you. Don't think I'm not watching!" The two Schoenberg boys, exasperated by his attitude, once gave him a thorough thrashing, but he won their respect by not reporting it to their mother. This was pure calculation. Jay had guessed that sooner or later the girls, always at odds with their brothers, would report his beating to Cousin Florence. When this happened, as he had predicted, he got credit both for his maltreatment and his silence.

Cousin Florence's decision to send Jay to Pulver Academy,

largest of the New England boys' boarding schools, brought the final break with his now aging father. Grumpy and suffering from a failing liver, Jesse drove out to Stamford and talked to his son on the terrace while Cousin Florence, her blue-gray head visible in the greenhouse window, pretended to be working over her pots.

"It is the final degradation," Jesse exclaimed solemnly. "The final bathos in the long, unseemly scramble from the ghettos of Germany to the pews of the Episcopal Church."

"Pulver is not a church school," Jay pointed out.

"Of course not, it can't afford to be. It has too many Catholic and Jewish grandparents whose feelings must not be violated. We need the nondenominational school as a step between the Irish parish priest and the bearded rabbi, on one side, and the sanitary sanctimoniousness of the Protestant bishop on the other. Pulver, my boy, is a tub where we wash the dirt of the European emigrant from our feet!"

But Jay was not impressed. At sixteen he knew perfectly well that his father's philosophy had no sounder basis than an envious hatred of the family which Cousin Florence had graced by her marriage.

"You've always sneered at the Jewish religion. Why do you care if I go to a non-Jewish school?"

"I've always sneered at *all* religions!" the old man shouted. "I haven't brought you up a free soul to have Florence Schoenberg turn you into an ass-kissing, plate-passing vestryman!"

"You haven't really brought me up at all," Jay retorted. "And I shall certainly do whatever Cousin Florence asks me. Even if it's to become a Jehovah's Witness!"

At this the old man broke down and wept. After some minutes of this, while Jay looked coldly on, he roused himself to the grandeur of a paternal curse. In later years Jay was to realize that his father must have been groping into the past for the aid of some prophetic, denunciatory tradition. But at the time he could not see any reason to feel sorry for him, and he was simply surprised, when Cousin Florence at last joined them, that she made such a fuss over the silly old windbag. After Jesse had departed, cursing her in turn for her pains, she tried to explain to Jay that, however indifferent a father might seem, he still had a spot in his heart that a child could hit and hurt, and that no parent could so totally forfeit the respect that was due him as to merit such a blow. Jay did not contradict her, for that was not his way with Cousin Florence. Anyway, it hardly mattered. His father died less than a month thereafter.

Here again Cousin Florence, and all the Schoenbergs with her, behaved very oddly. They acted as if they actually cared. A man like his father, apparently, could curse and drink and borrow his way through sixty-five years of a totally useless life, neglecting his wife and son, supported by charitable relatives, a mere pimple on the patient skin of the universe, and yet, if his wails were loud enough, if his self-pity had enough eloquence, his family would try to find a dignity in his protests that had some dramatic relation to the dignity and agony of man. And what was more, it was vitally important for everyone in that family to go along with any such effort. Jay learned within a day after his father's death that the Schoenbergs would forgive him anything but the open admission that he had never loved his father. And why should he make such an admission? A solemn face, after all, was as easy to put on as a black tie. Grown-ups really asked very little of one.

His own contemporaries asked a bit more. At Pulver Academy, in the autumn, he found himself, for the first time, in an environment on which he seemed unable to make any kind of impression. It was not that he was lonely or homesick or badly treated. It was simply that instead of being one boy he found himself a unit of twelve hundred in a big, clean, healthy organization that seemed to exist for the sake of being organized. He made his first acquaintance with the sports-worship of an all-male community, with the domination of handsome, athletic boys and with anti-Semitism.

The boy in the adjoining cubicle told him that his family had had to sell their home on Long Island because the neighborhood had "gone Jewish." Yet there was no animosity in the boy's tone, nor did he seem in the least to know or care that Jay might take his remark personally. The boy's family had merely moved away as they might have moved if a highway had been built too near their land or if the house next door had become a funeral parlor. But Jay also observed that a good 10 percent of the boys in the school were of Jewish origin, and that many came of families which had changed their names. He saw quickly of what gossamer qualities prejudice was made up and understood that only a perverse loyalty could stand in the way of one's easily getting around it. At the same time, however, he saw that he was committed to this loyalty, for Cousin Florence, though a renegade to Jewish orthodoxy, remained devoted to her Jewish origins and would never even give a house party without a certain minimum of Jewish guests. Jay supposed that she was misguided in this, but he was perfectly clear that while she lived and supported him he would be guided by her misguidance.

All that fall he studied the school carefully to determine how best to cope with it. He was too small to hope for athletic preeminence and not sufficiently of an academic persuasion to put in the time needed for top marks. He lacked the looks and personality for real popularity, in the "Pulver" sense, though with his easy bantering and his store of big city knowledge he obtained the respect of less sophisticated boys. He decided at last to try for the school literary magazine, and he obtained a small campus distinction with a short story about bootleggers and New York cops which he pretended to have based on "inside" information.

The Christmas and spring vacations he spent at Stamford where he continued to manifest, to all but Cousin Florence, the distrust that sprang from his fear of being patronized. With the boys and girls of the neighborhood he was cocky, wise cracking, never truly at ease. As at school he had partners — in sports, in expeditions, in story-swappings — but no intimates. His mask of "cheek," like his gaudy ties and sports coats, was so habitual as to have become a part of his personality. Yet he rarely felt lonely, for he believed that his lot was the common lot of man. He never, for example, considered that other boys' friendships were deeper than his own, or that "love" was a term to describe more than a tepid affinity. His feeling for Cousin Florence, of course, was different, but then Cousin Florence was different. He was only sorry that she would not accept his worship of her for the unique thing that it was.

"Jay, dear boy, you're too standoffish with the world. Particularly with people who try to do things for you. You act as if you were afraid that the least expression of gratitude would compromise you."

"I'm always grateful to *you,* Cousin Florence. I owe you everything in the world. I'm not ashamed to acknowledge that."

"To me, no. You're perfect with me. I have no complaints. But you have made an exception for me. Oh, I see that! I *like* it, it's true. You're my faithful hound. But that is vanity in me, as it is evasion in you. You have still the world to face. You may become disillusioned with me . . ."

"Never!"

"Or I may die, then. You must not put all the eggs of your human charity in one basket. You must love other people, too."

He threw himself on his knees and plunged his head on her lap. If she said nothing, if she so much as touched his hair with her fingers, it would be the sign that she had given in, that she would allow him to love her in his own way. But she did no such thing, and he knew in his sorry heart that she was stronger and more truly Cousin Florence for not doing so.

"Get up, you silly boy," she said. But at least she dropped the subject.

In the spring Jay made a serious effort for campus distinction. He submitted a story for the Prize Day issue of the school magazine that he had tried to make striking enough to win him an editorship for the following year. It was a departure from his usual fantasies of underworld life in the wicked city, a pastoral idyll of the sort popular in the early depression years, dealing with a farmer's wife in the Middle West who had to support a family of eight after the death of her husband in a haying accident. Jay had made up for his lack of experience by cribbing extensively from a story of Kansas farm life that he had discovered in an old bound volume of the *Century Magazine*.

The decision to do this had caused him no great difficulty. He assumed that detection was virtually impossible and told himself that he was doing no more than Shakespeare had done with Plutarch and Holinshed. And, more importantly, the whole business of stories and magazines struck him as simply another school sport, another game. One would be a noodle not to play it as it was played.

But was it worth playing at all? Was it worth taking even the tiniest risk for so small a thing as an editorship, which carried little enough real prestige in a school that was so heavily oriented to athletics? Jay had now to recognize that he had grown fond of the school and wanted to leave more than just the simple imprint of his name in its archives. In the long summer that followed there came over him an unfamiliar softening, an unaccountable "mushiness." He went much to the movies alone. He met a girl whom he liked a bit more than the ones with whom he had drunk filched whiskey and necked in Cousin Florence's garage attic. He made a friend of the Schoenbergs' superintendent's son who penetrated his crust of jokes and show-off and walked with him on Sunday afternoons by the river where they discussed sex and the choice of careers. It all seemed to amount to nothing less than the discovery that what had once appeared the foolish conceits of the poets in English class actually corresponded to an inner truth, that the heart offered joy as well as the eyes and lips, that his sexual energy was a force not necessarily confined to giggles and gropes in attics, but one that permeated all of life and gave color to girls, to friendship, even to ambition.

His story of farm life had been accepted, and Jay started his second and final year at Pulver with respectability, if not with glory, as an editor of the school paper. And then, against the unbelievable golds and reds of a perfect New England fall day, the gently opening doors of his new earthly paradise slammed shut forever.

A telegram warned him that Cousin Florence was driving up to lunch with him on a weekday, sufficient indication of a crisis, and he waited anxiously on the porch of the deserted Parents' House for her sky-blue Packard town car to appear. When it did and came to a stop, she hopped quickly out and, taking Jay's elbow, propelled him down the road beyond hearing distance of the chauffeur. It was like her not to wait a single minute for her bad news, which was this: an old bachelor cousin of the Schoenbergs', a devotee of the literary lost and found columns, had spotted the origin of the Kansas story which Jay's proud patroness had left by his bedside on a weekend visit at Stamford. Dazed and silent, Jay made out what Cousin Florence now expected of him. It was nothing less than a full confession to the editor-in-chief of the school magazine.

"If I do that, can I leave school?"

"Dear boy, it's only a question of holding out until spring, and then you'll graduate and go to Columbia, and all this horrid business will be forgotten."

"I couldn't take it. Please, Cousin Florence, I'll do anything you ask, but let me leave school. I can tutor for college. I can get a job."

The sadness in her beautiful blue eyes was painful to behold, even for him, even then. "Why did you do it, Jay?"

He shrugged. "I wanted to get on the board."

"But didn't you know it was *wrong?*"

"Sure. I guess so."

"No, Jay, that won't do." Gently she made him turn about and face her, a hand on each of his shoulders. "That won't do at all. I want to know if you understand that you have done a dishonorable thing. If you *really* understand that and are sorry, then I don't care a fig for anything else. It's only the future that matters. There isn't any point being alive, Jay, unless you're straight. Life is too short to be shabby."

"Oh, Cousin Florence," he protested with a sudden sob. "It's impossible to be like you!"

And then he wept freely as they walked arm in arm down the dirt road. Never had he more felt, in their very closeness, that she was more angel than mortal. He saw that he himself was made of shabby stuff, base alloy to her white gold, and he wept with a relieving resignation at the fine fullness of this new guilt. Now he could proceed to fabricate the tale of his motivation with composure in his heart, because he had a consoling feeling that it might be truer, after all, than he thought, that it might indeed *be* true, that nothing was ever irretrievably beyond redemption, that passion might give a gloss even to the past.

"I couldn't bear not to be anything at school!" he wailed. "After all you'd done for me! Taking me in and making me practically a member of your family over everybody's objections. Who else has ever given a tinker's damn about me? And after you'd gone to all that trouble and expense — flying in the face of Cousin Peter and your own children — what sort of figure would you cut with them if I ended up at Pulver not being a monitor or a member of the football team or even with a first in any subject? Think how they'd sneer at you! No, I wasn't going to have it. I tell you, I wasn't! If I had it to do over again, I would."

Perhaps the most wonderful thing of all about Cousin Florence was that she didn't believe him. Not a word of it! What would have been the point of a goddess who was taken in so easily by a piece of clay? Her greatness lay precisely in her being able to recognize the compliment in the lie. She saw it because she, too, had a glimpse of the beauty that *might* be, in a world of men, as it existed around them in the autumnal world of nature.

"Your motive doesn't make a smitch of difference," she said firmly. "There isn't anything in the world that would justify taking another man's story and passing it off as your own. The thing was bad, bad in itself. Admit it, get rid of it, and there's an end to it. I'm sorry about your humiliation, and if it's too much for you to stay in school afterwards, I'll take you out. But what you must do now is go to your editor-in-chief and make a clean breast of it. Now. This very afternoon. Then we'll see what can be done about picking up the pieces."

"But Cousin Florence, if you only *knew* . . ."

"It doesn't make any difference, Jay, what I know or don't know," she continued remorselessly. "Any more than it matters whether I would find it harder to confess than you. There are still some things in the twentieth century that are simple, and one of them is how to correct a shabby thing. Whether it's painful or not cannot matter. What must be done is clear. Do you agree?"

"I suppose so."

"And will you do it?"

"If you say so."

"But, Jay, I *do* say so."

As soon as he had promised, Cousin Florence dropped the subject, and they returned to the Parents' House for lunch. With the totality of her understanding and sympathy, she knew when not to hammer a hammered nail, and she chattered about family matters with a gentle continuity that required no response on his part. After the meal she did not remind him by so much as a hint of what he had to do. She simply kissed him on the cheek, a rare gesture with her, even for her own children, and stepped quickly into the blue car. Always afterwards he was to remember the little trusting shake of her hand from the window as she drove off.

One hour later her life was extinguished by a traveling salesman who, having been up all the previous night, fell asleep at the wheel of his car, crossed the dividing line of the parkway and collided with the Schoenberg Packard at a combined speed of one hundred twenty miles-per-hour. Even at that, death for all parties was not instantaneous, and Jay was long to be haunted by the vision, conjured up nightly in his anguished mind, of Cousin Florence, half-conscious and faintly moaning, laid out on the side of the road. His grief was very terrible, because in the first glut of his sorrow, when he was contemplating, with the natural human underside of pleasure, the pitifulness of being alone in the world, he suddenly realized that it was true. Then his tears were sincere and passionate; they were all for himself.

He went to Stamford for the funeral, and the family on the whole were very decent to him. Nobody seemed to know that Cousin Florence had had a special reason for going up to Pulver, so the fussy old bachelor cousin must have either forgotten the schoolboy's plagiarism or deemed it too trivial to mention. Only Elias Schoenberg, the family lawyer, a dry, grudging man of multiple nasal and throat noises and baggy suits, seemed overtly hostile. He had never made any secret of his conviction that Jay, like his father before him, was a sly opportunist, and, interviewing him alone in Cousin Peter's study after the service, he seemed, by the very loudness and insolence of his respiratory sounds, to be trying to drive Jay into repudiating the family generosity.

"I must tell you at once that Florence made no provision for you in her will." Here, a deafening throat-clearing. "Not, of course, that she was under any obligation to do so. After all, she had, in addition to her own posterity, a host of closer relations." Here, a stertorous catching for breath. "But nonetheless it was the consensus of the family meeting held yesterday that she had planned to add a legacy to you in the next testament that she should execute. Poor soul, she could hardly see that she would never have the occasion!" Here, a deep booming cough. "We have a note of hers to indicate that she was considering a legacy in the neighborhood of ten thousand dollars. A pretty good sum, you will admit, for a boy of your age. Eh, what, sir? Eh, *what?*"

Jay pursed his lips tightly shut lest the smallest involuntary noise should escape to be counted assent by the enemy.

"Well, sir, I tell you what. Your Cousin Peter intends to make good that legacy. What do you say to *that?*"

Tighter than ever were the lips pressed.

"No comment, eh? You understand, of course, that the family are under no legal obligation to do this? Nor even a moral one, as Florence's intent was far from clear. No word of gratitude, young man?"

"Pardon me, sir. I shall be glad to express my gratitude to Cousin Peter. Why should I express it to you, when I take it you opposed this 'generosity'?"

Elias Schoenberg eyed the young man before him now with something like respect. His final cough was like the last culminating burst of fireworks on a Fourth of July entertainment.

"No, sir, I did not oppose it. Nor did I oppose the further family resolution to pay for your college education. I believe, sir, that we Schoenbergs must look after our own!"

Jay left the room without a word. It would have been a magnificent gesture to fling the generosity of the Schoenbergs back in the teeth of their appointed representative, but he could see already that it was going to be a very long time before he could afford such gestures. Nonetheless, he learned that day that a life where one could not afford to make them might be a life of drudgery.

Back at Pulver he resigned from the board of the Literary Magazine, giving as a reason his need to devote the whole winter to preparing for the college entrance examinations. He explained to the surprised and indignant editor-in-chief that he owed this industry to his late patroness. He almost persuaded himself that the ghost of Cousin Florence was satisfied.

But what if it wasn't? What could Cousin Florence do for him now? Jay, lying awake in his cubicle at night with damp eyes, did not console himself or frighten himself with thoughts of her hovering spirit. He did not believe in spirits. He believed that Cousin Florence, goddess though she had been, was now quite nonexistent. She had left him in a world where he would very definitely have to fend for himself. It was not up to her — now a nothing, a beloved nothing — to tell him how this should be done.

The Schoenbergs also would be nothing to him now. He would have no family, certainly not a Jewish one. In the fall, when he had satisfied himself, by talking again to Cousin Elias, that the money for his tuition would not be prejudiced by his act, he enrolled as a freshman in Columbia under the name of Livingston.

6

At Columbia Jay's personality underwent a considerable change. Now that being alone in the world had become a fact as well as a pose, he dropped his old defiance in favor of an attitude of dogged conciliation. He went out of his way to meet the prominent members of his class; he pursued them about the campus, always ready with a joke or a funny story or a bit of college gossip, for the moment when he had their attention. He cultivated his professors as well, asking questions, sometimes officiously, in class and afterwards, calling at their offices and even at their homes. His bright, persistent presence became a kind of trademark of his class. He was laughed at, even sneered at, but he was not ignored, nor was he really disliked. His sharpest critics had to admit that there was a tough, rubbery quality about Jay, quite inconsistent with obsequiousness. He could be snubbed but he could never be crushed.

And, after all, was his attitude not basically complimentary? What, really, was wrong with his determination to squeeze the last drop out of the orange of Columbia? Was that not what they were all there for? His classmates did not have to know his motivations. They did not, for example, need to know that he had selected an English major for its social opportunities, having noted the affinity of the better fraternities for Shelley and Keats. As Jay had little inner preference among the subjects, it hardly mattered which he picked. Biology, history, economics, art: he was competent in all, brilliant in none. He could like

Rembrandt's "Polish Rider" or Tennyson's *The Princess* or Plutarch's *Lives* well enough, but he relegated them entirely to these college years, with little or no carry-over for the future. In this he differed from the bulk of his class only in that the act of relegation was a conscious one. Jay had a very definite concept of his world, and he was bored by those who found it a mystery.

Where college *did* have a post-graduate value, in his eyes, was in the opportunity of useful friendships. So long as one started from nothing, one might as well aim high, and in sophomore year the particular threesome to which he aspired to engraft himself, as a kind of urban d'Artagnan, was that of Hilary Knowles, Martin Shallcross and John Grau. Grau, a surly, industrious youth, whose bleak gaze seemed to bar even the friendliest approach, was not much of a magnet, but the other two represented everything that Jay thought that he wanted in social life. Knowles was a big, handsome, laughing fellow who was popular with everyone and seemed to like everyone, and Shallcross, if smaller and soberer, came of an old and distinguished New York family that Jay imagined capable of dispensing a financial or political fortune to any young man who happened to please them. It was through this scion that he decided to "crack" the trio.

Martin Shallcross might have been playing the average student in an educational film designed to promote college life. He took notes conscientiously in class; he was polite, if formal, to everybody; he had the right flannels and pipe for a seminar and the right white shorts and spotless sneakers for squash. Yet there was a detachment in his air of patience, a veiled suspicion in his attitude of faint exasperation, that was attractive to Jay. He made a point of tagging after Martin when he found him alone and occasionally succeeded in lunching with him in the cafeteria. Martin had none of John Grau's hostility or of Hilary Knowles' not quite sincere over-friendliness. He appeared to accept Jay with a total lack of snobbishness that at the same time committed him to nothing. When they talked of their futures, Martin was frank and cynical.

"You hear a lot of chatter of what you're supposed to contribute in life," he told Jay. "I get it here, and I get it at home. Yet what does it all add up to? My old man is a lawyer, and a successful one, but he's made his reputation defending a parcel of pretty shady characters. When I point this out, he makes the obvious rebuttal that every man is entitled to counsel. No doubt. Garbage must be disposed of, but we don't urge our brightest youths to go into the Department of Sanitation. My mother's family, on the other hand, love to boast of their long tradition in the textile business. But what, basically, have they accomplished but buy from the Scots and sell to the Jews? Conceding that it took a bit of talent to squeeze a living out of *that* transaction, where is the basic 'contribution'? No, when it's profit you're after, why go about it the hard way? I intend to be a stockbroker, my friend. It is a profession that is devoid of hypocrisy. One attempts to make the most money with the least work. It is clean. It is pure. It is without cant."

Jay was impressed. For a young man to talk in that way of the stock market in the late 1930s was unusual. It was still, with the nation's youth, a discredited organization. But he wished that Martin would be more personal in his talk. Although the latter spoke freely, almost intimately, of himself and his family, Jay suspected that he would have spoken with equal freedom to any other classmate. And it was perhaps not without significance that he never once asked Jay about *his* family or *his* future.

When he discovered that Martin was having a birthday party at the old family homestead in Queens, he decided that the time had come to make his first serious effort to achieve his goal. He told him that he would be in the neighborhood of Shallcross Manor that afternoon and asked if he might drop in to drink a birthday toast. Martin was surprised, but he did not allow his surprise to be offensive.

"Come in at cocktail time," he said. "I'm having some people for dinner, but I'm afraid we've reached Ma's capacity. However, there's always plenty of gin."

So it was that Jay had his first vision of Shallcross Manor, and he was dazzled. The people, old and young, who gathered on the terrace and lawn, seemed to him to have the easy, aristocratic grace of characters in a novel about the ante-bellum South. The Judge, so distinguished looking, was splendidly benign; his wife was vaguely gracious, mistily affable; the young guests seemed entirely at ease with the older generation. Inside the house, the dignity of the perfectly polished, impeccably cushioned, quaintly ugly mid-Victorian furniture gave him a museum-like sense of the restraint and decorum of an earlier New York. True, things had been very much more splendid at the Schoenbergs', but theirs had been a glinting darkness, a heavy opulence, a noisiness that seemed vulgar in retrospect. The Schoenberg men were inclined to shout in argument and to laugh boisterously, and for all their cultivation and self-importance they had never fully escaped the tyranny of the bandied wisecrack. Furthermore, they were full of enthusiasm. Jay now felt that his very enthusiasm for the lack of enthusiasm in the Shallcross milieu betrayed his own closeness to a rather smelly soil. Would a decade of cold showers and huge, soft, old-fashioned towels make him as fresh and cool as the Judge? Jay did not have to remind himself that Shallcrosses were inherently no better than Schoenbergs; he knew that human beings were basically the same. But it was the stage-set that mattered, and Martin's father was a master designer!

Alas, their manners were no better than the Schoenbergs', and, of course, he deserved what he got. He had pushed his way into the party, and he was treated accordingly. Martin nodded pleasantly enough, but Martin was busy being host. Hilary was the center of a laughing group, and John Grau was absorbed with the Judge. Mrs. Shallcross called him "Mr. Livinsky," betraying the label which covered his image in the bland area of her mind. But it was Elly Shallcross, the older daughter and spoiled beauty of the house, who gave him the worst time.

When he took his timid stand before her, she deigned to chat, but in the cool, mocking tone of the popular girl who has no intention of being monopolized by lesser guests. She addressed him solely in his capacity of brother's classmate, as if for her he could have no other, and asked, obviously without expecting an answer, if he were as "lazy and party-loving" as Martin and Hilary. When he started to comment, she interrupted to state flatly that men's education was a farce and moved abruptly off. In her high, bold, superior manner, she had seemed intent on demonstrating to him that she was not in the least afraid of snubbing him, that his social inferiority laid no claim to her sympathy, that her truer sense of democracy entitled her to select her companions with no regard for their need — no matter how humbly shown — of herself.

Jay was obliged in the end to content himself with the company of Sophie, her thirteen-year-old sister, plump, pigtailed and perfectly pleased to talk to any man, who dragged him to a sofa and told him about her school course in American history. Did he know that Benjamin Harrision was the only president to become a father *after* he had left the White House? Poor Sophie, her company was worse than none, for her exclamations made people turn, and they saw to what he was reduced. When he had taken his leave of Mrs. Shallcross, he suffered the final humiliation of hearing her say to the guest departing immediately after him : "Oh, do stay for supper, please! There's *heaps* of food."

Back in his room on Morningside Heights he passed a desolate evening. He even wondered if a weaker man might not have committed suicide. Another sophomore had shot himself the week before in the cellar of that same dormitory. Who knew if the dead youth's anguish had been anything greater than loneli-

ness followed by a snub? Yet Jay knew even then that his hold
on life was much too tight to be loosened by any number of
Shallcrosses. What had happened that afternoon was simply another example of the tiresome monotony of life. It was like the
plot of *A Midsummer Night's Dream,* one character pursuing another who in turn was pursuing a third. There were men, after
all, at Columbia who sought *his* friendship and whom *he* was
careful enough to avoid. Did he expect Martin Shallcross or Hilary Knowles to be any different? Once in a lifetime there might
be such a thing as reciprocation, as when Cousin Florence had
loved him. It might come again; who knew? In the meantime
there was still a world to be conquered. For Jay, in his very
lowest moments, never lost sight of the fact that the Shallcross
world *could* be conquered. He was even shrewd enough to see
that in the long run it might not be a very difficult matter.
When he went to bed, he did the only thing a man in his
position could do. He made brutal fantasy love to Elly Shallcross.

Not long after the Shallcross party Jay received an invitation
to supper from a family that *did* want to know him. They were
the Robert Isaacsons, his mother's brother and sister-in-law.
They lived with their daughter Hulda in Queens where his
uncle owned a number of tenements, and their apartment, large
and dark and bare, with brown matted walls and sparse, expensive department store furniture, bespoke a moderate prosperity.
Jay was glad, after all, to have some sort of family, for the
Schoenbergs had dropped him altogether with his change of
name, and he saw — as his sonless uncle intended him to see —
that a business opening might be in the offing. It took only a
month to establish the habit of his going regularly to the Isaacsons' on Saturday nights.

Uncle Bobbie supplied Jay with his first vision of the dedi-
cated, middle-class American businessman. He was appallingly
dry. Outside of his small real estate domain and an occasional

baseball game, he had no interest in life other than to sit for an evening in his shirt-sleeves sipping beer and listening to comic programs on the radio. He loved to relate how, on his only trip to Europe, he had looked in vain for the scrubbed, boxlike comfort of the Miami hotel that was his sole idea of luxury. He was bored by his wife and bored by his daughter, but it never occurred to him that any other relationship was possible with the women of one's family. Indeed, it never occured to him that he was missing anything in life at all — except a son.

Aunt Tessie was even drearier to Jay than her husband, for she lacked the redeeming feature of a comparable interest in her nephew. She was totally concerned with the comforts of her large white placid body and the occasional problems of her housekeeping. Her discourse was apt to deal with the drop in quality between the object in the shop window and the object in the purchaser's hand, between the respectful maid in the employment agency and the sullen slut in one's kitchen. But nothing surprised her, nothing excited her, and, like her husband, she considered herself and her reactions, or lack thereof, as fair samples of the tiny world that she inhabited. Jay paid as little attention to her as she to him, and they got on well enough.

In Hulda, alone of the family, there was a spark. She was of a dark complexion with a full figure, rapidly and fatally verging on the stocky, with roving, suspicious black eyes and a certain magnificence of manner. She was the kind of woman whose period of sexual attractiveness lasts hardly more than a year, and that year was already over, though not long over, when Jay met her. She was bright but lazy, critical but disoriented, yearning for love but so fearful of rejection that she was immediately rude to any man who was even passingly polite. Her parents were afraid of her, and she, a philosophy major at Hunter College, scorned their intellectual poverty. She had few girl friends, for those who managed to break through her barriers were clutched so fiercely to her bosom that they only wanted to get away again.

Hulda, passionately proud, was constantly humiliated by her anticipation of humiliation.

She sized up Jay quickly and shrewdly, torn between the jealousy aroused by her father's obvious, if tepidly demonstrated partiality and the pleasure of having a weekly male visitor. She saw that he was out to get what he could from her parents and that marriage would be the condition that her father would stipulate before taking him into the business. Determined to make it plain from the outset that she would not go along with any such bargain, she took a high tone with her cousin and sneered at what she considered his intellectual pretensions. She pointed out that men went to college only to get degrees and that the English majors at Columbia were all philistines at heart. Jay would retort that she was a bluestocking, that women took to books only when they couldn't find husbands and that as a wife (were she ever to become one) she would have to learn to conceal most of what she had learned. But even when she lost her temper, he never lost his. He always managed to keep smiling that maddening smile, even when he uttered or received insults, and Hulda went to bed every Saturday night, angrily convinced that she had managed once more to make a fool of herself. Yet she could never resolve to be absent when he came.

Painfully and reluctantly, with much sobbing in pillows and ranting at her image in the bathroom mirror, fighting herself futilely every bit of the short way, gulping down the hard morsel of her awareness of how easily she had fitted into her father's cynical plan for her future, she came at last to accept her violent attraction to this bright-eyed, compulsively smiling young man. And yet he had not taken her out on a single date! He had not, by so much as a wink, given her the excuse to regard their relationship as other than that of cousins! Another in her position might have considered it a mercy that her state was not officially known to the uncommitted male. But Hulda did not care a fig for official knowledge. She knew well enough that Jay knew what he had done to her! She knew that he knew that he had only to reach out to pluck, and hers was the final bitterness of knowing that he would not until he had to! She was almost relieved when the war intervened to take him away.

It did not at first take him very far. Uncle Bobbie had unexpected connections and got him a commission as ensign in the Navy Supply Corps in Brooklyn. Jay was inclined at first to regard this as a satisfactory berth. The more active war was certainly not going to do anything for Jay Livingston except possibly kill him. As the months passed, however, and as the first victories began to be recorded, it struck him that he might be passing up a good deal of excitement, maybe even some glory, for a very small amount of risk. He was at least as thrilled by the news of American advances in the Pacific as he had been by nineteenth-century English poetry. So he applied for sea duty, and despite the vigorous resistance of the old disbursing captain to whom he had made himself indispensable, he was assigned as supply officer to an LST Flotilla Commander in Plymouth, England, six months before the Normandy landings.

Jay now had the joy of discovering for the first time in his life what he could do with human beings. The flotilla staff and the officers of its amphibious vessels provided a perfect little seminar for the study of that post-war world that was already beginning to loom before him. They had too much of everything, too much food, too many guns, too many men, too many orders for the simple job of carrying tanks and troops across the Channel. They lived, in consequence, as true American bureaucrats, in constant friction with each other and in constant fear of paper. Jay, who had learned in the Navy Yard to thread his way through bulky official mail and to plumb the mysteries of supply depots, who knew just which forms were read at headquarters and which were ignored, became the gray eminence of the flotilla staff and the right hand of the grateful but naïve Commander. He was sent on missions to London and to the various units of the groups which, properly speaking, should have been entrusted only to a line officer. He got a fierce little kick out of the expression of shock and irritation that he would catch in the eyes of the sleepy LST skipper whom he awakened on an early call as they took in the oak leaf on his collar. It was a satisfying tribute, in a hierarchical world, to what a bit of ingenuity could accomplish.

Yet he never forgot that this was only one side of war. There was also death, about which there was no point thinking, and there was also glory. Glory was "The Battle Hymn of the Republic"; it was bugles and trumpets; it was parade. It was not worth much, but it was worth something. Everything was worth something, and for one ineffable moment on the beaches of Normandy he thought that it was going to be his.

It happened two weeks after the invasion, on an early evening at low tide when a dozen of the flotilla's LSTs were sitting, like the stranded corpses of whales, high and dry up on the beach. Jay was on the bridge of the LST A-31, the messiest and least disciplined of the flotilla and a constant headache to the staff, delivering a reprimand from the Commander to the officer-of-the-deck, when, way down the beach, unbelievably low over the ground, hardly more than a hundred yards up, he spotted a German bomber moving toward them. A glance at the deck showed him that the guns were unmanned. General quarters would be too late. Dashing to a 20-mm. he spun it around to aim it at the oncoming bomber and started firing. It was a moment of choking ecstasy. It seemed impossible to miss that black, lumbering, clumsy mass which came straight at him, very slowly, yet rapidly enlarging to monster size, and he had a vision of heroism so intense that there was a biting, snapping pain in his loins. Then in his roaring ears, over the deafening retort of the gun, he heard the even louder roar of the plane's engines, and he became so tense that he thought he must vomit. But the big plane simply smashed its way through the evening air above him as it made its contemptuous way down the beach, out of sight, not even bothering to waste a bomb on the emptied sea trucks sitting helpless on the sand below. And Jay, falling to his knees by the gun, burst into bitter tears of anguish and humiliation. He knew at once that if he lived into the hell of Armageddon itself he would never have such another chance to become a legend.

*

After the war, a thinner, more disciplined Jay Livingston went to work for his uncle. He did not smile so much, but he smiled when needed. He had learned in Europe what he could do; he looked back on the war years as the last chapter of his practical education. And the job was a good one. Isaacson was no great landlord, but he owned a couple of good corners and a whole street on the eastern border of Queens which had possibilities. It was obvious to anyone who looked about him that the swelling populace was going to need every square inch of the city's five boroughs. So long as a man had a start and a sharp eye, there was no excuse for him not to do well.

Within a year he had won his first major struggle with his boss-uncle. Rent control was depriving Isaacson of three-quarters of the income on his land. To lick it, the buildings had to be razed or modernized; to accomplish this they had to be emptied of holdover lessees. Jay proceeded to make himself an expert in the methods of inducing stubborn tenants to go elsewhere. He learned just how far they could be pushed. It was a kind of stagecraft. He studied the art of pesky bell ringing, of noisy party giving, of simulating muggings in corridors, of creating the impression (sometimes more than that) of dope rings and prostitution in the immediate neighborhood. When he started putting these courses into practice, his uncle objected violently, and Jay took a firm stand.

"Look, Uncle Bobbie. This is a question of survival. Either you give me a free hand or I quit. You can write me any memoranda you want about how lawfully the buildings are to be run. They'll be your evidence if there is any trouble. I'll take the rap."

Uncle Bobbie was unhappy about it, but he went along. In truth, he did not know what else to do. In two years time Jay had cleared out every holdover. There were appeals to the police, appeals to courts, but he won them all. His strategy was foolproof. When his uncle saw the profits he was dazzled. He took in his brilliant nephew as an equal partner, except that now there could no longer be any true equality. The one who had been passive in the risk-taking would eventually be passive in everything.

Jay was not much troubled by what he had to do. He did not mind the heat, and he had no intention of getting out of the kitchen. Occasionally there was a genuine hardship case among the evictions, and this was regrettable, but he had taken sides with the future, and this was the way the future would be brought about. He could see nothing sacred in legislation that he deemed obviously unconstitutional, passed by what he considered political hacks at the beck and call of pressure groups. The masses had to be moved into new housing; the shabby old crumbling city had to be rebuilt. The world was divided into two sorts: the men who got things done and those who obstructed them. Sometimes the latter were successful; sometimes they even put the former in jail. But the moral issues were largely illusory.

"You think there's no beauty in Isaacson Oval," he told his cousin Hulda one night when she had sneered at the plans of a small, three-story apartment house development that he and her father were backing. "But that's because there's no beauty to you in cheap, obvious utility. To me there is."

"Even your ivory tower is made of plastic!"

Time had improved neither Hulda's temper nor her looks. She was stouter and moodier and blamed her old maidhood on the loss of a "betrothed" in the war, a story which nobody believed, based, as it purported to be, on a passing flirtation with a neighborhood boy who had been drowned in a transport. She still hankered after Jay and still abominated him. When her father at last yielded nominal as well as actual control of the firm to his nephew, she, too, had reached the point of surrender. She agreed to go along with the offered terms which included herself. Jay had to marry her. But it was the very last thing that he ever had to do for the Isaacsons.

They lived together for six months, without a single happy day. He had no illusions; she had had the desperate one that he might learn to care for a shrew. When she heard of his first infidelity — or what she supposed was his first — she made a halfhearted attempt to stab him with a kitchen knife, and he returned her to her parents. There she continued to live for years, stubbornly refusing him a divorce, except on ruinous financial terms, and banking the large allowance that she exacted of him. Jay, to the consternation of the neighborhood, blandly continued his habit of supping on Sunday nights with the Isaacsons, and the curious myth, so brazen that it came ultimately to be almost believed, was circulated that Hulda lived at home because her husband "traveled."

Jay found the arrangement perfectly satisfactory. He had no wish to be any more married than he was. He knew that he had given the Isaacsons more than they had had any right to expect. He had made them rich and married their daughter. It was hardly *his* fault that he had had to supplant his uncle to save him from bankruptcy and to leave his wife to save her from manslaughter. Humanity continued to be made up of the loving and the loath, but this gave the latter no special duty toward the former.

Hulda, on those stiff Sunday nights, would stare across the table at him like a brooding Cassandra.

"I should love to see you get your comeuppance," she would

mutter again and again. "But how does a man ever get *that* unless he cares about something?"

Yet Jay cared about lots of things. He cared about his business and all the new businesses that he hoped to go into. He cared about the working out of seemingly insoluble corporate problems. He cared about his girl friends, that long succession of compliant creatures who were difficult only at the break-off. He cared about dancing and baseball and theater. He cared about his automobiles, his clothes, his parties in the big bare penthouse over the East River hung with the most fashionable Tamayos, Klines and Rothkos. He cared about painting and playing the flute. He cared about being in control of his destiny. There was always the danger of boredom, of course, but boredom could usually be avoided by distraction and movement. It was not always easy, but life was not easy.

When he had first run into Martin Shallcross again, on a small housing deal underwritten by Thaddeus Kay & Sons, he had felt nothing but a mild surprise that this plodding customer's man should ever have impressed him. He had looked back to his sophomore year when he had been so dazzled by Shallcross Manor and Elly Shallcross as to what must have been a time of jejune susceptibility. He had assumed that he must have been taken in by some tricky appearance of decayed aristocracy. So it was more kindness than nostalgia that induced him to take Martin out to lunch to discuss their old days at Columbia. He had even given him a couple of brokerage orders.

And then he had learned a few things. He had learned that Martin was much more than an ordinary customer's man, that he had the shrewdest kind of business nose. And that his sister Elly, with the instinct of self-preservation so often found in the females of old families, had married none other than Thaddeus Kay himself. The Shallcrosses were in fact in 1959 what they had simply seemed in 1939! Jay found that he was very glad indeed to be asked back to the Queens manor house for dinner.

Judge Shallcross, seeming not a day older, a reward of the prematurely white, was as pleasantly waspish as ever, and his wife as serenely unconcerned. Jay was even amused when she once again called him "Mr. Livinsky."

After dinner, which had been on a warm fall night, with only Martin and his parents present, Martin had taken Jay outside for a stroll over the lawn to the water's edge while they smoked their cigars. When he then first broached the idea of the sale of Shallcross Manor, Jay found that he was actually shocked. There seemed to be no getting away from the fact that he had fallen in love with the farce of those old white columns a second time in what he liked to consider a sophisticated lifetime.

7

Sophie, at last, had what her mother called a "beau" and what her father, always at war with modern slang, referred to with icy scorn as a "steady." When Jay picked her up in the evening, he would swing his cream-colored Cadillac into the narrow drive of Shallcross Manor, come to a shuddering stop by the front door and blast away with his horn. He considered this a permissible liberty because the sound was meant to be pleasing, being a duplication of Siegfried's challenge to Fafner. But this only made the Judge more furious. "Impertinent jackanapes!" he would cry. "Does he think the place is already his? Siegfried, my eye! If he's got to be a character in the *Ring*, why not Mime!" And Sophie would rush to the front door to forestall a second tooting, and off they would speed for an evening in Manhattan where Jay had the magical touch in tables and tickets and garages. It sometimes seemed to her that he could make the Cadillac disappear with one clap of his hands and reappear with another. Always before them, over the heads of surly, waiting queues, seemed to be hovering the raised hands of waiters, ushers, guards, beckoning them to come around corners, to use special doors, to slip past prohibiting velvet cords. To Jay the means of night life were almost more diverting than the ends.

Sophie was in a fearfully agitated frame of mind, determined to eradicate from her thinking every last trace of her family's prejudiced conception of Jay. What she had to keep brightly in the forefront of all her fancies was the hard little nugget of a fact that Jay, and Jay alone, was saving Shallcross Manor. It was all very well for her parents to talk and shake their heads, like Christian Romans of the late Empire, about heathen barbarians, but when it came to the point, who was the person who was saving the monastery with all its treasures which *they* had surrendered without a blow? Oh, yes, Sophie knew well enough what to think of the Shallcrosses. What she had to bring herself now to accept was the crudeness as well as the generosity of this new world that she was trying to see as brave. She had plenty of proof that the past was mean. What had she to risk in building her faith in the future?

Indeed, it seemed the only salvation. She could not hope to find in any new apartment that her family might take, surrounded by familiar faces in which she was disillusioned, the new inspiration that she needed for living. If she were not to retreat again to Dr. Damon, if she were not to live in idle memories and idler dreams of Hilary, it was certainly high time (the *highest* kind of time!) to find something new. And what was more indicated than this friendly, cheeky new friend, this taker-for-granted of everything that she had always been terrified even to *think* about, this rusher-in ahead of inhibited angels, this man who so flatteringly assumed that she was just another girl?

Was that presumptuous of her? Was it presumptuous to think of herself as a girl, a date, a steady, even as the wife (oh!) of a man whom her father would as soon welcome into the family as an adder fanged? Even allowing for the absurdity of parental prejudices, even rating Jay as high as he rated himself, wasn't she still, in sober fact, good enough for him?

God, what a nervous life!

Happily, he was so easy to talk to that their "dates" (well, that *was* what he called them!) were the easiest part of the relationship. One night at the theater, in a little dark bar where they had gone for an entr'acte drink (he did things like that, which Shallcrosses never did, not even leaving their seats) she got up the courage to ask him about Hulda.

"Are you and she ever going to get a divorce?"

"How can we?" he demanded. "Hulda's too greedy. She figures that the gift of her fair white body was worth a million bucks! And her price goes up as her looks go down."

"I should think you'd pay it to be rid of her."

"I haven't got it, Sophie."

"But everyone says you're so rich!"

"All my capital is working, and Hulda wants cash. Why should I want a divorce, anyway?"

"Well, don't you want to be free to marry again? Don't you ever want to have children?"

"Do *you?*"

"I suppose so," Sophie replied faintly.

"Well, you'd better get started," he said with a crude laugh. "You don't have as much time as I do."

Sophie at this silently prayed that it was time to go back to the theater. But Jay continued to sit there, twirling his brandy glass by the stem.

"Or is it me you're thinking of marrying?" he suggested.

"No!"

"Why should you want to marry me?" he continued with relentless playfulness. "Wouldn't you have hell to pay with your family?"

"I doubt it," she said, turning away from him with sudden bitterness. "They'd be only too glad to get rid of me."

"Well, that's fair warning!" he exclaimed. Then he actually had the impudence to put his hand on her chin and turn her face. "No, seriously, Sophie, why shouldn't we marry? Didn't I suggest it the first time we met?"

"Don't be absurd," she muttered, getting down from the stool. "And let's go. It must be curtain time."

"I suppose it would be one way to get back what I was stuck for Shallcross Manor," he joked, following her to the door.

Sophie hoped that they were through with the subject, at least for that evening, but she was wrong. When he had driven her home after the play, he stopped his car a hundred yards down the road from Shallcross Manor.

"What are you doing?" she demanded.

"I want to give my fiancée a proper good night kiss."

"Hadn't *my* fiancé better get rid of his wife first?"

"Now, Sophie." He shook his head and frowned. "I don't care for that bold, sarcastic tone. I believe a girl should act shy when a man wants to give her a kiss. A *nice* good night kiss."

And when he had given her just that, he promptly started up his car and drove her to her door. Upstairs in her room, sitting by the window and staring up at the full moon, with tears in her eyes, Sophie tried to make out what was happening to her.

Was it not shocking to be kissing and talking about marriage with a man whom she didn't love and who almost surely didn't love her? What were they like but two people who had met at a marriage bureau, exploring each other? And yet, who was she to be proud? Didn't thousands mate that way? And hadn't she been rather titillated by that kiss?

But, oh, what a sorry thing it was to be thinking of mating when one had once dreamed of love! Hilary, Hilary! She thought of the terrible night of the picnic and the bottle of *vin rosé* and reflected with a hot shame that she had told the whole miserable story to Jay on their very first meeting.

Yet what had there been to tell? It was not that she had really said anything to Hilary after the *vin rosé*. It might almost have been better if she had. She had simply drunk too much and giggled too much and sat too close to him and allowed her hand to touch his and looked at him damply and then . . . oh, God of Gods! The *look* that Hilary had given her! It had been hardly more than a glance, really — it couldn't have lasted more than a second, and then he had resumed his eternal laughing, but the import had been unmistakable. He had reacted as if she had been . . . his sister. That look, for that second — and in such matters it might as well have been an eternity —

had seemed to brand her with the stigma of incest. It had made no difference that for the rest of the evening Hilary's intensification of solicitude, brought on by her deep drop to somberness, had been a form of apology, quite possibly sincere, for the imputation. It had only made things worse.

The morning after her theater evening with Jay she felt too low to go to his office to work on the model of Shallcross Manor. It was almost finished anyway. She stayed home all day, feeling wretched, and by the time he telephoned to ask if she was all right, she was so lonely and grateful that she agreed to have dinner with him.

In the restaurant Jay put on his business frown. "There's something I want to talk to you about. I want you to tell me about Hilary Knowles."

"Why?" she demanded in instant alarm. "Why does Hilary interest you?"

"Because he's the roadblock between you and me."

"No more than your wife!"

"With Hulda it's only a matter of price. With Hilary it's a question of sentiment."

"Oh, sentiment." Sophie shrugged, restless, embarrassed. "Yes, I suppose there's some sentiment there, but what does it matter? Hilary couldn't care less. Let's not talk about him."

"How can we avoid him? He seems to be the key to everything. Why didn't he ever care for a pretty girl like you? Is he a homo?"

"Certainly not!" she cried indignantly. "Why, Hilary's even been married!"

"Does that make him a stud? Who was his wife? A New York girl? Old family?"

"Oh, no, the very opposite. Some blowsy, sexy type. Hilary met her in the Canal Zone, when he was in the Navy during the war. She trapped him into it."

"You mean it was a shotgun wedding?"

"Except she only pretended to be pregnant!"

"How shocking!"

"And his poor old parents had to pay a monstrous sum to buy her off."

"Well, it was probably their fault, anyway. Isn't that what the analysts say? Tell me about his literary ability."

"Oh, he's top notch!" Sophie, aware at last that he was laughing at her, still warmed to this worthier theme. "His *Reading Shakespeare in College* has become a standard text. The only trouble is that he's too much a perfectionist. Do you know he wrote a whole book on his theory of Shakespeare's sonnets and bought it back from the publisher after it was actually printed just because he'd changed his mind about one date? How many people do you know who'd do that?"

"None," Jay conceded with a chuckle. "What a funny couple you and I make, Sophie. You with your Hilary and I with my Hulda. You with your torch and I with my wet blanket. But we get on, that's the great thing. And it makes sense, too, damn it. Isn't that how marriages have been arranged through the centuries?"

"But by parents," she protested feebly.

"Well, I don't have any, and yours don't care, so we have to do the job ourselves! But that doesn't mean I'm forcing myself, I *like* you, Sophie, I . . . ."

"Please, Jay!" she cried. "You must give me *time!*" She raised her hands to her cheeks in dismay at his suddenly darkened expression. "That's all I need, maybe, but I *do* need that. Give me time."

"Sure, honey," he replied with a shrug. "All the time you want."

She thought he would not kiss her that night when he took her home, but he did. He gave her a kiss on the lips, a long and very wet one, hugging her with both his arms, bearlike, about her neck. For a moment she had the sensation that he, for all his jaunty independence, needed her. Then, abruptly, he bid her good night, not even getting out of the car, perhaps ashamed at having betrayed, even for a second, that he cared at all. It was obvious that any development in their relationship was a matter that he felt concerned only himself.

And supposing it were true? Supposing he decided, after all, to marry her, what should she do? Tell him she couldn't love him? Everything they had both said seemed to imply that love was at least irrelevant, perhaps actually indelicate. On the night of their first kiss she had dreamed that she *had* married him and had awakened in panic. For the terrifying thing about this odd new friend, this jack-in-the-box lover, this uncongenial, congenial companion, was that he fitted into no experience she had ever had. It was as if he had bought her when he had bought the house, an educated but still essentially useless slave, a Greek acquired by a barbarian. If he wanted to put her to some use, was he not the only man in the world who did? And was he not, far from being a dream, only too much a reality? Surely, her past was the dream; surely the boys and girls who had picnicked by the Narrows and under the George Washington Bridge were the dream; sure, Hilary himself, dear, maddening Hilary, was the dream. If reality proposed to her, how in the name of Freud and all his cohorts could she find the way to say no? She could only pray that reality would never ask her, and, running into the house, she prayed very hard that it would not.

*

The next day she went shopping in Manhattan with her mother. The Shallcrosses had now rented an apartment in Elly Kay's building, and many things had to be purchased for the impending move. Sophie, who took little interest in this, trailed idly behind her busy parent, nodding automatic assents to questions about samples, and she was relieved when it was over, and they had to go to Elly's for tea before returning to Queens. For it was unthinkable that Marian Shallcross should spend a whole day in the same borough with her older daughter without making a call.

Every day, it seemed, was Elly Kay's *"jour."* She was always in between five and seven, and there were always half a dozen callers in the long parlor that looked, as Sophie had once told Hilary, as a French eighteenth-century salon might have looked had it had the advantages of Elly's passion for wax and varnish. Elly herself, as impeccable as her chamber, now gingerly presented a cheek to be pecked by her mother and sister.

"What absolute darlings you are to drop in! But I'm afraid it's a dull day for callers. Sophie, my dear, what have you done to yourself? You look simply stunning! Having a beau seems to agree with you. I wish you'd brought him. Ma, you should have made her!"

Sophie flushed. "If it's Jay you're referring to, I doubt if he'd get on with your set."

"Don't be so sure. We're not living back in Grandpa Chalmers' day, you know. Everyone's on his own in my little group. We're cosmopolitans. Keep up to date, Sophie! Prejudice has become vulgar."

Sophie turned away from that walled stare and soothing tone. It was impossible to tell when Elly was trying to be kind, for one doubted if she knew herself. Elly was always crouching, suspicious and defensive, behind the bolted grill of her beauty.

"You might at least be civil," her mother hissed in Sophie's ear. "Elly always makes such a fuss over you, and you treat her like a beggar in the street!"

"I hope I'm nicer to beggars!"

Marian Shallcross hurried back to Elly, and Sophie went to sit by herself on the sofa and smoke the last of her quota of cigarettes for the day. As she did so, she saw Hilary Knowles in the doorway.

She decided at once with a pang of remorse — for it seemed

somehow disloyal to poor Jay — that he looked wonderfully handsome and distinguished in his dark suit and claret-colored tie. His thick, brown, gray-streaked hair rose over his scalp like a musician's, but his high white brow and large fine nose helped to restore the initial impression of patrician discipline. Hilary always entered a party with mild gravity; his first greetings were formal and restrained. Only later, among his friends, did he become vivacious and give vent to his noisy but contagious laugh. Then his whole exterior seemed to crack into lines of friendliness.

She tried to harden her heart, making a wager with herself that he would seek out the most important person in the room, but he came directly over to her.

"I understand you're trying to save the manor house."

"I'm doing my best."

"Do you really think it can be done? I believe in letting things die a natural death when their time comes."

"That's easy enough with other peoples' things."

Hilary looked more astonished than hurt. "Why, Sophie, what's eating you? You know I love Shallcross Manor!"

"Enough to let it die."

"Well, I can't go along with this modern theory of making public toilets out of old libraries and laundromats out of abandoned churches. They become poor shells of their old selves. Like grand duchesses working in beauty salons."

"But shells can be important architecturally," Sophie corrected him. "Your theory would consign our whole past to the bulldozer!"

"It's true," he conceded, shrugging. "I'm a hopeless romantic. I can't compromise. When Shallcross Manor ceases to be a symbol of gracious living, I turn away from it. I don't want any part of a Livingstonized version . . ." He stopped himself. "But I shouldn't say that, should I? You and Jay have become great pals, we hear."

"Partners, anyway," she said, and despised herself for evasiveness.

"Of course, he's the future."

"So everyone says."

"Unless he's the present," he continued, looking at her more searchingly. "Is he *your* present, Sophie?"

But Sophie found she could not bear to answer his question or even to brush it off. Deliberately, with a visible effort, she changed the topic. "Have you done any more work on the sonnets?"

He threw up his hands. "God no! When I got to the point where I was waking up in the middle of the night trying to make out what Shakespeare had meant by the mortal moon's eclipse, I decided to quit. Who in this world of bulldozers, as you put it, cares whether it refers to the death of Elizabeth or the Lopez conspiracy or even the defeat of the Armada?"

"Lots of people!" she exclaimed. "There's a tremendous interest in Shakespeare today."

"Oh, Shakespeare on the stage, yes. Noise and trumpets." Hilary shrugged again. "Lustiness. Vigor. Modern parallels. All that crap. I want him in his own century or not at all."

"You live in the past."

"Care to join me there?"

And then, suddenly, inevitably, as they looked at each other, almost seriously, he had to make a joke. "Come on in. The water's fine." At the same time he laughed. Oh God, Sophie 'iought with a clutch of panic at her heart, would there ever be : ı end to his laughing? She had a vision of Hilary in a box, a l ndsome grinning jade figure in a teakwood box, with a sliding panel for a cover, stuffed to the bursting point with cotton to keep the jade from cracking. And what was the cotton but laughter, suffocating, insulating, life-denying laughter?

"Oh, Hilary, you must always be joking!" she cried with a near sob.

"No doubt Jay is more serious," he retorted with sudden sharpness. "That's the modern note, isn't it?"

But Sophie, weary of combat, was simply relieved when she saw her sister approaching to carry him off.

*

In the back of the old Packard town car, moving slowly north in the evening traffic to the Triborough Bridge, Marian Shallcross glanced at the brooding countenance of her younger daughter. It was always difficult to tell whether Sophie's silences invited some comment that Sophie might wish to rebut or simply invited further silence.

"I still don't see why you had to jump on Elly so," Marian observed. "She was only trying to be nice."

"She was only trying to be odious! Talking that way about Jay!"

"I suppose Mr. Livingston must be an interesting man."

Sophie said nothing.

"Martin seems perfectly devoted to him," her mother continued.

"He makes it worth Martin's while. As a matter of fact, he makes it worth *all* your whiles."

"Do you suggest that's why I find him interesting?"

"Well, isn't it?"

"You may as well give it up, Sophie. You're not going to catch me in an anti-Semitic remark."

"Why don't you come out with it, then? Why don't you say you don't mind a Jew who's proud of being a Jew?"

"Why on earth should I say that?"

"Because you all sneer at Jay for changing his name!"

"Not I. As a matter of fact, I think it most appropriate. So many of them are called Livingston now, it's really almost a Jewish name."

Sophie's laugh was shrill. "Ma, you're peerless! I suppose you wouldn't mind if he called himself Shallcross?"

"I shouldn't mind in the least. As a matter of fact, if you marry him, I think he'd better. Your father would much prefer to have his grandchildren partial Shallcrosses to bogus Livingstons."

"Who's talking about marriage, for God's sake?" Sophie cried in a strangled tone. "Really, Ma, what's got *into* you today?"

"I'm trying to be modern, my dear. As long as you tell me nothing about yourself, you leave me to my own speculations. After all, a mother can't help but be interested."

With this the silence between them was resumed, and Marian settled back to one of her favorite reveries. It was the one she assigned to her daily drive in the old Packard; to other parts of the day were given other fragments of her childhood. The automobile was naturally associated with the black, musty Victoria in which her Grandmother Chalmers had taken her driving on Newport afternoons. They would start on Washington Street where the Chalmers house, a Gothic edifice, had faced the harbor, and trot slowly out to Lands End and back along the ocean. Wars and fashions had no effect on Mrs. Chalmers. Small, smiling, soft, huddled in black with a widow's cap, giving forth biblical quotations and kitchen recipes, kind, impersonal, consigning the heart to an ordered mourning for perhaps forgotten loves and the mind to the routine of domestic habits, she had treated the present as she must have treated the 1850s. Even when, as a young woman, Marian had gone up to Newport to take the drive and tell the old lady of her engagement, the vision of Eben Shallcross had been absorbed, all but obliterated, on that gently rocking ride.

Later that night, sitting before her dressing table, looking into the mirror held in a tall mahogany frame, Marian observed her husband as he sat in bed with a brief.

"Sophie's going to marry that man."

She saw his lips automatically framing the question: "What

man?" Then he saw that she was watching him and gave it up.

"What makes you think so?"

"A woman's intuition."

"Do you mean to imply that she can actually *love* him?"

"What does that matter? She's at the end of her rope."

"My daughter!" he exclaimed, giving way to sudden wrath. "So much at the end of her rope that she'll marry a climbing little realtor parading under a false name! Why, he's even married!"

"He needn't be, next week."

Eben lifted his eyes to the ceiling in mocking appeal to her Presbyterian deity. "What about his being a Jew?"

"Well, he's not really, is he? He's nothing. Anyway, everyone marries them now."

"If your father could hear you! I remember his saying that he'd as soon see his daughter in her coffin as married to a Hebrew!"

"Well, he also used to say there was some question about the Shallcrosses. Wasn't your great-grandmother a Miss Rosen?"

Eben sat up in bed now to thunder at her image in the mirror. "God, woman, everything about you is superficial, even your prejudices! What did the son of a Scotch weaver like your father know about New York society? The Rosens were Junkers!"

But Marian had long been immune to his dramatics. "You can't put yourself in the shoes of a girl who's over thirty and unmarried," she said. "I certainly make no claim that Mr. Livingston is a catch, but I suggest *you* find us a better. You've always gone on about Sophie being your darling. Let's see what you'll do for her now!"

Saying which, and dropping an abrupt curtain on the stage of her husband's forensics, she rose and strode past him to her closet. She was glad of the little train on her velvet evening dress which gave an added emphasis to the totality of her rejection of his pleas.

8

THE SPECULATION about Sophie's possible engagement to the vandal of Shallcross Manor came as a shock to everybody outside the family, but to Hilary Knowles the effect was devastating. He had not really believed it possible. Ever since her nervous breakdown, three years before, he had cherished the idea that she would one day be his wife, that he and she would ultimately convert their near sibling intimacy into that long-delayed, last-chapter sacrament so popular in the Victorian fiction of which he was an addict. Eben Shallcross, with his accustomed acerbity, had chosen not to leave him in ignorance of the role which he had played, albeit unconsciously, in Sophie's collapse, and Hilary, stricken, had secretly postulated this marriage as an atonement for his stupidity in not sooner divining her feelings. But was it not also the obvious solution to his own emotional aimlessness? By the end of Sophie's term in the sanatorium this image of an ailing sweetheart who would one day be restored to health by love had become his principal fantasy. Then, suddenly, she had emerged, and all of his old caution had reasserted itself. But *had* it been just his old caution? Might it not have been also the fear of unduly exciting a convalescent? And then, before he had thought it really proper so much as to press her hand with amical warmth, the horrid news had crashed in upon him of her rumored attachment to Livingston.

He was in such a state that he had to go back to Leo Silverman, who had supposedly completed his psychoanalysis the year before. Stretched out again on that drearily familiar green couch, looking bleakly up at the faded chromolithograph of Battery Park, Hilary felt something akin to panic at the idea that medicine could do no more for him, and panic made him sententious.

"Of course, it's nobody's fault but my own. I realize that. I've lost Sophie the way I've lost everything else in my life by waiting too long. And now, as my fortieth birthday approaches — on heavy robot feet — I can't help wondering if my only accomplishment in life won't be a handful of elegant phrases and a few *bons mots* wasted on fools." He paused, but there was only silence from the desk behind him. "Do you hear me, Leo?"

"Of course, I hear you. What's elegant about 'robot feet'?"

"Well, there you are," Hilary said gloomily. "Even my language has become banal. How could a man be a greater flop?"

"What about your *Reading Shakespeare?*"

"What about it?"

"How many men write a standard college text before they're thirty?"

"Maybe I burnt myself out." But Hilary was gratified, even though he deplored Leo's own articles for medical journals on the neuroses of Shakespeare's heroes. An analyst was like a mother; even his crassest reassurance had its function. "Maybe I was a one-book man, and my mission is over."

"You don't believe that."

"*You* don't, I know," Hilary came back at him. "You believe I could write anything I wanted. An analyst has to believe that. But what you *don't* believe is that I really love Sophie."

"Now, Hilary."

"You don't, Leo! You think it's all wishful thinking. You think it's all staginess and romanticism. And maybe originally it was. But I tell you, now it's different! There's no mistaking the real thing when it happens to you. I haven't been sleeping at night. I've been hugging my pillow and weeping aloud. Oh, it's

been shameful! I know all about the satisfactions of self-pity —
who better? — but I tell you this has been different. This has
been . . ." Here he raised himself suddenly up on the couch
and jerked his head around to catch Silverman in the act of fill-
ing in a space in the *Times* crossword puzzle. "If you think I'm
going to pay for this hour, Leo, you have another think coming."

"I'm sorry. It was the word 'staginess.' It gave me the clue to a
five-letter word for 'catafalque.' "

"I'm glad somebody's getting something out of this session."

"You're awfully touchy this morning. Suppose we discuss
why?"

"Because I know you're sick and tired of hearing about me
and Sophie again. No doubt you'd rather talk about the
'bard.' "

"Oh, speaking of that, did I send you my piece on Hamlet's
procrastination?"

Before Hilary could retort that Leo spared his patients nothing, the telephone rang, and Silverman conversed at length with
another doctor about a patient who had attempted suicide. In
the days of his regular visits Hilary had bitterly resented these
interruptions. He had seen no reason why Silverman should
chat, even in an emergency, on *his* time. But now he was glad of
the respite to look over his synopsis of the conclusions drawn
from his old analysis which he had written out to submit to Silverman. He had hoped it might help in the present crisis.

His parents, of course, had done the initial damage. Parents
always did. They had been too old, too dear, too soft, too high-
minded (a legal scholar and a poetess!) for an only son, born
after twenty years of a childless union. Hilary had been mortified from the beginning by their cackling adoration, their summoning of friends to view his every progress, their smothering
osculations. As a boy and as a youth he had been actually embarrassed by his own physique and virility that had seemed to

justify their tedious extravagances. But for every minute of concealed boredom and resentment he had paid another of sweating
guilt over his imagined ingratitude. He had given up boarding
school and summer camp to stay home with the old couple; he
had chosen Columbia over Yale because they had lived on
Morningside Heights; he had even stood by while his father had
used pull in the Navy Department to get him a desk job in intel-
ligence. For his mother, a pacifist, had persuaded him that his
death at sea would be fatal to them. They would have richly
deserved it!

After that, everything had fitted into its vengeful psychiatric
order. In the Canal Zone he had been made to suffer the exquisite torture of watching from a front-row desk the transit of his
shipborne friends to an area of combat which had proved fatal
to some of the closest. Deprived, by his sentimentality, perhaps
by his cowardice, of the chance to prove his manhood among
men and guns, he had sought in despair to prove it among
women and bottles. This period had ended in the affair with
the blonde daughter of the Zone engineer who had gone to the
Admiral himself with her shrill tale of seduction. He had been
ordered to the altar, in the interests of Navy-Canal Zone relationships, and his final humiliation had been the revelation that
his mocking bride was no more pregnant than he. After the war
his parents had had to pay half their principal to buy her off.
When they had died, within a year of each other, leaving him
all the poor remnants of their little fortune, he had wondered if
he had not killed them, after all. But had they not asked for it?
Had they . . . ?

"What did you think of it?" Silverman had finished telephoning at last. "Of the Hamlet piece, I mean?"

Hilary had to search his mind for a moment until he recalled
it. "How can I think anything about it," he asked, a bit testily,
"when I can't even concede its basic premise?"

"You mean that Hamlet procrastinates?"

"Well, when does he? He has to check on the ghost's story, doesn't he? And the first chance he has to do that is the play scene. Then he strikes. But he strikes the wrong man and gets shipped off to England. His next chance to kill the king doesn't come till the duel scene, when he does it! How could he have acted any faster?"

"What about the time he passes the king at prayers? When he says: 'Now might I do it pat!'?"

"Killing the king is only part of the job. He has to damn him, too. He does the same thing to Rosencrantz and Guildenstern. You might even say it's an obsession with Hamlet. He says he can think of no greater horror than the prospect of seeing one of his foes in heaven."

"What becomes of your hero then? He's a monster!"

"Elizabethan heroes are often monsters. Don't be a Victorian sentimentalist!"

"What about the ghost then?" Silverman insisted. "Doesn't he speak to Hamlet of 'your almost blunted purpose'?"

"Well, of course! The ghost can hardly be expected to be pleased with the time Hamlet wastes checking *his* story."

"Anyway, you can't deny that Hamlet regarded himself as a procrastinator."

"I don't. But that doesn't make him one. What he really is is a botcher. He checks on a story that turns out to be perfectly true and then kills the wrong man. But it's hardly procrastination."

"All right, then, what *is* the play about?"

"Anything you want!"

"And what do *you* want?"

"I suggest, Leo, that we get back to Hilary Knowles and his neuroses."

"But we're right with them!" the doctor exclaimed.

Hilary was struck by this. He settled back on the couch and thought for a minute as he stared at the Battery print. "There may be something in what you say, Leo. We live in a world that can survive only by forgetting. Who cares that Gertrude has remarried? Or that she enjoys sexual intercourse with her brother-in-law? Or that Claudius is a usurper? Isn't that all status quo? Isn't the king a perfectly good king? The Poloniuses and Osrics of this world don't want any black crow of a stepson haunting the feast with all his horrid memories and suspicions, turning over stones and looking for skeletons in closets. Why can't he leave well enough alone? And, indeed, when he *does* set things to rights, isn't it at the price of a general holocaust? Doesn't it result in the crown passing to a traditional enemy? Some help! The Osrics are perfectly right. They're as right in 1960 as they were in Elsinore. Who but Hilary Knowles cares that Jay Livingston started his career as a blockbuster? Old Shallcross himself would give Sophie away to him. Yes, Leo, I am Hamlet! I dine out, in the highest society, with ex-bootleggers and ex-call girls, and I alone remember!"

"But you don't have to kill anyone, do you?"

"Ah, of course, there you have me," Hilary retorted bitterly. "I am not, as Eliot says, Prince Hamlet. I am an attendant lord, a jester. I suggest we get back to my free association."

He took a deep breath and made an effort to relax. He adopted his old discipline of imagining his mind as a white screen and waited for an image to appear. Almost at once it did. The big, bland countenance of Leo Silverman filled his screen like a grinning Buddha. Another long silence elapsed.

"What are you thinking about?" Leo asked.

"I was thinking what a pitiful knowledge of Shakespeare you had."

"Go on, go on. Get it off your chest."

"And what a big nose you have."

"And how plain I am. And how Jewish."

"And how like a Jew to use my time to get material for your silly Shakespeare articles!"

"That's not fair, Hilary."

"Oh, of course, it isn't." Hilary jumped up from the couch and came over to sit opposite the chosen arbiter of his psyche. "But look here, Leo. Man to man and not patient to analyst. I *do* have a criticism of you. A real criticism, not just a fantasy one. I think you're part of the whole rotten society we live in — like Ophelia and Laertes and Guildenstern and all the rest. Because you're perfectly willing to accept me as I am!"

"And what is that?"

"A half-man! A driveling dilettante who goes to too many parties and makes half-love to bored matrons! I think you're basically immoral. You ought to be encouraging me to be a man and lead a man's life!"

"I don't care about men and men's lives. I care about you leading your life."

"Well, that's going to be marrying Sophie!"

"Fine!"

"But you're not working with me."

"I'm not working toward any specific goal, Hilary, no. I'm simply working to make you free to choose it — *if* it's what you really want."

Hilary got up again impatiently to walk to the end of the green office. "You're so slippery," he protested. "You can skip responsibility for anything. All you want is for me to be myself. But what 'myself' is you don't care. That's why I say you're immoral. You don't care if I have affairs with married women. You wouldn't even care if I had affairs with boys. As a matter of fact, I think you might prefer that. You might think it's more my type!"

"Look, Hilary, all I want . . ."

"Shut up! I tell you, I'm going to marry Sophie!"

"I'm delighted to hear it."

"No, you're not! You don't believe it. You don't really believe I love her at all. You think I just want to see myself as a romantic, and that the longer Sophie isn't available, the happier I'll be. But you're wrong!"

"Indeed I would be. If I believed those things."

"Oh, go to hell. You always have to have the last word. But you'll see. I'm going to marry Sophie and live happily ever after!"

"Hilary . . ."

"Sorry, my hour is up. If I stay another minute you'll probably charge me for two. Besides, I'm sure some sex-starved society bunny with an impotent millionaire husband is rubbing her hot pants against that closed door right now!"

"Which reminds me. You may know the next patient. Would you mind using the side door and leaving the office the back way?"

Hilary hurried out the side door and through the back corridor to the street. He then almost ran around to Dr. Silverman's main door, on Park Avenue, and opened it just in time to see Elly Kay disappearing into the green office. He scandalized the receptionist by his loud hoot of laughter.

In a booth on Madison Avenue he telephoned Sophie at Jay's office.

"I want to see you!" he exclaimed. "I want to see you today. How about lunch or dinner?"

"I'm afraid I'm having lunch with Daddy. And I'm going out tonight."

"With Livingston?"

"Really, Hilary. I hardly see that's your business."

"What else is my business? Look, Sophie, *please* let me see you. I'll meet you downstairs in your building for a cup of coffee. In fifteen minutes. Okay?"

When she met him in the lobby at the appointed time, she said that she did not want coffee, and they walked instead to Central Park. Sophie was silent and severe, but apparently willing to give him the time he wanted. In the park, they sat on a bench; it was a warm November day. As he talked, she kept plunging her hand into her coat pocket and pulling out small pieces of bread. One by one she tossed these to the clucking pigeons. Her expression was grave but perfectly calm; it was comprehending but not committed. Never had she seemed lovelier to him.

"You can't marry that man, Sophie. You just can't, that's all. And don't tell me you're not thinking of it, because no woman goes out with a man without thinking of it. The whole thing is ludicrous. Preposterous! He wants the respectability of a Shall-cross alliance, and you're simply scared of being an old maid. You think you're never going to do any better. But you are!" Sophie still said nothing. She did not even look at him, but simply threw more bread to the now dense carpet of clucking pigeons at her feet. "Damn it all, Sophie, forget those birds, will you?" He got up and stamped his feet until the pigeons, angry but hardly scared, waddled a little way off. "I'm telling you something important!" Then he sat down again in rather lame conclusion, and the pigeons returned.

"Have you finished?" she asked.

"I suppose so."

"May I talk now?"

"Please."

"You must remember, Hilary, that two people are involved in this. Two people, I mean, besides Jay. There's me, as well as you. You are thinking of your duty as an old family friend. That duty is to warn me. Very well. But what about *me?* Three years ago I was very deeply involved with you. We have never discussed that, but, of course, you know all about it. It took me a long time to get over what happened then — small though it may have seemed to you — and I cannot afford to go through it again. Life is a question of alternatives, and I do not know at the moment what my alternative is to Jay. Now perhaps you are going to offer yourself. But if that is so, please, Hilary, my dear friend, look before you leap. Be sure you know your own mind. Don't sacrifice yourself for the honor of the Shallcrosses. Don't play with me. Don't practice with me." She had now turned very white. "For I can't stand it, Hilary! And if you're *not* going to offer yourself, for God's sake don't be a dog in the manger!"

He felt the small, hateful, caressing little waves of fear eddying out from his heart to move, like saucy fingertips, across his epidermis. The whole day seemed to be suddenly darkening, as if a big, suffocating cloud had been pushed into the face of the pale sun. How had he the gall, with all his deficiencies, with all his hysterical self-doubts, to sit on a bench like two-and-twenty and raise false expectations in the heart of this injured, trusting girl? Was she not right? And Silverman right? None of them, none of his friends, expected him to be any more than Hilary Knowles, the good friend, the laughing friend, even more seriously, the kind friend. Was it not the devil himself, like Hamlet's ghost, that tempted him to the disaster of a fabricated love? The groan bursting from his heart seemed so loud that he was surprised that he could not actually hear it. For what was she saying but that she *would* love him? And what was that but the last, the very last hope of his life?

"Oh, Sophie, Sophie," he moaned.

"You see what I mean, Hilary. I'm going to take a walk now. By myself."

He watched her figure in the gray coat until it disappeared behind one of the red brick buildings on the outskirts of the zoo. Then he suddenly sobbed aloud, to the scandalization of an English nanny who rose from the neighboring bench with a "Well, I really!" and pushed her perambulator irately past him.

9

MARTIN SHALLCROSS was a rather jaundiced guest at the farewell party for Shallcross Manor. As the engineer of its dissolution, any tears that he might have shed would have been bound to be termed a crocodile's. Sophie had tried to persuade their parents to make it as gay an occasion as possible and to strike, as much as they could, the note of the future. She had set up in the middle of the front hall, so that no arriving guest should miss it, the model of the housing development that showed the proposed new role of the ancestral home, and she had insisted upon champagne and an accordionist. Some hundred Shallcross friends, including many of Elly Kay's smart crowd, now moved through the downstairs rooms to congratulate the Judge and his wife for saving a landmark.

Martin could hear his father holding forth to a little group of men, mostly fellow members of the bar, of whom John Grau, the youngest partner of MacManus & Shallcross, was an obviously dissenting unit.

"Don't talk to me about lawyers' ethics," Eben was saying. "They don't exist any more, not as the word was used when I was young. How could they? With legislation as complicated as it is and our ineffable high court always on the alert to muddy the waters, how can the modern client afford old-fashioned honor? He's got to engage in a certain amount of clandestine price-fixing and trade-restraining in order to survive at all. He may even have to claim dubious tax deductions and set up a less than totally philanthropic foundation. He will surely have to indulge in a bit of perjury to get through the million forms in which Uncle Sam tries to strangle him. Every successful lawyer knows this. Don't blame the bar for the erosion in the moral code. Blame a slaphappy Congress and nine would-be Oliver Wendell Holmeses!"

"I'm afraid, sir, you'll have these gentlemen thinking we're all shysters," John Grau reproached him. "I certainly have found no difficulty conforming to the Canons of Ethics."

"Oh, the Canons." The Judge gazed up at the ceiling as if to find them there. "The Canons are like the Constitution. They can be interpreted."

"You know you and I construe them strictly, sir!"

The Judge winked maliciously at his little circle. "We have an ivory tower in the New York Central Building where we keep John Grau."

John moved angrily away in the general laughter, and a very old gentleman, a Shallcross cousin, proceeded, with the immunity of his years, to interrogate the Judge on a more delicate subject.

"This fellow Livingston, Eben. Is he a client of yours?"

The Judge looked around, with elaborately exaggerated caution. "Not so loud, Tom. He's supposed to be here. However, I don't see him." Here he reduced his tone to a conspiratorial whisper. "The answer to your question is *no*. I said the bar had lost its honor. I didn't mean to imply it had lost its honesty!"

The old man exchanged looks with others of the group. "I'm surprised to hear you talk that way. We heard he might be going to marry Sophie!"

Eben Shallcross chuckled and, glancing around again, still pretending to be confidential, replied: "In that respect, let me tell you gentlemen a little story. In Napoleonic days, when the poor old exiled Queen of Naples was told that her granddaughter was to be served up in marriage to the Corsican usurper, she

cried: 'The final humiliation has been reserved for me! To become the devil's grandam!' "

It was now Martin's turn to leave the group. He did not in
the least care what his father said about Jay, but, being in business with him, he thought it more fitting to remove himself
from the paternal sarcasms. Besides, hypocrisy bored him. He
found his mother in the doorway to the library, and her face
brightened when she saw him. "Oh, Martin, thank heavens,
you're here!"

"Is something wrong?"

"I need you when Mr. Livingston comes. It's so difficult, Sophie's wanting him here, with your father feeling as he does, and
so many of Elly's friends coming."

"Don't be ridiculous, Ma." Her concern for Elly's friends had
promptly aroused his sibling rivalry. "What do you expect him
to do? Pee on your Aubusson?"

"Don't be disgusting. You know he won't know anybody.
What does one talk to a man like that about?"

"What Elly's crowd talk about. How much money people
have and who's sleeping with whom."

"Martin, you're terrible!"

"Well, they're always in such a tizzy about who's who. Suppose they get ahead of the game today and consider who *will* be
who?"

"Ah, there he is now. I'd better keep him as far away from
your father as I can."

Martin watched her hurry over to Jay, who was wearing a suit
of too light blue, with wry amusement. Would there never be an
end to the hypocrisy of his world? None of the things that he had
most enjoyed as a schoolboy — chess and bridge, debates and geo-
metric problems, laboratory and bell ringing — had ever been
supposed to be as amusing as football and fishing and dirty talk.
And this dichotomy had persisted through his life. The things
that he now cared about — his tidy bedroom at the Hone Club,

his long closet of tailored suits, his uncluttered desk at Thaddeus Kay & Sons and the chance to make money at it — were hardly fashionable enthusiasms. Oh, no! Fashion dictated that a man should prefer an easy informality and should constantly yearn for the great outdoors. And what disgusted Martin most was that even the men (a majority) who preferred the things that he preferred dared not admit it. Walking down Wall Street on a bright spring morning, looking forward to a full day of money-making, he could count on every last vapid mother's son of them to greet him with the chant that it was a "tough day to be chained to a desk"!

Well, the world had to be accepted, and Martin had tried to be wise. He had adapted himself to the men about him and had learned to control statements in which dissent might be revealed. So long as he had the stock market to study and a family on which to vent the irritations that he had to conceal from others, he had been able, by discretion and industry, to attain a partnership in his brother-in-law's brokerage firm and, unknown to anybody, a fortune of half a million dollars.

But Martin was by no means as detached as his mildly sardonic smile purported to imply. He was engaged to be married, at last, to a girl whose failure so far to arrive that afternoon seemed to suggest an independence that he had not fully anticipated. He had expected her on the dot of five-thirty, and the old cousins were already demanding where she was. What a surprise they were in for! Martin knew that his relatives had always considered him a cold fish who would one day marry some plain little heiress. Wait now till they saw Alverta, so big, so handsome, so splendid and so poor! They would learn that Martin, sober, slighted Martin, had as much fire and passion as any of *them*. More!

Ah, there she was now. She loomed up in the doorway behind shorter guests, and he hurried across the room to greet her, a sudden anguish of disappointment in his heart. Why in God's name did she not realize that the cue for a large woman of dark complexion was a splendid simplicity? Why did she have to wear that lamentably fussy green hat that made her small eyes seem smaller and those wide horizontal stripes that made her big hips seem bigger? The fact that she was obviously scared, scared of his family, scared of the party, scared maybe of him, was now only irritating.

"You mustn't leave me," she said tensely as he took her hand.

"Darling, I have business to do."

"Business? With these old blue-heads?"

"You're just like my mother. You think business is all done at a desk. That it's a game men play downtown, with telephones and pretty secretaries."

"Well, isn't it? And I'm *not* like your mother."

"Business is wherever money is. And, of course, you're not like Ma. But why in God's name did you wear that hat?"

"You don't like it? I bought it just for this party!"

Martin sighed. Alverta was surely a lady, more so than any at the party. She was a van Schaake, after all, older New York even than the Shallcrosses. But working as a salesgirl to support an old bitch of a mother who was drinking herself to death (alas, not quickly enough) in a two-room flat of faded elegance had not given Alverta even as much taste as poor Sophie. "Of course, I like it, darling," he said, correcting his tone. "But I like your hair more. You should never cover it."

Alverta at once took the silly hat off and put it on a table by one of ancestor Peter Shallcross' Buddhas. "Is that better?"

"Much better. Go talk to Ma. She's over there by the window. I have to speak to someone."

"Martin! You haven't even kissed me." But when he moved to touch his cheek to hers, she drew indignantly back. "No, properly."

"Honey, I can't kiss you that way in front of all these people! Our engagement hasn't been announced yet."

"Very well, I'm going home!"

"Alverta, be reasonable!"

"Then take me into another room and give me a proper kiss."

Martin, casting a guilty look around, led her down a corridor to the downstairs guest room. As soon as he had closed the door, Alverta flung her arms around him and kissed him violently. She bit him on the lips so hard that he bled.

"Really, Alverta!" he protested, disengaging himself. "Be careful, will you? I'll have to see if there's a styptic pencil in the bathroom."

"I'm sorry!" she cried, overcome with remorse. "Darling, really I am! My Grandmother van Schaake was an Italian. I suppose I should have warned you. Sweetheart, what can I do? Shall I get a Band-Aid?"

"You can go back to the party before people wonder what the hell we're up to," he retorted testily. "I'll douse this thing in cold water till it stops bleeding. If it ever does."

When Alverta had gone, Martin stared at his image gloomily in the mirror, touching a dampened washrag to the rapidly re-emerging stain, and wondered if his engagement had been wise. He had fallen in love with the image of an Alverta who had been hardworking, courageous and gay, devoid of the self-pity that her situation would have engendered in most girls. He had been only too willing to concede that she might have found the security that he offered as appealing as himself. But it was certainly not fatuity in him that made him now suspect that Alverta was not marrying him simply to escape from bondage. The joke was hollow that he made to his friends: "People have always said I would marry for money; now I'm being married for mine!" Alverta was all passion, frustrated passion. He wondered if he might not have preferred some of her attention directed from his body to his purse. What did *he* have to do with biting and Italian grandmothers? He could only take comfort in the absolute inevitability of his marriage. As it was unthinkable to get out of it, so it was futile to worry about it. His tensions ceased as he saw now that the bleeding was less. After all, she was a van Schaake. Even she could not take that away from him.

*

It was the first and last party at Shallcross Manor for which Sophie had ever been responsible, and she was so nervous about it that she had stayed in her room to the last possible minute and had several unwise but fortifying gulps of whiskey. Then her mother had rapped indignantly on her door and demanded that she come down, and she had obeyed, in rather a haze. Already a group of family friends were gathered about the model of the housing development, and opinion seemed to be unanimous that it was a splendid solution for the old house. Sophie found herself congratulated by all. Such remarks rang upon her bewildered hearing as:

"It's what I've always said: landmarks can't be saved as sterile monuments — they have to be put to use."

"Sophie, you've proved you're the only really modern member of the family!"

"A toast to you, my dear!"

Jay came up to her, in his light blue suit, with shining eyes; and Sophie, who had expected him to stand out from the crowd, perhaps to his advantage, perhaps even to theirs, was disappointed to find that, despite his suit, he seemed so easily to fit in. But why not, after all? Was he not — were they not — of the same genus? Only she and the old house were something else. They shared the dignity of inanimate things.

"You've done it, honey!" he exclaimed, taking both her hands in his. "You've really done it. I think half these old dodos understand that we've actually improved Shallcross Manor!"

He was soon too busy meeting her father's friends to have further time for her. He already had an option on the land adjoining Shallcross Manor and hoped to interest some of the richer guests in another development. Sophie moved vaguely about, lulled by the chatter and the general enthusiasm. She had a sense of new detachment, not from her family and her family's friends, which was an old, familiar sense, but from Jay and their plans for the house. For now that the crisis was actually at hand she was beginning to see that the ancient alliance between herself and those rooms might admit of no partners or changes. When she encountered Alverta, she had the relief of being with someone even less at ease than herself.

"I'm sorry that you and Martin will never be able to live now in Shallcross Manor."

"Oh, Good Lord, don't worry about that!" Alverta exclaimed. "It's hard enough entering such a close-knit family as yours without having to fight a landmark, too!"

"Are we so close, do you think?"

"My dear, I find it actually spooky. I feel that you all understand each other, just by glances."

Minutes later, when Sophie passed her brother carrying drinks to somebody, she stopped him.

"Alverta thinks, as a family, we're very close-knit."

Martin glanced about to see if his fiancé were near. "It's a compliment to me," he whispered. "She thinks I'm such a catch that you all want to hang on to me. Don't let her know you've been peddling me to every skirt in the neighborhood for the past fifteen years!"

"I've been peddled, too."

"You?" His face was suddenly serious. She had always been closest to Martin of all the family, but this had never been very close. He eschewed intimacy, and it was in crowds, as now, that their understandings most frequently touched. "I thought you had Jay all sewed up."

"Is that what you'd like?"

"Wouldn't you? He's going places, that boy. Take it from one who knows."

"But I'm not sure I want to go anywhere!"

She walked on, feeling a bit unsteady and reminded herself to have nothing more to drink. In the front hall she found Hilary, a champagne glass in hand, standing alone contemplating the portrait of Peter Shallcross. She had not seen him since their meeting in Central Park, and she was immediately heartsick. The hum in her head made her think of the long-ago night at the picnic and the fatal bottle of *vin rosé*.

"Do you think Peter Shallcross would approve our plans?" she asked in a voice that rang out unexpectedly loud and challenging.

"He?" Hilary whirled around to face her, and she was taken aback by the hostility of his tone. "Don't tell me you're leaving *him* with your marina?"

"Of course not. He goes with everything else to the new apartment."

"Well, do him a favor, will you? Just for me. Put him with his back to the East River so the poor old bastard can never look across and see the desecration of his home."

She stared. "You really think it's as bad as that?"

"Don't you? Deep down in your heart?" The bitterness of Hilary's tone rang harshly in her ears, as he pointed scornfully at the marina. "Can you really convince yourself that the soul of Peter Shallcross, sailing across some fleecy heaven in the ghost of a beautiful clipper ship, will look down with any benignity on *that?*"

Sophie's cheeks burned as she conceded, all at once, in a single, searing moment of truth, the stunning justice of what he said. As she gazed now ruefully at the model, she saw it for the first time, yet saw it as she had really always seen it, from the very beginning, in the back of her mind. There it was, poor old Shallcross Manor, painted a gaudy pink, dwarfed by six giant cubes, like six pink candy sticks, and dotted with tiny gala flags to indicate its renewed marine connection. And what did those little toy yachts and motor boats remind her of now, those "stinkpots," as her father had always called them, tied up along its banks, but so many ferocious cubs sucking greedily from the tired dugs of a dying mother who lived only to give them one last meal? She turned back to Hilary.

"It's grotesque," she murmured.

"Of course it is. It's like some poor tragic imbecile dressed up as a clown by Arabs and made to do a crazy dance to amuse the multitude. How could it be worse?"

Never had Hilary seemed stronger or more right. She understood now the alliance, or even merger, that she had thought she had imagined between Jay and the family friends. Old New York, new New York, what was the difference? What was the distinction between the ratty furs and seed pearls of the old-maid Shallcross cousins and Jay's blue suit and ruby cuff links?

"How indeed?" she murmured in response to Hilary's last question. "How indeed could it be worse?" She gazed about the room as if looking for some means of instant atonement. As she did so, Jay came out of the living room, escorting old Miss Jay, aged ninety, to see the model. Sophie went quickly up to it and put her finger on the roof of the Shallcross marina.

"Tear it down, tear it down, please!"

"Tear it down!" Jay had flushed with surprise and vexation. "Why, I thought the whole point was to save it!"

"It was, it was. *Please*, Jay, don't think me ungrateful. I'm not. You have been the very kindest friend in the world. But I didn't think this thing through. I've been insane! I see now that it may be better not to compromise. Let the old house *go!*"

"You don't like it?"

"I think it's horrible!"

"Well *I* think it looks fine! Don't you, Miss Jay?"

"It's perfectly lovely! So ingenious."

Sophie groaned. "I'm afraid I must beg you to raze it. I can't bear to have the house look that way. So forlorn and out of place, with all those ghastly fat men in skippers' caps, watching television, tied up to a dock!"

"What fat men?" Jay demanded, staring at the model.

"You didn't have to put them in. I *see* them all too well. Oh, please, Jay, do this for me now!"

Seeing that he simply thought she was drunk, she put her hands suddenly on the model of Shallcross Manor, tore it out of the plan and flung it on the floor.

"There! Forgive me for a crazy fool! Forgive me and forget me!"

"Sophie!"

She was aware now of the silence in the hall and all the staring faces. Miss Jay looked actually frightened. It was like a party in an opera.

"I'm sorry, everybody!" she cried wildly. "But that is the proper end of Shallcross Manor!"

She ran out through the party, past the hired waiters, through the old kitchen with the tables of heaped sandwiches and out the back door. She ran down the lawn and stopped before the black, troubled water. It was bitingly cold, and she had no coat. But it had been worth it! Oh, yes, it had been worth it! There was redemption in cold, salvation in biting wind. Now she was shivering all over, but still she would not look around. Someone would have seen her from the house. So long as it was not her mother! Please God that it should not be her mother!

She felt the blessed blow on her back as a coat was wrapped firmly about her.

"Am I late?" Hilary hissed in her ear. "Am I on cue?"

"Oh, Hilary!"

"Such a hammy actress needs a hammy leading man," he continued, and then he laughed, but this time it was all right. It wasn't her mother! Oh, she would *learn* to be grateful! "In ham, you'll find, Jay is a rank amateur compared to me!"

"Oh, Hilary!" she repeated. "Hold me, Hilary! What a fool I've been. What a bloody fool! Hug me, darling."

As she felt his arms tighten about her, she realized, with a sudden frenzied exhilaration, just how great a fool she *had* been. For should it not have been clear as the cloudless sky above her that her warning in Central Park had been just the thing to freeze him? Where, in the name of ignored, insulted Venus, had her female intuition been? What did she care for promises or commitments if she had this moment, even just this moment?

"I love you, love you, Hilary."

"What can I offer you compared to Jay?"

But she felt immediately the new confidence in his tone and knew that she had to say nothing. And then he laughed again, but not the loud guffaw of his party jokes. Oh, no! For it did not exclude her. It was a lower laugh, a kind of gleeful chuckle, and she was part of it.

"What is it, darling?" she asked.

"You've had it now, poor creature. Jay just peered out the door and saw us."

"What did he do?"

"I'm afraid you won't be complimented. He smiled and waved his hand. I'm not quite sure he didn't make an obscene gesture."

"Oh, he won't care. Is he gone?"

"He's gone. With all his millions. I've cost you a fortune, Sophie!"

He kissed her now on the lips for the first time in all the years of their cheek-to-cheek kisses. Then she flung her arms around him again and put her head on his shoulder. There might be years in which to improve those kisses.

"Oh, darling, I'm so happy!" she cried. "Now I won't have to care about the old house. Like you, I'll turn away from it. Let me go back and do research for you, the way I used to, years ago, when I was at school. Do you remember? Oh, Hilary, I'd love it so! All I'm going to care about from now on is how many knights Goneril dismissed and *did* Lady Macbeth have children and what happened to Lear's fool!"

"Now you're being sarcastic."

"I swear to God I'm not!"

"What about me? Aren't I even to be a minor character in *Locrine* or *Sir Thomas More* or one of the apocryphal plays?"

"But you're to be the whole canon!" she said with an almost hysterical laugh. "Come on, I'm getting cold."

"Back to the house?"

"Oh, I'm never going back to the house! Don't you know that? I can stay at Elly's till they pull it down."

And, arm in arm, they walked around the doomed old manor house to the empty lot where the cars were parked.

10

ELLY KAY's practiced party eye noted that her sister's little scene had actually enlivened the gathering. Fifteen minutes after Sophie's appalling eruption the talk was louder, the laughs more frequent, the drinks more rapidly consumed. One was never very far, she reflected sardonically, from the days of the Roman arena. What people really yearned for was disaster, so long as they were safe themselves.

Not that she herself was concerned about Sophie or in the least bit sorry for her. Sophie, like their father, always behaved as badly as she felt inclined and always got away with it. And Martin, she was sure, had simply shrugged his shoulders, while their mother had looked the other way. No, the only person at the party who had minded, really minded, was Elly Kay. For she could never avoid the mocking elfin counterpart of herself — yet distinctly independent of, even hostile to, herself — an embodiment of the world's observant eye which ironically took her own shape and appeared every time anyone connected with her misbehaved.

Oh, yes, she knew just the spot in the living room from which that other Elly would be watching! It would be on the portico over the big double doorway into the hall that the little elf would sit, careless and impudent, chewing gum and letting one long, adolescent, unstockinged leg dangle over the heads of arriving and departing guests. It was obvious, Dr. Silverman had told her once, that this elfin Elly was no more than a remembered vision of herself as a little girl spying, as all little girls will, on her parents' parties at Shallcross Manor. But then a great many things were obvious to Dr. Silverman that were a good deal less so to other people. Actually, she had no memory of being a spy on parties, and, besides, that watching Elly was not watching the guests. She was watching Elly herself and sneering at her!

If only she were alone in that! But that room was full of sneerers. Elly's gold puff-sleeved dress, her long, high-piled gold hair, her big, searching blue eyes that gave such smiling animation to alabaster loveliness, her low, lilting voice, what were all these perfections but a row of gold spittoons into which the passing multitude could expectorate?

Oh, she was very clear about it, at times almost too clear! If she could have assembled the scattered spite in that long room into one coherent block of judgment, she would have interpreted it thus: "The funny thing, my dear, about Elly Kay, the *real* reason she never quite comes off, is that she's absolutely sexless. It's curious, isn't it? Because she has everything else: the figure, the complexion, the manner, even the clothes. And, of course, she has oodles of brains and capability. She made thirty thousand for St. Agnes' Hospital on that Modigliani benefit. But my Harry (aren't men *awful?*) says he'd as soon go to bed with a wax doll . . ."

Dr. Silverman said all this was nonsense, that people didn't say that sort of thing about her at all. But how did he know? He didn't live in her world. Far from it! And wasn't it his job to build her up? And wasn't he very well paid for his efforts to shore up the failing purpose of her life? Was it *likely* that he would respond, in that flat neutral voice: "Oh, yes, I'm sure that's what they say, Mrs. Kay. For, after all, you *are* sexless. You struck me, from our very first session, as an absolutely sexless woman"? Would that be the way to hang on to fifty dollars an hour?

But, oh dear, *now* she was in for it. At the very next session her free association would be totally blocked until she had confessed to the doctor that she had been accusing him of mercenary motives! God! Did anyone really imagine that psychoanalysis was *fun?*

There were the John Graus. Addie Grau was the kind of frump who would expect Elly to snub her, who would probably *want* Elly to snub her; she noted how resentfully Addie's flitting eyes took in her dress. But if Elly could only now follow her heart (Silverman kept telling her she had one), she would pull Addie Grau over to a corner and tell her what a dear she was and find the kindest pansy in the room to make up to her. And now she would do just that. She would *make* that heart come out!

"Hi, Graus!" How that party voice mocked her! "Can either of you tell me, when every last soul of one's acquaintance absolutely swears how they loathe and abominate cocktail parties, why we continue to give the damn things and go to them? Now what sense does that make? Eh? What sense does that possibly make?"

Who had said that? The Elly on the portico heard it all. She saw, too, the serious Graus, rebuffed by the chiming hardness of their hostess' daughter's tone, move uncomfortably off, seeking refuge at the bar table, reinforced in their ancient view that she was the silliest creature in all New York. And the most sexless, too!

There was Thad now. He *had* come, after all. He was listening to old Miss Jay, smiling the vague, amiable smile that was the surest indication of his mental blankness. He was not so drunk as not to recognize his interlocutor, or not to be aware that she was a cousin. Oh, he would say nothing wrong! And Miss Jay would be perfectly satisfied, too; she would be glad to supply all the talk while he supplied the looks. To *her* age he might still seem the glorious figure he had been once, before the erosion of gin, the accumulation of body. Everybody liked

Thad, as everybody liked Laura and Lila, his two duplicates (if they would *only* stop growing!) now in love with horses and boarding school. Kays were never blamed for anything; Kays were lovable. Thad could fish and sail and drink away his early promise, and people would simply nod and wink and speculate: "Everything might have been *so* different if he hadn't married a frigid wife."

Naturally, Silverman disagreed. There was no such thing as a frigid woman. Oh, no! Only an unaroused one. Hadn't Thad been a clumsy lout? Hadn't he turned to cruder, easier women? But, really, what was the difference between one's analyst and one's hairdresser? One could always buy flattery.

"Angeline, you're a dear to come. Of course, we all loathe cocktail parties, but we can't do without them, can we? How could one have a crowd like this to dinner? And if we didn't ask darlings like you, the ones we *don't* ask for dinner might get the idea. Thanks, sweet!"

Who was the man across the room staring at her? Who was the man across the room grinning at her? Where had she seen him before? Oh, yes, Mr. Livingston. But he was more attractive than she remembered. That light blue suit was too light, but it fitted perfectly, particularly about his rounded, muscular shoulders. He was short but compact. And those mocking eyes — why was he staring at her? Were Jews, blond Jews, better in bed, or was that just a fantasy? She would ask Dr. Silverman . . . well, perhaps no. Oh, hell, now she would have to!

He came straight across the room to her.

"You don't remember me, Mrs. Kay."

"Of course I do. At Dad's office."

"Oh, I don't mean then. I mean long ago. Nineteen years ago, to be exact. At your brother Martin's birthday party, right here, at Shallcross Manor. I remember thinking you were the most beautiful girl I'd ever seen."

Elly gasped and tried to smile. What kind of a game was this, from a man staring at her for all the world as if he meant it? Those yellow-green eyes might have been laughing, but were they laughing at *her*?

"You're very gallant, Mr. Livingston. Is that why you bought the old place? Was it the effect of my beauty?"

"Possibly."

"And is that why you want to save it?"

"Oh, your sister's changed all that. Didn't you see her?"

"My sister's unpredictable. I envy her that quality. Everyone knows just what I'm going to do. It's so flat." But he was still staring at her. "What did we talk about at that first meeting? Was I inspiring?"

"Oh, you weren't inspiring at all. You were very snotty. Very short and clipped and snotty."

"Really! I guess it's lucky I was beautiful."

"Oh, yes. And you still are. Just as beautiful."

"Still! A beautiful ruin?"

"You're not a ruin. You can't be more than thirty-eight. I suppose marrying young and having children young, as you did, makes a woman feel old. But if I were your husband, Mrs. Kay, I wouldn't spend so much time hunting and fishing."

"What on earth do you know about my husband, Mr. Livingston?"

"Quite a bit. He's the titular head of the firm that does my brokerage."

"Titular? Don't you think you're being rather impertinent?"

"I'm being honest. Do you object?"

Again she gasped. "No, I don't suppose I do." She realized with astonishment that he was angry. Actually angry!

"I've put up with a lot from your family, Mrs. Kay. First, with your snottiness at Martin's birthday party. Then with all your father's sarcastic cracks that he thinks aren't repeated to me. Then with the general attitude that I was some kind of hun to buy this old shack that all of you were itching to sell. And now with Sophie making me the laughing stock of this idiotic party. Who the devil do you think you all *are?* Or rather who the devil do you think *I* am to take it from you?"

Elly found anger exciting; she was never afraid of it. It was only concealed anger that she feared, concealed anger and hidden contempt. "What do you want me to do, Mr. Livingston?" she asked boldly. "Apologize?"

"What good does that do?"

"None. But what else is there?" She moved quickly to the aggressive. "I suppose we could pay money damages, but they say you're rich."

"Does it never occur to you that I might want to be treated like a human being?"

"Ah, now you're asking for the moon!" she cried passionately. "Who can expect to be treated like a human being? Have I ever been?" She was suddenly so indignant that she had to pause to swallow. "All my life I've wanted to be treated like a human being! And has anyone ever tried? Has my mother? My husband? My daughters? No, never! I'm a doll, a silly artificial doll that everybody wants to pet and kiss. And then do you know what they do with that doll, Mr. Livingston? They hurl it on the floor. They stamp on it! Why? Because that doll is prettier than they are. Because that doll has better manners. Because that doll is kinder and nicer! So there, Mr. Livingston! You can feel as sorry for yourself as you want, but the boat you're in is so jam packed it will probably sink!"

Mr. Livingston's ire seemed to dissolve altogether before hers. He even clapped his hands. "Bravo! Do you know what you've just done? You *have* treated me like a human being. I bet you and I could be friends, Mrs. Kay!"

"I have no friends. No real friends. People type me as soon as I open my mouth. The type has friends, I suppose. Types usually do."

"But don't you think we could even try?"

"You can try if you like. But it won't work. People have tried before."

"May I call and ask you to lunch sometime?"

"Of course. Anytime. But I warn you, I can't talk. I don't know how." She turned away now to pick up a cigarette, with a shaking hand. "Well, I've enjoyed our badinage, Mr. Livingston. It's not every day that one hears such nice things. There! Do you hear me? Do you see what I mean? If you'll excuse me now, I must get back to my job of helping Mummy."

Her mind a chaos, she crossed the room to her mother. Even the elf on the portico had stopped sneering.

"You'd better take Mr. Livingston around and introduce him," she said breathlessly. "I don't think he knows many people."

"Really, darling, I can't face him after the way Sophie's behaved. I'm too mortified to face anybody."

"Oh, Mother, nobody minds that kind of thing. It's considered 'honest.' Unless *I* indulge in it, and then everyone screams."

"My dear child, everyone adores *you.*"

There it was again, that constant, boring, valueless maternal faith that she was so ashamed of still having to evoke!

"Thanks, darling." She took her mother's hand and kissed it, knowing how Marian hated dramatics from anyone but her.

"You must get back to our guests, dear."

"I'm going to sit right here with you till the party's over."

"Elly! You can't."

"Wouldn't you like it?"

"What difference does *that* make? Everyone depends on you, my child!"

There was no point arguing, nor did Elly even want to. Being with her mother was only a better way of being alone, and now, quite suddenly, she could be alone anywhere. She rose and crossed the room, but before she had reached the throng of guests she had to pause and put her hand on the back of a chair to steady herself. She was giddy, superbly giddy.

She joined the group around old Miss Jay. She laughed shrilly; she joked. She was aware of Mr. Livingston, standing by the door. He was watching her.

It was fantasy. It was free association. She could feel the buttons of Dr. Silverman's couch in the small of her back. It was the sheerest ecstasy to suppose that between the tinsel affair of her daily life, her tinsel duties, her tinsel family, her rather better than tinsel manners, and the black, turgid drowning tide of passion there might be no barrier. She had told Dr. Silverman of the dream-world Elly who rang for the elevator man at midnight, who urged sturdy taxi drivers to park in dark streets, who had brief, frenetic couplings with house painters and window cleaners, who abandoned her husband and children, her money and fame, leaving all to lie naked on an empty Caribbean beach by the side of a huge naked Negro.

But could one graduate to reality? Her throat thickened so suddenly that when she turned to Miss Jay to answer her question, no sound emerged. She coughed and recovered herself. She shook her head and glanced defiantly in the direction of Mr. Livingston. He was leaving. Thank goodness! He would be stripped of his flesh and blood and relegated to the ghostly cast that performed three mornings a week at eleven o'clock in Dr. Silverman's green office.

Part II

1

HILARY HAD PERMITTED himself the illusion that, at forty, with an unearned income of twelve thousand a year, a very decent living for a bachelor in 1961, and with the prospect of some additional help from Sophie's small trust and the sale of an occasional literary article, there was no reason that his approaching marriage should disrupt unduly his present schedule. His three-room garden apartment would prove quite adequate for two, and two, in view of the gentle pace that would undoubtedly be necessitated by Sophie's mental history, was the only number that he should for a time have to consider. But in his very first after-dinner library interview with Judge Shallcross, he discovered his error.

"That might be all very well for a year or so if you were a young man," the Judge pointed out, in his airy-pleasant manner. "It might give you a chance to mull over yourself in relation to the suddenly shrunken world of lawful love. But at your age, my dear fellow, you can't afford the time. You have to get started. You and Sophie don't begin to have an income to live on."

"We won't require much, sir."

"Don't fool yourself. An eligible extra man, like yourself, gets used to receiving things — parties, weekends, yachting trips. Oh, *I* know! But all that is shut off, bang, at the altar. You hardly reach the door of the church after the ceremony before you're dunned for charities, for country clubs, for summer cottages. And don't fool yourself, because Sophie professes a fine scorn of the world, that she can't spend money. You'll find she's a true member of her sex there!" Here the Judge dragged deeply and contentedly on his cigar and then comfortably coughed. "Not to mention, of course, her occasional psychiatric charges."

Hilary reflected dismally that, with the removal of the threat of Jay Livingston, the Judge felt no further need to "puff" his younger daughter. Hilary Knowles was welcome enough to Sophie, but welcome to her on Shallcross terms.

"I pride myself that she won't need Doctor Damon any more," he said stoutly.

"You never know, my friend, you never know. It always pays to be prepared. We'd better have a look about and see if we can't fix you up with something in Washington."

"But I have no experience in government, sir!"

"Don't be an ass. These are the 1960s. You don't need any."

Hilary felt very low after this. He had to admit that the Judge had some justification in refusing to take too seriously his literary career. In sober truth, it amounted to very little. He had been too unconcerned with politics for the *Partisan Review* or *Commentary* and too much of a literary historian in the school of Van Wyck Brooks for the "new" critics. With his elaborate, image-laden sentences, he sometimes reminded himself of the ghost of Walter Pater lost in the bleak prose of the twentieth century. Except for the near fluke of his popular *Reading Shakespeare*, a short biography of Elizabeth Gaskell and a few articles included in critical anthologies, what did he really have to show for the past fifteen years?

Sophie was much upset when he told her of her father's proposal.

"Daddy's afraid he's going to have to support us!" she exclaimed. "He should have more faith in me. I'll never go to him for money! Anyway, we have all we need. We don't have to live in New York. We could go abroad, or to some little New England village, and I could do the housework and cooking while you write."

Hilary was at first much touched and pleased by this, but as the days passed and he began to take in that she was entirely sincere in her offer to abandon New York, even anxious to do so, he was troubled. Cut away from his other occupations, isolated with paper and pencil, might he not be putting too great a strain on a slender muse? Suppose he were even to revise and successfully complete his unpublished book on Shakespeare's sonnets, might not the long hours devoted to further research and speculation serve to emphasize to his only too easily disillusioned mind how few persons, even in the literary game, cared whether "Mr. W. H." was Pembroke or Southampton?

At his lowest point help came from the very source that he would have considered — had he considered it at all — the most unlikely. For what call did Jay Livingston have to play his god from the machine? Jay telephoned him early one morning to ask him, in a voice as cheerful as if Sophie had never been an issue between them, to be his guest for lunch at Twenty-One. When Hilary arrived there — for he could imagine no reason to decline — he found that his host had ordered a splendid meal in advance with two kinds of wine. Like the true businessman that he so notoriously was, Jay came straight to the point.

"I want you to know that I have no hard feelings about Sophie. I don't think she and I were ever really meant for each other. Besides, she was stuck on you from the beginning, and girls like her don't get over that. So there's no reason we shouldn't be friends. I know at Columbia you thought I was too pushy about trying to get into your set, but I'm sure you've seen enough of the world by now to know that people like me don't get anywhere unless they push. Even people like you have to shove a bit."

"Ah, that's my trouble, of course. I don't."

"Do you know something, Hilary? I've been watching you for a time now, and I think I've discovered something. I think you and I are almost exact opposites. And exact opposites ought to be able to help each other."

"Well, I suppose you could help *me* easily enough," Hilary conceded with a shrug. He made it, however, a good-natured shrug, for he was touched by Jay's interest. Jay, he was beginning to see, was an unusual man. "You could loan me money if I needed it, which happily I don't. But how could I help *you?* From where I sit, you seem on top of the world."

"Oh, you could do a lot for me. You could help me round off my rough edges. You could polish me up. You could help me get on with the people of your world. I'm sick of banging around with business types. Living from day to day and night to night. I'd like to belong to a group. A social group. People who do things with some kind of order in their lives."

"Have you any particular people in mind?"

"What do you think of the Kays?"

"The Kays? Elly and Thad? What makes you think there's any order in *their* lives?"

Jay for the first time in his candid revelations seemed embarrassed. "Well, Elly struck me as being unusually gracious, if that's the word."

Hilary winced. "That's *not* the word. Lesson number one." But he found already that he was developing a sympathy for his openhearted host. And what Jay had said about his having learned to tolerate pushers was perfectly true. Hilary was always ready now to help a social climber who had the candor to admit what he was. "If it's dining at the Kays' you want, I think we can arrange that easily enough."

"It's not just dining with the Kays," Jay objected, reddening. "That was only an example picked at random."

"Don't kid yourself. I've been analyzed, and I know that examples are never picked at random. But it's no business of mine

why you want to go there. You have to start somewhere, and
the Kays are as good as anyone. Besides, once you go to the
Kays', you can go to a lot of better places."

"I don't want you to get the idea that I mean to be a social
butterfly. I'm a very busy man."

Hilary held up a warning finger. "Lesson number two.
Never boast how hard you work. The really big men always
manage to give an impression of leisure." And then, during the
balance of their meal, Hilary descanted, freely, vividly and at
times rather maliciously, on the ways and means of appealing to
Elly Kay and her friends.

"What do you think *I* most need?" Jay asked at the end of his
talk. "And please don't spare me."

Hilary glanced at the check suit with the green stripe and
shook his head disapprovingly. "A new wardrobe."

"Would you help me pick it?"

"Why not?"

"Right now?"

"Sure, if you want. The sooner we get rid of that tie, the
better."

At Benson's, an hour later, while Jay was being fitted for a
suit, one of Hilary's Knickerbocker Club friends paused behind
the chair where he was waiting. "Who's your protégé?" he
drawled, jerking a thumb toward Jay across the room. The man
was old, thin, red, one of those afternoon tipplers whose whole
morning went into dressing perfectly.

"A friend of mine. Jay Livingston."

"Livingston?" The man dismissed the fitting scene with a
gesture. *"Plus ça change, plus c'est le même juif."*

Hilary turned away angrily, but not without the uneasy reflection that it was, after all, to impress just such asses that the
suit was being bought.

When they left Benson's, Jay, already putting into practice
the hint that big men never boasted how busy they were, agreed

to accompany Hilary on his weekly visit to The Arden Book Store. Hilary was ashamed of his secret hope that Jay might buy him a volume in return for his social tips, but when it came to old editions he suffered from an avarice that he found almost impossible to control.

"I'm always interested in a new racket," Jay told him.

"You'll find this a very old one."

Certainly, Jay was an odd, bustling presence in that quiet, dusty back room, picking over a table littered with catalogues and old sets, peering into an open safe with rows of gleaming backs, climbing a ladder to inspect an upper shelf. But Shellabarger, the owner, who never budged from his desk, a vast, bald, gravel-voiced man with tiny lenses perched on the tip of a round snub nose, seemed to take his new visitor entirely for granted. In his day, no doubt, he had turned odder candidates into avid collectors.

"The only Shakespeare item I have since you were last in, Hilary, is a good copy of the 1711 sonnets. The Lintot one. I've put a $500 tag on it."

Hilary examined the little volume, in near mint condition, and decided, with a sigh, in view of his talk with Judge Shallcross, that he had better limit his extravagances. "It's a beauty. Mine is the third issue with the Congreve ad. But I guess I'll make do with it."

"Isn't 1711 awfully late?" Jay demanded from the stepladder. "I seem to remember from my school dates that the bard died in 1616."

Shellabarger glanced up to give all his attention now to his customer's friend. "Precisely, sir. Yet Lintot's is in fact only the third edition. Really, the second, when you consider that the 1640 was a bowdlerization of the original 1609."

"How much would a 1609 be?"

"There are only thirteen known copies. I'm afraid none of them is likely to come on the market."

"But *that* would be something to have!"

"I see that if your friend should become a collector, he would not do things by halves," Shellabarger said with a smile to Hilary. "So much the better. We need more such, with museums and libraries taking everything off the market."

Jay came down off the ladder. "Why do men collect, Mr. Shellabarger?"

"Because there isn't much else a millionaire can do with his money," the proprietor replied promptly. "As you will find out, Mr. Livingston."

"What makes you think I'm a millionaire?"

"I have an infallible instinct in such matters."

Jay laughed, and Hilary was amused at the immediate congeniality between the two.

"But I like to start things," Jay said. "I like to get things going. I don't see myself buying old books to place on shelves, if you'll pardon my frankness. I'd rather put my money in authors. I'd rather put it in Hilary, for example."

"Well, of course, I deplore your taste in preferring people to books," Shellabarger replied benignly. "But if you must, I agree that Hilary's a sound investment."

"What would you do with him?"

"Just a minute, you two," Hilary objected. "You seem to forget I'm here. What do you think I am? A quarto on an auction block?"

"Pay no attention to him, Mr. Livingston. I know just what he needs. I've told him for years that he ought to start a magazine. All he lacks is an angel, and why should that seraphic role not be yours?"

"What kind of a magazine?" Jay asked, interested.

"Really, gentlemen!"

"Hilary, be quiet!" Shellabarger said sternly, turning all his attention now to Jay. "I mean a first-class monthly magazine about the cultural life of this city. The painters, the writers, the museums, the theaters, the ballet, the opera, the galleries, the auction houses, the bookstores, even the zoos. We're no longer the business capital, and one fine day the U.N. will move out, and then we'll really be in the soup. *Unless* we hang on to our culture. Hilary knows everybody from the Mayor down, and he's the man who could get you the articles, and *keep* getting them, which is more to the point."

"That kind of thing never works for more than a couple of issues," Hilary objected. "Then everyone gets sick of it. Besides, half those people can't write."

"Oh, of course, you'd have to have a staff. Don't you believe in ghosts?"

At this point a very famous collector entered the shop, and even the independent Shellabarger was required to give him his attention. Hilary and Jay left and walked to the latter's office building while Jay asked his new friend questions about the proposed magazine. Then they parted, and Hilary walked home, musing over the afternoon's experience and wondering if Jay would follow any of it up. He decided that the probabilities were against it, but that night, in his apartment, as he was dressing for dinner, he received a package by special messenger. It was, of course, the Lintot sonnets, with this note from Jay:

> *Please accept this small token of my thanks for what you have done for me today. And if you could be induced to think seriously about starting a magazine and want that angel, come to my office and talk about it. I'm just capable of sprouting two small wings. Perhaps I'd like to prove to myself that there isn't anything Jay Livingston can't make money out of!*

*

The following Saturday night Hilary spent in Bronxville, with John and Addie Grau. For them he would give up all but the very grandest parties. At midnight, with all five of the Grau children in bed, the three of them were sitting about a very adequate drink tray, talking about themselves.

John and Hilary had always maintained their college friendship, and Addie had taken Martin Shallcross' place in the old Columbia trio. It was not that Martin had been excluded, but he had tended, in the years after the war, to concentrate on the formal rather than the intimate side of his human relationships. And the Graus and Hilary were certainly intimate. Their Saturday night sessions, hilarious though they sometimes were, had some of the characteristics of a group analysis.

Contrast provided some of their congeniality. The Grau's life was almost totally domestic; Hilary's almost totally social. The former were amused by Hilary's accounts of the great world, without in the least wishing to have any part of it, and Hilary was warmed by the proximity of the Graus' family happiness, and compensated, at the same time, by a defensive, secret feeling that they, poor darlings, were irredeemably provincial. Addie Grau could never remember to wind a clock or repair a cigarette hole, and the faded lithograph of Winterhalter's Empress Elizabeth in their dining room had a twenty-year-old crack in its glass. But if she did few things other than work for local causes and take adoring care of her five children, and if she saw few people, she cared passionately for what she did and for whom she saw. Hilary, endeared to her by his willingness to prefer her to the greatest hostesses, was her particular favorite, and she protected him aggressively from her husband's sometimes rather brutal bantering.

John Grau was a broad-shouldered, hulky man with a tense, quiet manner. His chin was stubborn, his eyes small, slate-colored and usually faintly weary; his face was broad, with small, regular features. His hair, at forty, was still thick but very gray. Although not a trial lawyer, there was apt to be more than a touch of cross-examination in his questioning.

"What the hell are you and Sophie waiting for?" he demanded. "You don't think either of you are too *young*, do you?

I could meet you both at the Municipal Building on Monday morning, and we could pick up the license and have a champagne lunch. Then you could get married on Thursday. How about it?"

Hilary finished his Scotch and stared with one eye at the shriveled ice cubes at the bottom of the glass. He did not like the sudden feeling of depression that John's words had evoked in him. Nor had that feeling slipped into his being like a stealthy, unbidden guest as such feelings usually had in the past. It had knocked, on the contrary, quite boldly at his gate, and he was trying to meet it with such mental defiances as: "Oh, I know all about *you*. You're my old friend, Peter Panic, and you're battening on John's proposed acceleration of my marriage. But don't kid yourself. Your being here doesn't mean I'm afraid to get married. I couldn't expect you not to make one last try. But, oh, *do* go away. Please go away!"

"It's all very well for *you* to take that attitude, John," Hilary answered aloud now, a bit testily. "Everyone likes to play the part of the shrewd, realistic old grandmother in the third act who urges the young couple to elope. But you forget that Sophie is less than a year out of a sanatorium and that only a scant few weeks ago she was practically engaged to another man. I'd like to give her at least till spring to get accustomed to the idea of me."

"I don't forget any of those things!" John retorted. "They're precisely what I'm thinking of. Marriage will wipe out the nightmare of the sanatorium. Not to mention what I should regard as the rather worse nightmare of Jay Livingston!"

"Not to mention the nightmare of *me*," Hilary muttered as he leaned forward to mix himself another drink. He took advantage of the pause to make another effort to dispatch his mental intruder. "I know just why you're here," he again silently addressed the specter in his mind. "Leo Silverman and I know all about you. You want to make me think that my reluctance

to abandon my irresponsible bachelor's life, my post of peren-
nial observer, my position of uncommitted guest in the Graus'
Saturday nights is evidence that I don't *really* want to marry
Sophie. But it's not true. I *do* want to marry Sophie!"

"There's been entirely too much ratiocination about the
whole thing," John continued. "Entirely too much lying on
couches and spouting to bearded Freudians about your sordid
childhood antipathies. God! When I think of the hot air that
you and Sophie, between you, must have exuded at all those sessions! It would float the Navy blimp corps! And all for what?
To accomplish the simplest of animal functions, to bring about
an act that will occur as soon as you open the gate that keeps the
stallion from the mare! An ordinary, everyday act of sexual
union. Well, unite, for God's sake!"

"Listen to him!" Addie Grau broke in indignantly. "Would
you believe, Hilary, that it took him a whole *year* to propose? I
was at my wit's end, thinking up new tricks to get it out of
him!"

"We were very young," John said complacently, "and neither
of us had a bean. Those conditions hardly apply here."

"Why, I never heard such talk! Hit him, Hilary. I regard
Sophie as *very* young. And why should you and she have to
creep off to City Hall as if it was a shotgun wedding? Naturally,
any normal girl wants to be married in a church with brides-
maids and cake and everything. I expect to sit right on the aisle
and weep buckets of tears!"

Hilary blew a kiss to Addie and immediately felt better.
There had been a distinct, reassuring erotic shudder in his
groin at John's image of the horses. For a few moments he had
thought warmly of himself and Sophie in equine character, and
then he had felt ashamed. How could he compare himself to
such a symbol of virility as a stallion? But why not? Wasn't he
as much of a stallion as Jay? Ah, but *was* he, that was it! Damn
these doubts!

"There's another reason for waiting a bit," he told the Graus, "and that's my big news tonight. I may have a new job."

"Hey!" cried John.

"This will come as a bit of a shock, so prepare yourselves. It's with Jay Livingston."

"No!" Addie almost shrieked.

"God, man, are you going into real estate?" John cried.

"Now hold your horses." Again those equine images! "Jay called me up the other day and asked me to lunch. I wondered if he was going to threaten me with a suit for alienation of affections. But not at all. He was very cheerful, almost bouncing, the way he used to be in college. He reminded me how he'd always wanted to be friends with us . . ."

"How did all this end?" John interrupted. "Did you give Sophie back to him?"

"We hardly mentioned Sophie. He couldn't have been more tactful. Even you will have to admit, John, the guy can turn on the charm when he wants to."

"I admit nothing! What's the job?"

"You remember Shellabarger's and my old scheme for the New York cultural magazine? Well, he's going to finance it."

"So Jay thinks he can buy the arts now!"

"As soon as a man makes any money, everyone starts shouting that he's trying to buy things that can't be bought. Like happiness or beauty or health. It's pure jealousy, that's all. But yes, John, I think Jay *can* buy the arts. In fact, I think he's bought them."

"He's bought you, evidently."

"John!" Addie exclaimed.

"Oh, let him grouse, Addie, I don't mind," Hilary said magnanimously. "The world is full of sour apples."

He rose and went upstairs, tiptoeing down the darkened corridor past the children's bedrooms to John and Addie's room. He sat on their bed and dialed the Shallcrosses' number.

"I'm sorry, Judge," he said perfunctorily, when he heard his future father-in-law's sleepy "hello." "Is it horribly late? I wanted to speak to Sophie."

"Confound it, man, do you know it's after midnight? Why, I thought something terrible must have happened!" There was a pause while Hilary, chuckling to himself, pictured the old man debating the prudence of telling him to go to hell. This would pay him off for trying to push him into a Washington job! "Oh, all right, I suppose 'young love' must have its way," the Judge continued grumpily. "I'll get Sophie. But if this is going to be a long engagement, I shall certainly give her her own phone and number. And charge it to you, Hilary Knowles!"

When Sophie came on, on the living room instrument, for he heard the click as her father hung up, she asked at once: "What is it, darling? Are you all right?" and he knew instantly that it would be a mistake to tell her what he had called to tell her.

"I just had to say good night. And will you promise me something? *Never* let me go out without you again. Even to the Graus'. Do you promise?"

"Of course, I promise. Are you still at the Graus'?"

"Yes."

"Well, then promise *me* something. Go home as soon as you've finished the drink in your hand. It's late, and you've obviously had plenty."

"Do I sound that bad?"

"No. But you'd never have dared wake up Daddy if you hadn't."

"Good night then, my darling."

When he had hung up, he sat for a moment on the Graus' double bed feeling so happy that he wondered if he had ever been happy before. Then he went downstairs to have another drink. There would be plenty of time in which to follow out her instructions. And plenty of time in which to tell her about Jay.

2

WITHIN A MONTH after the farewell party at Shallcross Manor
the old house was leveled to the ground. Jay followed the procedure from his office and in the newspapers with a faintly acid
detachment. He had been perfectly willing, after all, to leave
the marina plan as proposed, but Martin Shallcross, as soon as
Sophie had abandoned the idea, had insisted on immediate dem-
olition.

"There's no point losing money over sentiment now that Sophie's pulled out," he had argued. "That crazy marina would
have taken up the space of two shops and a garage."

Jay saw no reason that he should be more Shallcross than the
Shallcrosses. Had Sophie been more receptive, he would have
been willing to make her a present of the house. Had she been
ready to consider marriage, he might even have agreed to live in
it. But Sophie had chosen to be a goose, and geese had to be
allowed to fly their own way. Besides, the momentary anger and
humiliation aroused in him by her conduct at the party had
faded before the luminous vision of her older sister.

"Do what you want with it," he told Martin. "It's your family's house, after all, not mine. But don't let people blame *me*
for what happens."

Yet that was exactly what happened. People did. The preser-
vation societies got wind of the impending destruction, and a
public clamor was raised. Martin, alarmed that some kind of
injunction or stay might be obtained, brought in a truck with a

wrecking ball without even instructing his partner, and Jay found himself vilified in the public prints under large photographs of the shambles to which the poor old manor house had been almost instantly reduced. In another mood he might have laughed at the fantastic hypocrisy of the family's press statements.

The Judge issued the following: "Our tax law having reached a parallel to that of France just prior to the Revolution of 1789, where the honest wage earner pays greater imposts than the oil tycoon or the millionaire bondholder, we old families who still live by the sweat of our brows must surrender our heritage to the iconoclasts who enjoy the fickle graces of a tasteless Revenue Service."

The beautiful Mrs. Thaddeus Kay, interviewed by the *Mirror* in her apartment, contributed this threnody: "I simply can't imagine Flushing Bay without the old house. Something beautiful and precious will have gone out of our heritage. I know we must all live in the present, but I shall never be able to drive by the site without looking the other way."

Reading this, Jay decided that he had better, after all, try to laugh. Strengthened by his talk at Twenty-One with Hilary, he telephoned Elly Kay to ask her if she would stand by her agreement at the party to have lunch with him one day. He was a bit surprised, not only that she answered her own telephone, but that she seemed not to consider his request in the least impertinent.

"Why, certainly, if you want," she replied. "I don't suppose Sophie could possibly mind *now* if we met for lunch. I love Ludovico's. Suppose we meet there on Tuesday at one? I go to my analyst that day, and it's practically next door."

When he arrived at Ludovico's, just one minute after the appointed time, she was already seated at the table he had reserved, pulling off a white glove and studying the menu. It was obvious that she was devoid of the common female vanity of making men wait, but he was nonetheless disappointed. Her attitude seemed to strip their meeting of the least possibility of romance.

"I adore clams," she said, looking up as he took the seat opposite her, "but I hear they give you hepatitis. Do you believe that?"

As she proceeded, in this same tone, after they had ordered, to chatter about the ball that she was running for cerebral palsy, and what company would give the liquor and what the flowers, he stared at her with renewed surprise. For truly, her beauty was astonishing. She might have been much nearer to thirty than forty. Everything about her was as perfect as in a model for a facial cream advertisement: the golden hair must have been set, the nails manicured, the eyebrows plucked, no earlier than that very morning. It was hard to believe that she was real, except for her eyes, which were large and evasive, like her brother Martin's, but, unlike his, of a rather cold blue.

"You were wonderful when you were angry the other day," he said, in the first pause of philanthropic details. "Are you often angry?"

"Dear me, I hope not. What an odd thing to say."

"But I think I prefer you angry."

"Isn't that what I told you at the party? People are always wanting me to be something I'm not."

"Don't you ever want to be that? I do."

She waved suddenly to an acquaintance. "Perhaps you're right. Perhaps that's the real reason I go to Doctor Silverman."

"He's your analyst?"

"Yes."

"Does he help you?"

Elly's blue eyes became a bit colder at this. "I pay Doctor Silverman very adequately for the privilege of talking about myself. He quite satisfies that urge, thank you. I don't need other ears."

"But I'm so interested! In you, I mean."

"Well, I'm not."

With this she turned to the clams that she had, after all, been persuaded to order. Clams were never easy for a lady to consume delicately, but Elly did not even try. She ate them greedily. Jay wondered if he had ever seen so curious a combination of affectation and bluntness.

"Why do you care for society?" he asked.

"What makes you think I do?"

"One's always reading about you at balls and parties."

"I like good manners," she replied, after a moment's consideration. "I like good food. I like elegance."

"Even when it's artificial?"

"It's always artificial."

"Isn't that like liking insincerity or hypocrisy?"

"If I may say so, Mr. Livingston, you are still in the ranks of the psychiatrically uninitiated."

"Won't you please call me Jay?"

"I'll try." She did not counter with a similar invitation.

"Do you really mean that you can know something's just a front, a facade, a hollow thing, and still care about it?"

"Certainly."

Jay contemplated her expression of bland earnestness with perplexity. "But don't you ever want to feel committed? Would you prefer a valentine to true love?"

"Ah, there you go!" she exclaimed, suddenly moved. "True love indeed! Not everyone wants true love. Lots of people are afraid of it. Doctor Silverman says lots of people like society for the very reason that it offers only the appearance of love. They're perfectly willing to settle for that. That's why ladies of the fashionable world kiss when they meet and exchange elaborate compliments. It doesn't mean anything, but it's not supposed to mean anything. It's a kind of charade."

"But what's the point?"

"It *works*, that's the point. It protects one from loneliness and fear!"

"And *you* need a defense against loneliness and fear?"

"At times. Everyone does. Everyone I know, anyway."

"Well, I think it's the limit! Here you are, the most beautiful woman I've ever seen, with charm oozing out of your every pore, with money, children, social position, everything, and you have to go to parties to play at love and not mean it, like Marie Antoinette!"

Elly's eyes became blue-yellow now, as they had the day of the party. "See here, Mr. Livingston. If you don't like the way I do things, you can leave this table right now. And never mind about the check. I can charge here."

"I was only joking."

"Some joke. I'm sick and tired of always hearing about my advantages. About my beauty and my charm. What do they do but make people envy me? Well, do you know something? I hate envious people! I want to shout in the face of the whole ugly world: 'Damn you, you *deserve* to be ugly. It serves you jolly well right!' "

"Believe me, Elly, I'm sorry."

"Oh, skip it." Spoiling for a fight, she was disappointed at the speed of his collapse.

"Will you forgive me?"

She had returned to the last of her clams. "Come now, Mr. Livingston, you're making too much of it."

"You won't call me Jay?"

"Oh, all right then, Jay."

"And may I call you Elly?"

"Call me Butch if you like!"

Jay had been enchanted by this second display of her temper. He returned now more tactfully to the subject of charity balls and did not change it for the rest of their meal. He even volunteered to contribute, through a press in which he had an interest, some of the printing expenses. Elly was delighted at this and at once became very friendly. In parting, when he asked when he could see her again, she was unexpectedly precise.

"Come to dinner next Wednesday, if you're free. Eight-thirty and black tie."

Walking back to his office he wondered if she always had a dinner party to put a man off with.

*

The Kays' apartment, in a spacious old building on upper Fifth Avenue, had an eight-window view of Central Park. Jay, the first to arrive, had the living room to himself for ten minutes before even his hostess appeared, and he studied it with a practiced broker's eye. Obviously, Elly was a spender. He had a shrewd idea of what Thad Kay was worth, and he was sure that the provider of that room had not done it out of income alone. The furniture, all French eighteenth century, was not only the finest but in the very best condition. The upholstery, in vivid pinks and yellows, was absolutely spotless. The chairs were probably recovered every year. There was not a crack in any of the porcelain, not a smudge on any of the glassware. The room was as perfect as its mistress.

The only jarring note was her portrait over the marble mantel, done after the style of Dali by a fashionable artist. It showed her, in what looked like a pink nightgown, standing before a flat, green sea on a beach strewn with fantastic shells. Jay laughed aloud.

"That's a fine start for my evening! To hear a man laughing at my portrait."

He had never seen her so assured. She was clad in gold mesh, with a necklace of rubies. He was immediately aware that Elly Kay at home was a very different person from Elly Kay abroad. The room backed her up.

"All those shells made me think of your clams. I take it they didn't give you hepatitis?"

"That's a quick recovery, Mr. Livingston. Jay, I mean. It's

Jay and Elly now, isn't it? Well, Jay, so long as you were good enough to come so promptly, you can help me with my *place-ment.*"

"Your what?"

"The seating, dear boy, the seating." She was holding a little board with slits in which place cards had been inserted, and he sat down by her on the sofa while she checked these. She was treating him, all of a sudden, as if he were an old friend, an intimate of the household. She explained the peculiarities of her guest list, as if he and she, alone of the party, were normal human beings.

"Can I be next to you?" he begged.

"Oh, no, I've given you to Mrs. Lydig," she whispered, for the first arrivals could now be heard in the hall. "She always wants to meet the coming people. So you see how I rate you!"

The party, made up from the current world of high fashion, was of mixed ages and professions: a young actor, an old New-port widow, a hugely rich oil man, a homosexual decorator, two editors of women's magazines (one of each sex), a British diplo-mat, a sprinkling of Orientals and (to supply an audience) two neutral, well-dressed, middle-aged couples from the legal and banking world. Jay noted that all the women shared the com-mon denominator of expensive clothes and that all the men de-ferred to the oil man. He decided that Hilary had been right. It was not, after all, going to be so difficult a group to understand.

The only person to whom he took an immediate dislike was his host. Thaddeus Kay was a big, beefy man with thick, blond, curly hair who might once have been strikingly handsome. His velvet evening coat and emerald studs showed that, like his wife, he still cared about appearance, but in every other way he seemed intent on divorcing himself from the party. He greeted Jay with a casual comradeship that was almost insulting. "God knows what gang of fairies and hairdressers my wife has assem-bled tonight!" he muttered. "A gentleman is hardly safe today outside the Brook Club." The only two people he talked to all evening were the oil man and his wife. He, too, was not going to be so difficult to understand.

Everybody else, however, was polite to Jay, a bit formal, perhaps, a bit brisk, but still polite. It was a world, he suspected, that would have no prejudices except against failure, and it would assume, from the simple fact that he was there, that he had not yet failed. At dinner he was given a social lecture by the Newport widow, Mrs. Lydig, a magnificent old ruin with staring red eyes, whose big nosed, over-powdered profile retained a certain chiseled handsomeness.

"We don't care any more who people were born or even how much money they have. All that's as archaic as European titles. I'm prouder of the fact that my grandson is playing the trumpet with Sandy Redskin's Band than I am that my great-grandfather was minister to the court of Louis Philippe. That's the note of society today. The *new* society. We care either for people who *do* things or people who amuse us. Mere money isn't the open sesame it used to be."

"You mean I'm too late?"

Mrs. Lydig blinked her eyes at him. "Not necessarily. Money always helps. But Elly tells me you're amusing. At least, it appears you amuse *her.*"

"I wonder if that isn't going to be my goal in life."

How those red eyes took him in at this! "Well, I'm glad to hear it, Mr. Livingston. Darling Elly needs a good friend. She may not look it, but she's a highly nervous girl. And a very unhappy one, too, I'm afraid. Of course, he's a brute to her, and always has been." Mrs. Lydig did not indicate, either by a glance or a lowering of her voice, that she was referring to their host on her other side. "I have always been devoted to her, and I'd give anything to see her happy. But take my advice, young man. Go *slow.*"

Jay accepted the hint that Elly did not have a lover, perhaps had never had one. It was as he had suspected. "Do you think her analyst does her any good?"

"Of course not. But all her friends have one. It's the thing. I'm of the old school. I think love is best."

"So do I."

"Well, I hope you'll do," she said with a grunt, "but I'm not sure. Frankly, you're not the type I would have picked for her. You *look* amiable enough, but then I gather from Elly you look younger than your years. Such people are usually mean."

"Then you must be very mean, Mrs. Lydig!"

Her stare at this was glassy. "Do you mean I must be very old, Mr. Livingston?"

"Oh, we're all old," he said airily and turned to the lady on his other side. He did not have to be afraid of Mrs. Lydig. She *was* old. Exuberant, he saw ahead of him the decades that he would have and she would not.

He had no chance to talk with Elly after dinner, but she made him feel, with a couple of friendly glances, that this was only because of her duties as hostess. When he left, avoiding a possible chance to escort the amiable woman editor and declining the warmly proffered lift of the decorator, he walked home happily through the cold night air. The first round was certainly his. He *had* become her friend.

3

THAT HE was not on the threshold of any ordinary affair had been apparent from the beginning. The whole business had an odd, dreamlike quality, a passing through a social looking glass into a stiffer, but still welcoming, world of reversed values. He was not sure that he wanted to go through altogether, but he was very sure that he did not want to turn back. He had been coming, for some time now, to the end of his various roads, not only in his personal life, as he had explained to Hilary, but in his business career as well. He had come to the end of his satisfaction with small deals and minor triumphs, to the end, in short, of the kind of ambitions that were patterned more on what men were supposed to like than what they necessarily did like. It was high time to look around, to take stock, in the most personal as well as the least personal things. It was time, if ever, to be bigger.

He felt it even in his office, the suite of rooms rented in the name of his holding corporation, World Inc., on the top of the Barthman Building, that he had loved with so ascetic, so monastic a fervor. Now, as he suddenly saw it through Elly's eyes, he could imagine her disdain of the circular desk in which he could entirely enclose himself, of the gold knickknacks strewn about, even of his frameless portrait showing him in strong, if rather sinister, profile, with a pink and yellow sense of jumbled apartment houses in the background. No, she would approve of nothing but the view from Fifty-first Street sweeping down to the southern tip of Manhattan and exploding into the glory of New York Harbor. And looking out his window on the cold January morning after her dinner party, a morning so cold and clear that even the East River was blue and the cloudless sky a blue-gold, he decided that she was right.

Alone, with his door closed and telephone shut off, standing before that view, he was nonetheless working again. He was fitting in the pieces to the puzzle of Atlantic Corporation, and he had been doing so since eight o'clock that morning. After three hours of solitude and thought so concentrated that his hands and brow were still moist, he was inhaling deeply from the dollar cigar with which he always rewarded himself after arriving at a business solution. The nicotine and the elation gave him the momentary illusion that the top of his head was rising straight up in the air.

He had learned to savor such moments. That, like love, they were brief, was not to be fussed about. One had to expect transiency in big matters as in little. What did it matter if Jay Livingston tired of his office, of his dictaphone, even his portrait? Were there not other buildings, other machines, other painters?

And this new project, to justify his growing optimism, was not on the same scale as earlier ones. At stake, in his proposed raid on Atlantic, were the assets of its subsidiaries: a dozen parking lots, six movie theaters, a chain of cigar stores, three shopping areas, a bus line, all strung along the eastern outskirts of the Bronx and Queens at intervals that would mesh with properties that he either now controlled or influenced. His vision was to be nothing less than master of the boundary between the city and Nassau County, with magnificent bargaining power, between the political entities, as to what improvements were placed on which side of that line. At the very least it was a project worthy of his new love!

He picked up his telephone and asked his secretary to bring

him the mail. In it he discovered the letter that he was looking for from the editor whose opinion of Hilary's magazine he had solicited.

"I know Hilary well," the man had written, "and I think he might possibly pull off such a project — *with* the proper supervision. Hilary is unquestionably brilliant, but he is too literary, too other-worldly, to be trusted alone in any venture that is expected not to lose money, let alone make it. The magazine will need interviews, photographs, columns, reviews, and a great deal of indispensable personalization to give it the requisite flavor. For this you will need a co-editor with Hilary, or, better yet, one over him. Although I have enjoyed my present position, I am much interested in your idea, and would be willing to discuss a switch if a substantial salary hike could be arranged. All this, of course, is written in the same confidence of yours to me . . ."

Jay smiled and, handing the letter to his secretary, told her to make the necessary appointment. It was just as he had thought. Hilary was perfectly usable, if only properly controlled. The magazine could be started and pushed. Within a year, if all went well, it might be sold at a fancy price to one of those asses of inherited millions who were always hankering for something to do. After that . . . well, magazines were chancy businesses. But Hilary, at the worst, would have been given a start and publicity, and Jay would have paid his debt, as he liked to pay them, at a profit to himself. And there was no question now in his mind as to the existence of that debt. Hilary, without any knowledge of Jay's lunch with Elly, had told him the very next day: "By the way, I saw Elly at the Shallcrosses' last week and gave you a terrific buildup. I think I even went so far as to say you had fallen in love with her. I hope you don't mind. Did anything come of it?" So *that* was the reason she had not been surprised by the telephone call! He sent his secretary out of the room now and dialed Elly's number himself.

His need to communicate with her was suddenly so strong that he had to control himself to avoid snarling at the maid who told him she was out. Then he remembered that she had said she was going to Wildenstein's to look for a small French painting for her dining room. When he arrived there, a bit before noon, he was told that Mrs. Kay was in a private room, into which, considerably to his surprise, he was promptly ushered. Elly, seated in an armchair before a small eighteenth-century *fête* scene, seemed equally taken aback.

"Why, Jay! Whatever brings you here?"

"I just wanted to see you. Nobody asked me my name."

"They must have thought you were Felix."

"Thanks." Felix was the interior decorator who had been at dinner the night before and who had urged Jay to come home with him for a nightcap.

Elly laughed. "He sometimes advises me about pictures. But now you can. How pleasant!"

He sat down, still trembling from the excitement of his walk and the fear of not finding her. For the next half hour, warm in that warm chamber and utterly happy, he said hardly a word, simply staring from Elly to the canvases, brought out and placed, one by one, on the velvet-covered easel before her.

The simple mauve draperies and walls of the room, unfurnished except for two armchairs and the easel, had nothing to distract the customer from the pictures, which provided windows into the fantasies of the eighteenth century: lute players and clowns, ladies in swings, ladies holding up mirrors to their faces as they lay in bed, ladies on forest hunt picnics, gentle shepherds, laughing soldiers, gentlemen drinking at country inns, apple-cheeked children against lush backgrounds of very green, very leafy trees, or pavilions tinted with gold. Elly was obviously absorbed. The communication between her and that more decorative century must have been a strong one. Yet Jay had the reassuring impression that she still belonged more to her own day. Her lines and colors were never blurred or indistinct. She was very definite, very bright, perhaps even the least bit hard. He didn't mind that.

He could see now why she lost her temper whenever he mentioned her natural advantages. What good had they done her? How frustrating it must have been to have everyone always insist one was among the blessed! He wondered if the tie that was obviously forming between them had not been created at least in part by an intuitive feeling on her part that he understood this. As she began now to ask his opinion on the paintings, he was sure that she was not being simply polite. The funniest thing about this woman was that the one thing that all the world took for granted that she had to be — by birth, by marriage, by manner — a snob, was precisely what she was not.

Why did he keep thinking of Cousin Florence? She had been warm and full of understanding; her great sad eyes had embraced a suffering universe. She would have recoiled from the blond brightness of Elly; she would have called him an infatuated fool. And yet there was a happy sadness in his heart, a rich melancholy fullness not different from what he used to feel in thinking of Cousin Florence.

The man showing the paintings had gone in search of more, and they were alone. Elly was smoking, looking at a tiny Vanloo of a church interior.

"I love you," he said.

She did not turn, only shook her head quickly. "Please don't say it, Jay. I can't cope with that. Truly. I'm not being coy. Truly!"

"Does Doctor Silverman tell you that?"

"I don't know. Maybe. Never mind."

"But I will mind! I bet the hound wants you all for himself! Oh, I can see him, the lascivious bastard, just panting for that hour in the day when he has you there, helpless, on the couch in front of him!"

Elly's expression was so startled that he had to laugh. "Surely, you don't think I *undress* for those sessions?"

"I'll bet you'd have to if *he* had his way!"

"Now look here, Jay. You told me you wanted to be my friend. That's fine. I want to be yours. But you'll have to accept the fact that I'm a complicated creature and that I don't want to talk about love."

"For now."

"For now and a long time."

"All right, a long time." He laughed again, in the pleasure of scoring so ancient a point. "Just answer me one thing more, and then we'll go back to the eighteenth century. Have you told Doctor Silverman about me?"

"What about you?"

"Anything about me."

"I tell Doctor Silverman everything."

As he was about to admit that the last round was hers, the salesman came back, bearing, appropriately enough, the portrait of a princess.

4

THE FEW close human relationships in John Grau's life had not been of his own seeking. Hilary had had to do all the cultivating of their friendship in the early Columbia days, and Addie had been obliged to give up her own career as a law student to court and marry him. There had been just enough charm in this thick-set, sullen, hardworking, no-nonsense young man, poor as Job, the orphaned son of a Brooklyn accountant, who had educated himself by tutoring undergraduates in mathematics, to save him from the isolation that he stubbornly seemed to seek. But if he did not reach out to other human beings, he had the sense to cling onto those who reached to him. He made up for his lack of acquisitiveness in friends by a loyalty that verged on possessiveness. Hilary used to liken John's affection to the squeeze of an anaconda.

It was through Hilary that he had come to know Martin Shallcross, and through Martin that he had met the Judge. Eben Shallcross had spotted in this solid young man a promising law clerk, and John, in his turn, had been shrewd enough to see in MacManus & Shallcross, with its small group of aging stars and its large staff of patient hacks, his own perfect opportunity. In the next decade and a half, with toil and single-mindedness, he had succeeded in hatching the glittering egg of a splendid corporate practice in this large, littered nest of litigation and politics. Everyone knew now that when the Judge died, what was left of MacManus & Shallcross would be John's firm.

John, however, cared little for prestige and not much more for money. He was an artist in law and got the same satisfaction out of setting up the intricate plan of a bond indenture, with its elaborate flow of funds into pools for maintenance, for debt, for construction, as must have Le Nôtre in creating the fantastic fountains and waterways of Versailles. Time meant nothing to John on a job; he could work right through the night and the next day. Fortunately Addie, in addition to five children, had the capacity to immerse herself tensely in local issues — she was constantly in arms about the condition of the street, the quality of the water, ill treatment of stray dogs — and, no matter how late he came home, she was always barely ready for him. As far as the cultural life of the great city was concerned, they might as well both have lived in the Gobi Desert.

Hilary, with whom John regularly lunched, but always at a time and place fitting into the demands of the latter's work schedule, took one of these occasions to try his hand at psychoanalyzing him.

"What nobody's had the wit to see in you is that you're really a hedonist," he told John. "Basically, your law practice is the sheerest indulgence. You work the way you do everything else, excessively. When you start something, you can't stop. Like poker. Or drinking. You'll drink twelve Scotches on a Saturday night. I've counted them! I guess we're lucky the law takes up so much of your time."

"You might be lucky if something took up more of yours!"

"Ah, but then I wouldn't be the balanced man I seek to be," Hilary retorted. "Nothing in excess. It's funny, when you stop to think of it, how wrongly the world judges you and me. We seem the exact opposites of what we are. I, the literary person, am commonly deemed unworldly . . ."

"Not by me!"

"I said 'commonly.' While you, the corporate lawyer, are a veritable symbol of mammon. And yet what are we both, in reality? I am a fantasy statesman, power hungry and powerless, a frustrated materialist, while you are a kind of architect who has managed to erect, in the very fray of the corporate battle-field, your own little ivory tower. You're like a monk in the Middle Ages, deaf to the clangor of combat around you, intent on the salvation of your own grubby little soul!"

"First, I'm a hedonist, and now I'm a monk! Who is it who's been hitting the Scotch this morning?"

"But it's true! You're both!"

Yet John was far from being as satisfied with his professional life as Hilary implied. A year before he had had to spend a month in a hospital following the removal of a malignant growth in his side. The doctor had given assurance of its com-plete excision, but had also insisted on complete rest, and there had followed roomfuls of white, empty time in which the pa-tient had had little to do but consider, as from a moon, the frenzy of his interrupted planetary life.

He had been too shocked by this brush with death, which had struck him glancingly, like a rude old man in the subway slam-ming through crowds in search of a seat he would not take, to be overly disturbed by this subsequent mood of detachment. He found that he could think now of his five healthy children and accept the evidence that none of them had either his brains or his industriousness, that they were all like Addie: loyal, excit-able, lovable, perhaps the least bit uninteresting. And Addie herself appeared, in these new, neutral reflections, as the nicest kind of squirrel, running rather desperately in her revolving cage. And he? Oh, he didn't bother to spare himself! What was the religion or the worldly ambition (the lack of which attri-butes he had sometimes deplored in younger, lazier men) that kept *him* going but an obsession with solving conundrums? What did he have, with each completed job, but the dim little sense of futility at the end of a long wasted Sunday morning in contemplating the finished squares of a double acrostic?

This mood changed when he went back to work, but it never disappeared altogether. He continued to be nagged by what he had once contemptuously described as the typical first-year law student's suspicion that a lawyer's work could have no greater validity than the client's cause for which it was expended. He became irritable with his senior partner, Judge Shallcross, whose cynical denunciations he had once regarded as simply comic. "If I believed what you believe, Eben, I'd quit the practice of law!" he would snap at him. Certainly Eben did not believe, platonically, that there existed, apart and independently from the petty moneymaking of the normal greedy client, such a thing as an ideal profit system, existing in elegant isolation, like an eighteenth-century "folly," to romanticize a humdrum landscape. And yet why not? Might a great dentist not do his most spectacular work on the tooth of a morally rotten man?

Sometimes, lecturing at night at the Practicing Law Institute to his fellows at the bar, catching just the right question from the floor and answering it with a precision that drew spontaneous applause, he would feel a new kind of elation, but he would as quickly reason it away. If a lawyer was no more than his client, what more was a lawyer preparing another lawyer?

He had watched rather contemptuously, from his happily removed vantage point in the corporate department, the negotiations in MacManus & Shallcross for the sale of Shallcross Manor. The Judge had reminded him of Frederick the Great's description of the Austrian Empress who had joined him in the rape of Poland — weeping as she grabbed. In John's newly sour concept of his native city Jay Livingston seemed to typify the moral obstacles that beset him, and he was more than usually gruff when his old classmate, passing down the corridor from Eben Shallcross' office, stuck his head in the door and asked if they could have a talk.

"I'm pretty busy, Jay."

"Oh, I shan't be long." Jay took John's silence for assent and sat down, placing his brown derby familiarly on John's desk. "You think, of course, I've come about Shallcross Manor," he began. "But that's all buttoned up now."

John looked sourly at that trespassing hat. "What *have* you come about?"

"To ask if you'd represent me."

"What!"

"I want you to be my lawyer, John. I've outgrown Harris and Epstein, and I've told them so." Jay broadened his smile, as if he suspected that the other was already debating the wisdom of telling him to go to hell.

"Why me?" John asked instead.

"Because I'm going to need the best securities lawyer in town, and I'm satisfied you're it. Oh, don't bother to deny it. I've made my researches. If you're not the best, at least there's none better. And I'm bold enough to think we might work well together. Harris and Epstein — up to the moment of their recent discharge — have regarded me as the perfect client. I don't second-guess. I don't quibble over bills. I answer all questions promptly. And I'm willing to work as hard and as late as the hardest and latest lawyer!"

John stared in continuing astonishment. "Have you discussed this with Judge Shallcross?"

"Why should I? I don't want him. I want you."

"But I very much doubt, from what I've heard of your business, if I'm the man for you. We have only a small accommodation real estate department. It's hardly up to your big deals."

"Oh, I don't need you for my real estate. I've got a house lawyer at World Inc. who can take care of all the metes and bounds I can throw at him." Here Jay winked at him. "I wouldn't want to turn anything *that* tough over to a firm like yours."

John bridled. "Meaning that we're too soft?"

"Meaning that you're gentlemen."

"I think you'd better get one thing straight, Livingston. I don't represent clients with different layers of lawyers. If I'm too soft for the real estate, I'm too soft for the rest of it."

"You mean you have to represent me generally or not at all?'

"Well, I wouldn't go quite that far, but . . ."

"But I would! Take the whole thing, then!"

John saw at once that he had been outmaneuvered. There was nothing left but to be candid. "What I should have said right off is that I doubt you'd find it profitable to do business under the eye of counsel like MacManus and Shallcross."

"Meaning that you're too honest for the likes of me?"

John's frown deepened, but he had never objected to this kind of challenge. "Meaning something like that, yes, if we must dot every 'i' and cross every 't.' Not only would the transaction about which you consulted me have to be straight, but your whole business would have to be. In other words, I won't represent a client who has a special tax lawyer for questions John Grau is too finicky for."

Even as he said it, he could not help wondering if Judge Shallcross would subject himself to any such limitation. But he hoped that his face remained inscrutable.

"There would be no such special lawyer," Jay assured him. "My man at World Inc. would be under your complete supervision."

John at this relaxed a bit and let some of his bafflement show. "Why do you sit there and put up with my rudeness, Jay? Why don't you tell me to go to hell?"

"Because I've learned that when you want something in this life, you usually have to choose between it and your vanity. I'm not going to beat about the bush with you, John. I know you know that in the past I've done a few things that wouldn't be countenanced by a firm like yours. But that was housing. It's a special kind of game, and I played it the way it's played. Now that I'm in your bailiwick, I expect to be guided by your rules."

John laughed. "Meaning you're too rich now not to be honest?"

"If you want to put it that way."

"I like your frankness, anyway. Suppose you tell me what kind of counseling you need. We can put off for the moment the question of whether or not I'm your man."

As Jay proceeded to the question of his proposed raid on Atlantic Corporation, John found himself soon approving his lucid and succinct relation. There was not a detail supplied that was not relevant. When Jay entered on his exposition of the ownership of the common stock, John could not help jotting down an occasional figure in his tiny neat handwriting in the upper left corner of his large yellow pad. At the end of an hour he looked at his watch and stood up.

"I think that gives me the idea. I'll speak to Judge Shallcross and see if we can take it on."

"I'm afraid Judge Shallcross doesn't like me."

"I shouldn't worry about that. Eben is not a man to be concerned with personal feelings where business is concerned."

"But don't forget it's not him I want. Or any of your hired hacks. It's you, my friend!"

John noted from the assurance in Jay's tone that the latter now took it for granted that the lawyer-client relationship was already established. But very likely it was. He simply nodded as Jay took his leave.

When he told Addie that night, her reaction was characteristically violent.

"But you told Hilary he was a crook!"

"Well, that was putting it a bit strongly. Anyway, he seems to have turned over a new leaf."

"He's a leopard with spot-remover?"

"Perhaps."

"You mark my words, John Grau! He'll bring you right down to his level."

"You didn't object to Hilary's taking a magazine from him."

"That's different. Hilary's using his money. But Livingston's using *you*. Now that he wants to look respectable, he's got to have respectable counsel. It's as plain as the nose on your face."

"Addie, wait till you get to know the fellow. He's not a bad guy at all."

"Oh, you men, with your good guys and bad guys! You're the slaves of good fellowship. Why any man ever bothers to bribe another is more than I can see. All he has to do is buy him a drink and tell him a dirty story."

"Jay Livingston did not buy me a drink. And he certainly didn't tell me a dirty story."

"Then he must have told you you were the best securities lawyer in town!"

*

Jay proved good to his word about being the perfect client. Once John had cleared his calendar to be able to devote full time to the proxy fight, by which Jay proposed to win control of Atlantic, he found that Jay had done the same. The latter, in the planning stages, would arrive early in John's office and work with him right through the day and into the night. In less than a week's time they had formed their strategy and worked out how best to approach each group of stockholders. Jay's job, of course, was to be largely in public relations. He would visit stockholders, give lunches and cocktail parties, talk on the radio and generally conduct the public campaign. On John's shoulders would rest, in addition to the fundamental burden of keeping the procedure in line with the federal securities law, that of spotting weaknesses in opposing stockholders' titles through tax deficiencies, transfer complications or even anti-trust violations.

John loved a good fight and had a reputation among his associates for grim tenacity. But the grimness was only the mask needed to ensure the seriousness of his co-workers. Once he felt that Jay was as serious about his own affairs as a good client should be, he became as cheerful as his new friend. Clerks working late at MacManus & Shallcross were astonished to hear peals of laughter occasionally emanating from Mr. Grau's room in the early hours of the morning. It was quite unprecedented.

Addie, however, did not change her mind. John took Jay home for dinner one Saturday night, with two younger lawyers from the office who were working with him on the proxy fight, and it did not prove a happy experiment. Jay was too careless in his manners. He was obviously not interested in homes or in children, and he was probably not even aware that it was incumbent on any guest of Addie's at least to pretend to be. He talked business at table, without considering that this excluded his hostess, and John, seeing in his wife's darkening countenance the scene that was in store for him later that night, wondered, with an obscure little twist of envy, if Jay might not be one of those men who had no use for women outside of stenography and sex.

"I tell you, he's cheap stuff!" Addie exclaimed, as soon as their guests had gone. "They don't come any cheaper! You mark my words, John Grau. He'll lower the tone of your whole office!"

Yet to John his new client was already beginning to seem something very different from this. He was intrigued by the frivolity in Jay that seemed to go hand in hand with a judgment as settled as his own, by the constant amiability that reached out to become a part of his very toughness, by the laughter that coexisted with his ruthlessness. Jay appeared a very hybrid insect; he was the cricket and grasshopper combined; he sang as he worked. And John, hypnotized by this tireless, ebullient character who managed to remain the same through the long hours of toil, began to speculate that what Jay represented might be energy, pure and simple, energy unhampered by domesticity, by ordinary morality, by professional rules of conduct. Was not

what Jay possessed the very thing that John had become fussed
over *not* having: creativity? Was it not what he now at forty
missed: in his life, in his law, even in his home? Were the deni-
zens of his world, the lawyers, the accountants, the brokers, and
their wives and offspring, more than simple stagehands in the
show that Jay *alone* was putting on? And if that were so, what
in God's name was the show all about?

Late one night, when he and his client had gone out for a cup
of coffee, he asked Jay: "What are you going to do with Atlantic
once you've got it?"

"Do with it? But there are so many things. One hardly knows
where to begin. We're right in the twilight zone, between city
and suburb. It's probably the area with more problems than
any other zone in the country. You name it. We've got it.
Take, for example, the question of the traffic along Twenty-
eighth Street in to Avenue A . . ."

As Jay talked on, and at considerable length, John found that
for the first time in their new friendship (if that was the word
for it) he was only half listening. He suspected that the Jay who
was talking social betterment was only an echo of some editorial,
some scrap of dinner conversation, some quickly discarded appeal in the mail. He had very little to do with the Jay who
might soon be president of Atlantic. John even now wondered if he could not detect in Jay's tone a hint of disappointment that a realist like John Grau should require the recitation
of this part, the acting out of this old role required by a stubborn public in sole return for the onus of being forever neg-
lected. If he *had* required it, and if Jay was protesting, then Jay
was quite right. He had been a fool to break his old rule of not
expecting a client to be anything but a client.

5

MARTIN SHALLCROSS had found the pace of his life uncomfortably quickened by his association with Jay Livingston. It was not all Jay's fault. Hardly had the Shallcross Manor deal been legally consummated before they were deep in the struggle for Atlantic Corporation. But right between these two affairs Alverta van Schaake's old bitch of a mother had seen fit at last to die, taking with her, it seemed, the last remnants of her shrunken rag of an old New York fortune and leaving her daughter (in the way of resentful and imposed-upon adult children) so hysterical with imagined guilt and would-be grief that even Marian Shallcross had seen no remedy for it but an immediate marriage. So Martin and Alverta had been united at last in the presence of the Shallcrosses and one old sobbing hypocritical van Schaake aunt. There had been no reception and only a brief week's honeymoon in Bermuda. Then the battle for Atlantic had started.

The bride's recovery, however, had been quick, not to say explosive. She had even seen fit to underscore her renewed faith in the future by becoming pregnant with a rapidity that might have aroused her husband's suspicions had not other circumstances demonstrated beyond a doubt that she had belonged to no one before him. Alverta seemed avidly determined to have all the things that she had missed at once: a husband, a baby and (to everyone's surprise) a house in Greenwich, Connecticut.

Martin had always assumed that they would live in New York and that Alverta, who had been an art major at Vassar, would be happy, after the long years as a salesgirl at Bergdorf's, to take a leisurely advantage of the cultural opportunities of the city. Not at all. She had fallen gushingly in love with a white French bungalow on Round Hill Road, and there had been nothing for Martin to do but to lease it. Now, a scant three months after their plighted troth, she had converted herself so completely into the suburban housewife that she might have played the part of the spirit of Greenwich in a local pageant!

The proxy battle, under the circumstances, had come almost as a relief. Martin had moved from Thaddeus Kay & Son to the offices of World Inc. to act as Jay's first lieutenant, and found the work engrossing. In hunting down the individual stockholders of Atlantic, he found there was no period of his life and almost no connection of his family's that did not have some actual or indirect benefit. He found a cache of stock owned by an old Columbia acquaintance, another by a trustee for a Shallcross cousin, still a third in the portfolio of a Chalmers aunt. His new boss was duly grateful.

"One thing I've learned is never to underestimate the survivorship power of old New York families," Jay told Martin. "There must be some vigor obtained by caring so much and so long about money."

"Look who's talking!"

Martin had studied Jay for a long period before deciding that he had the qualities essential for success. He had found him clear and cool in head and in heart, utterly liberated from the terrible modern sentimentalities that had filled the vacuum left by the collapse of faith: love of youth, love of political theory, love of love. Jay's mind had seemed to Martin as devoid of cant as his own. But more recently he had become alarmed by some seemingly uncharacteristic behavior in his chosen champion.

"I trust you will bear in mind that my brother-in-law, Thad Kay, is in this Atlantic fight, too," he warned Jay. "Also, that he has purchased a considerable quantity of stock. Let us be quite sure that he votes it with us."

"Is there any question about that?"

"Until very recently I should have answered that question in the negative." Here Martin, who was standing in front of Jay's desk, stared down directly into the latter's already angry eyes. "But unless you and my sister Elly show some discretion in this new 'friendship' of yours, you may find that you have turned him into a raging bull. Just because he doesn't happen to care about his wife doesn't mean he won't be jealous. That type of sportsman is always a Victorian."

"I think my private life is my own affair, Martin!"

"It's just exactly what it isn't," Martin retorted. "Particularly when it happens to be an affair with my sister."

"It's *not* an affair!" Jay had jumped to his feet.

"What it isn't is *your* affair," Martin conceded blandly. "What it looks like is mine. I don't care what you and Elly are up to, except insofar as it affects Atlantic. But there I'm warning you. Watch out!"

Jay had turned a vivid red. "Elly means more to me than any damn company!"

"It's not a question of having to choose between Elly and Atlantic," Martin insisted coolly. "Rather it's a question of your having Elly *and* Atlantic or losing them both."

Jay seemed to hover for a moment between exasperation and self-containment. Then he turned his back on his visitor. Martin, perfectly contented with this effect of his warning, left for Grand Central.

That night he had a drink in the bar car. Usually he waited until he reached home, but any effort to mask his inner tensions always upset him, and he was now additionally upset by the prospect of having to tell Alverta that he would be spending three nights a week in the city. It was no longer possible for him to commute daily and help in the Atlantic battle.

Yet that evening, in the small living room still bright with the glazed hopefulness of some fifty wedding presents that seemed to match — chairs, silver, glass — as such things seem to match in department store windows, Alverta, drinking her whiskey from a Steuben goblet, showed little change of expression at his announced heresy.

"Well, I suppose I shall have to get used to the idea," she said. "You'll stay at your family's, I assume?"

"You wouldn't come in for those nights?"

"And stay in that ghastly guest room? No thank you. It would be enough to have Baby born with your mother's taste."

Martin finished his drink and waited, before mixing another, for Alverta to finish out her usual vivid portraiture of his mother. But when he looked up, after a few moments of silence, he was astonished to see that she had resumed her work on the cover of the basinette and was entirely preoccupied.

"Of course, what I'm doing will be for Baby, too," he suggested awkwardly. "If this Atlantic deal goes through, and I make anything like what I expect to make, I'll set up a trust fund that will make Baby an heiress."

"An heiress!" Alverta exclaimed in astonishment. "What makes you think she'll be a girl?"

"I don't know. I just said that."

"But it seems so funny," she pursued. "I should have thought a man would instinctively think of his first child as a boy."

"It doesn't matter, Alverta."

"Of course it does! It's fascinating."

As their one-sided discussion continued, passionately on her side, about the sex of the infant, the name of the infant, the schools and colleges that the infant might attend, and even, during supper, on the kind of man or woman who might one day be the infant's spouse, Martin relaxed with the realization that the subject of his nights in town was not going to be raised again. As he had, in a few months' time, replaced, in the steamy hallway of Alverta's affections, the malicious old mother whom she had so hysterically criticized and so irrationally adored, so had he in his proper turn, been replaced by a three-month-old fetus. Looking across the table at his wife's serene countenance, he understood, once and for all, that, armed with the capacity as she was, of channeling all her affections in any one way at any one time, she would be a perfect mother. As if to prove this, she had had none of the ordinary discomforts of pregnancy, not even morning sickness. She would probably want ten children. It was a dim augury.

Yet even more depressing, and enough so to blur the lines of his *Times* in the train the following morning, was the collapse of his secretly cherished romantic ambition. For Martin had never been fool enough to believe that man could live by bread alone. He had always known that the heart had its necessary function, and he had secretly regarded his long bachelor years, in this respect, as a time of preparation and exploration. It had tickled his fancy that nobody, not even his own mother, had guessed this about him. It had suited his plans that people should think him cool, self-sufficient, even at times hard. He had smiled to himself, imagining what they said about his matrimonial prospects: "Martin? You can be sure he won't lose his heart any faster than his head. Not that boy. Someday, before he's forty, he'll announce a discreet engagement to a girl who's eminently proper in every way — including the pocketbook." And all the while, deep within his guarded heart, was such a different ambition!

He had wanted a girl, all for himself, who would owe him everything. He had dreamed of a girl who would receive her first security and her first love from him. And Alverta, from the very beginning, had struck him as just what he wanted. She had been almost heartbreakingly pathetic in her patience, in her conscientiousness, in her industriousness, in her rather cowed bigness, in the splendor of her unabashed gratitude at his smallest attention. There had been no tiresome female coyness in her acceptance of his first invitation to go out to dinner — only a disarming surprise and a candid enthusiasm.

In those first weeks of their romance he had indulged in the most delicious fantasies. For every daydream had been sweet, not only those where he had pictured her as happy, better-dressed, appearing like a tall princess at his side, somehow apologizing for being taller than he, but those where he had seen her as gallant in disaster, as his widow, after an undeserved bankruptcy, working as a charwoman, scrubbing on her hands and knees to put their children through school and college. Idiot that he had been not to have learned that the speediest conversion of which the human being is capable is that to prosperity!

Alverta's way of showing her wifely love had been to possess him. If he had wanted her as part of himself, so did she, with the stronger personality, want him as part of *her*. He had been quite correct in divining that she had the makings of a great woman, but that woman was going to be a greater mother than wife. Arranging the wedding presents in the Greenwich house, she had reminded him of nothing so much as a bird building a nest. But when he thought of his own role in this drama of propagation, it was from a different branch of the animal kingdom that he drew his analogy. He tried not to think too much of the fate of a drone bee.

In the distraction of the office, in the frenzy of telephoning, Martin was able that morning to find his anodyne, and he was irritated when his sister Sophie called.

"I need your help. It's about this magazine that Jay's staking Hilary to."

"What about it?"

"I can't tell you on the telephone. Won't you lunch with me?"

"I don't lunch, Sophie! I know you consider yourself above these things, but Jay and I happen to have a war on our hands."

"You must eat something."

"I have a sandwich sent in."

"What time? I'll come down and have one with you."

At noon Sophie, woebegone, arrived at his desk and proceeded to pour out her problems as if no such thing as the Atlantic proxy fight existed. Jay, it appeared, was trying to corrupt

Hilary. Every time they met to discuss the proposed magazine, Hilary made a new concession at the expense of artistic integrity. When Martin interrupted wearily to suggest that this was Hilary's business and not his, she exclaimed shrilly that that was the terrible thing: Hilary didn't care! Hilary was actually now working on a profile of that old bag, Mrs. Lydig, which he had the nerve to defend as a piece in the manner of Sainte-Beuve!

"Oh, Sophie, grow up!" he interrupted her at last. "Who but you cares what Hilary writes or doesn't write? It's a living, isn't it? Let him work it out for himself, the poor guy. Don't be so damn bossy!"

"But I've got to think of Hilary's future if he won't!" she cried. "Someone has to. What do you plan to do with this magazine?"

"*Do* with it? Isn't that Hilary's job?"

"I mean ultimately. You and Jay."

"You mean Jay?"

"All right, Jay."

"Sell it, I suppose. Isn't that what Jay usually does with things he buys?"

"Sell it? Oh, Martin! Who to?"

Something in his sister's desperation reminded him of Alverta, the old Alverta, and he became brutal.

"The highest bidder."

"Do you mean it? Is that fair to Hilary?"

Martin turned away from her despairing look. "What's Hilary got to do with it?" he retorted. "He should know Jay. What does he think Jay cares about literature?"

"Hilary says he *does* care. He says he reads things now."

"Dream on, dear. Jay cares about profits. He's not under any illusions. He knows perfectly well that New York will never support an expensive, serious magazine. But he also knows that people will never give up the idea that it may. So to cash in on this he has to get up a fancy format, sprinkle it with colored

photographs (have you ever seen a *bad* colored photograph?),
stick in a couple of unusual interviews, with Lady Macbeth or
Pontius Pilate, and start the town talking. With any luck he
should be able to unload it by the third issue on some arty jackass who wants to be remembered for something besides his
wealth."

"And what happens to the jackass?"

"I suppose he learns a valuable lesson in public fickleness.
Besides, he can deduct it all from his income tax."

"And poor Hilary's out of a job," Sophie retorted bitterly,
"for the sin of believing in Jay."

"But what's he lost? He doesn't have a job now. He may even
pick up some prestige at the jackass millionaire's expense!"

Sophie now became irritated, too. The atmosphere was tense
with that mood of inter-sibling dislike that always hovered so
close to even the closest congeniality. "Don't you and Jay ever
wish you were engaged in something constructive?"

"I'm engaged in constructing a fortune. That's all I ask."

"You sound so grim. So desperate. You sound as if you'd
been so knocked about by life there was nothing left for you but
to make a fortune. Yet from where I sit, it would appear you
have everything a man could want: a loving wife, a baby coming, a nice home . . ."

"Oh, Sophie, don't talk rot!" He whirled about in his chair to
face her. "You ought to know *some* facts of life after all your
analysis. Alverta is everything she ought to be. If I expected
anything more, I was an ass. But as an ass I still have to face my
asininity. Love, I find, has very few satisfactions for me, love or
family life or arriving babies. I can't get away from the sense of
living in an ant-heap. Here, in Greenwich, in New York, wherever I am. And the only way to cope with an ant-heap is to have
so much money you *can* get away from it!"

Sophie put her fingers to her lips in the shock of receiving his
confession. "But, my poor Martin, how?"

"On Caribbean islands, in yachts, in private planes. In all the most vulgar, obvious things. Why do you think the rich put so much money into transport? Because they feel what I *know*."

"And do they find happiness?"

"Happiness? You talk like a green girl. When have *you* been happy?"

"I'm still trying."

Martin was about to apologize, but she had risen already and left the room, and his heart was full of the dry desperation that comes with having vented on an innocent relative the anger that belongs to another.

*

Sophie, waiting for the office elevator, moved to the window of the foyer to watch the rain that had just started to descend on the misty, cold island. Looking eastward over the thick swirling of the dirty river, over the docks to the stretching cubes of Queens, she was totally depressed by the prospect. Where things in the city were old, they were simply dreary; where they were new, they were simply grim, remorselessly utilitarian, bare of decoration, barren of hope. New York seemed to be moving into a future that was terrifying in its dullness, where every little tassel of imagination and gaiety had been sheared off, leaving nothing but walls and windows, squares and oblongs. And Jay Livingston was the lord of this new world! He loved it, he battened on it; he drew cheer from it, while she and Hilary, pale anachronisms, clutched a few precepts from the hysterical faith of the last century to comfort or console them as mere sentimental relics, not as legal tender for anything that had to be acquired. For one terrible gray moment she saw no single point in being alive. Then the elevator door opened, and she was rescued from nothingness.

6

MOST OF Jay's time he now spent roving the city in his red Cadillac limousine, his other office, paying calls on stockholders, in constant touch by automobile telephone with Martin. He called on trustees, on guardians, on executors, on widows; he called on the rich and on the poor, on the sane and sometimes on the near-incompetent. The bulk of Atlantic's owners were located in greater New York, as the company's activities were too local to have broad appeal beyond, but there were still several thousand of them. When not traveling, Jay worked with public relations men on the mailings, entertained at cocktail parties in hotels, gave press interviews. He orated about what he could do for Atlantic as president until it seemed to him that if he were running for mayor, he could not have been seeking more votes. Control of this corporation, like Elly Kay's heart, was a remote, elusive thing.

Many of his evenings were spent working on legal details with John Grau, who was devoting himself to the fight with an energy that seemed astounding in one who had only a fee and not a fortune to gain. John's identification with his client's cause was fierce: he seemed now actually to dislike the "gang of idiots" who controlled Atlantic. But fierceness only sharpened his ingenuity. He paralyzed one large block of securities in the enemy camp by lodging price-fixing complaints against a group of textile companies to which ownership of the Atlantic stock could be attributed by certain arcane federal regulations. Jay fully appreciated the intellectual grasp of his counsel's mind. He saw it as an exquisite product, a rare piece of art, wrought of the finest gold, proudly displayed on a velvet counter for preferred and trusted customers. Yet purchasable. Had he not purchased it? John was a trusty bloodhound who would change his affections with each new master. His world, like Elly's, was not, in the last analysis, too difficult to understand.

In that other world he and Elly had reached a plateau, a high, dry plateau, with rarefied air that seemed to have the effect, on her anyway, of nullifying the ambition for further climbs. She talked to him with rather too much candor now, and certainly too many details, of her never-ending psychoanalysis. She would, he grudgingly supposed, have been willing in return to hear about his, but he didn't have one to offer. She also discussed, at equally fatiguing length, the problems of her two daughters, fifteen and sixteen, and here again he had no ammunition to throw back at her. She put him, it was true, in a special category among her friends, but it was not at all clear that she would ever be willing to alter that category.

Yet he had gone so slowly! Even in the furor of the proxy fight he had found time to call with flowers on her boring old mother. Mrs. Shallcross liked him now; she would evidently like any friend of Elly's. But the visit had not been sprightly. He had gone twice more to the Kay's for dinner and submitted to the indignity of being obviously considered by Thad Kay as one of his wife's "pansy pals." He had taken a Sunday walk in the park with Elly and her sarcastic old father and suffered under the latter's barely veiled wisecracks. And all for what? All to be told by Elly, in that high, bright, brittle tone, with that serene blue gaze, that he was the only true friend she had ever had!

One morning, before lunch, he called at John Grau's office. "Let me ask you a question that's *not* about Atlantic. Do you handle divorces?"

"Thank God, no."

"Does your firm?"

"For regular clients — when we can't get out of it."

"Would you handle mine?"

John glanced up at him with an expression that seemed to suggest that his query was in the poorest kind of taste. "I imagine we could. I'll speak to Al Zimmerman. He does that kind of work."

"I've told you before; I don't want any of your hired hacks. I want *you*."

"But I've never handled a divorce in my life!"

"I don't care. You're my lawyer. I need your judgment and your bargaining power. I need you to hammer some sense into Hulda's crazy head. She wants my shirt." Jay almost smiled as he saw John's frown. He knew he could count on the inarticulate loyalty that exists between all males in any prospective battle of the sexes.

"Why do you want a divorce all of a sudden?" John demanded. "I thought your separation was mutually satisfactory."

"It was. But that was before I wanted to get married."

"You want to get married again? Now? In the midst of this proxy fight?"

"I'm in love, John! Is that so incredible?"

There was a question, among the law books, amid the proxy mail, under the dark prints of Marshall and Taney, whether this simple utterance would not be reduced to the status of a vulgar, private noise. But even John, the lawyer, even in his office, was touched at last. "You'll have to promise me you'll do right by your wife. Financially, I mean."

Jay spread his arms to indicate the totality of his abdication. "You know what I'm worth. You know what I've borrowed. You be the judge. Any agreement you make with Hulda I'll sign."

"You must be very much in love," John said with a grunt.

"May I inquire who is the Cleopatra that's done this to you?"

"Elly."

"Elly! You don't mean Elly Kay?"

"Certainly I mean Elly Kay!"

"Good God, man, she's my senior partner's daughter!" John's chin came forward aggressively as he jumped to his feet.

"What has that to do with it?"

"She's got a husband. She's got children!"

"She has a husband who's treated her like filth."

"She picked him!"

"And two daughters who live for horses. Half their friends have divorced parents."

"As if that made it any better! I'm sorry, Jay, I cannot share your attitude about these things. Marriage to me is sacred. Now maybe with you and Hulda it's different. You've been separated for years. There are no children to consider. But with Elly . . ."

"John, listen to me," Jay interrupted him firmly. "Like everyone else, as soon as you get into the field of morals, you snatch for a generality. I like you better in law, where you deal in particulars. Can you seriously believe that I'm going to pass up my one chance of happiness for some abstract formula about the sanctity of the home? And the *Kays'* home, at that? Stay with the facts, counselor!"

John's hardened countenance slowly relaxed. "I guess I've been a windbag. Nobody ever appointed me your guardian. I'll speak to Judge Shallcross. If he agrees, we'll go ahead."

"But he'll never agree! John, won't you do this thing for me on your own? Elly doesn't have to be involved, *or* her father. This is purely between Hulda and me."

"But won't Elly come here for her divorce?"

"How should I know? I haven't asked her."

"You haven't *asked* her?"

"I haven't asked her anything. How can I, until I'm free?"

This unexpected delicacy seemed at last to engage some part of John's active sympathy. "I've got to go to a meeting now on that textile companies' suit. Come back this afternoon, and we'll work out an offer to Hulda. I suppose, like any woman, she has her price."

"Sure. The moon!"

"Well, at least you're willing to pay off Hulda before you're sure of Elly. I like that." John's face rigidified again, but this time with what Jay recognized as his "protector of client" look. "Will Elly give up Thad's money before she's sure of yours?"

"Damn you, John, are you implying she's a mercenary bitch?"

"I'm implying she's a society woman," John retorted with a shrug. "Which has nothing whatever to do with the sincerity of what she feels about you."

*

Jay, walking the few blocks to Ludovico's, recovered the buoyancy that John had temporarily dashed. In the street he always fixed his eye on the horizon. Sometimes it was water, the yellow-black East River, the slate-colored Hudson; sometimes a golden morning over Queens, like a train's headlight in a subway tunnel, sometimes a sunset that seemed to show the Jersey shore on fire. As he turned down the street to the restaurant and looked ahead at the dead whiteness of the winter sky, a sky that promised neither snow nor rain, but threatened both, he planned his opening words to Elly. Standing in the velvety obsequious darkness of Ludovico's lobby, he watched her for a moment, sitting at their corner table, in a white blouse and purple toque. She was always ahead of him.

"You don't need a psychiatrist," he said abruptly, as soon as he had joined her. "It's all hokum. Just look at yourself in that mirror over there and ask yourself how many women look like that!"

Elly shrugged. "Looks don't bring happiness."

"They would if you'd let them."

"Perhaps, but I won't let them."

"Be really frank for once. Do you honestly think he's helping you?"

"Of course I do! I wouldn't have been capable of a friendship like ours a year ago."

"You mean you needed a Jewish doctor to reconcile you to a Jewish boyfriend? Poor little wasp!"

Elly shook her head. "I don't think that's it. My friends consider prejudice middle-class. In the smart world anything goes — Jews, Negroes, homosexuals, what have you."

"Thanks!"

"Well, you know what I mean. I still have a lot of my father's phrases in my head, and it's natural for them to pop out from time to time. But basically you know I'm not prejudiced."

Staring into those inscrutable, fixed blue eyes, hearing the click of her measured tones, he almost felt that he did know it. And hadn't he wanted her to be prejudiced? Wasn't that just his conceit? To overcome it?

"My superior airs are nothing but defenses," she continued. "Doctor Silverman says I was a rejected child."

"Rejected! By *your* mother?"

"Yes, even by her. Mummie has never really loved me. She dotes on me, as if I were some precious doll, some pink and white thing in silk and satin. Small wonder I've spent my life looking for echoes of love. Reading about myself in social columns that tell me how warmhearted I am!"

"But those columns are paid for, Elly."

"You're telling *me?* But I don't pay any more. Now I'm in the process of rejoining the human race."

Jay controlled his impatience at this final banality. After all, it was just the moment he had been preparing for. "But you must have had love once," he insisted. "What about the first days of your marriage? What about your honeymoon?"

"Oh, that was even worse. I never had any real love from

Thad. Not even in the beginning. Of course, *he* says the shoe's on the other foot. I'm sure there's no indecency about me he hasn't confided to his cronies at the Racquet Club bar. A man can say things that a woman would be called a bitch for saying. But I never told anyone what *I* went through! I never told anyone that on our wedding night he said I wasn't as good as the whore he'd gone to after his bachelors' dinner!"

Jay had to be very careful not to smile. "These 'old New York' gentlemen!"

"Exactly! These old New York gentlemen! For years now I've provided him with the excuse he needs for his failure in life. When I started my psychoanalysis I really believed I was. I considered myself a fraud, trapped in a world of sincere people. Now my danger is that I may come to think of myself as the only honest person in a world of phonies. But no! I mustn't do that!" Elly had worked herself up now to a state of considerable agitation. "That is the mad way out. Once you start hating, you're never very far from those ragged nuts who shout pointlessly on street corners."

Jay paused to give her time to regain her composure. Then he asked: "What do you think of me? Another phony?"

That ivory countenance had recaptured its impassivity, and the blue eyes, slightly softening, ever so slightly, took him in, turned him over, appraised.

"Not a phony, dear, no. But you have your illusions."

"Such as?"

"My family for one. Me for another. You see me as a kind of princess."

"It's what you are."

But there was no coyness in the slow, deliberate shake of that blond head. "It's just what I'm trying to stop pretending I am. Don't you see you're working against me? I don't want to be a phony princess. I want to be a woman!"

Her tone seemed to threaten him with a world where everything was normal, explicable, dead, where men were just men, and women, women. His need to repudiate the doctor was so great that for a moment the words choked him.

"You're very wrong if you think *I* don't want you to be a woman. And very wrong if you think I'm going to go on indefinitely playing this role of brother confessor."

Elly's equanimity instantly showed cracks, like blue ice hit by a rock. "What do you mean?"

"What do you think I mean? Or must you ask Doctor Silverman?"

The hand which reached for the untouched cocktail glass was not unsteady, but it was clear that she was making an effort. "You mean, I suppose, that we should become lovers?"

"Would he object?"

"Who? Thad?"

Jay laughed crudely. "Hardly."

"Please! Let's not talk about it."

"Why must we always talk about your past? Why can't we talk about your future?"

"Because it's so hard for me to!"

"Have you stopped to consider that this way it's hard on *me?* How do you think a man feels when he desperately wants a woman and is put off with the second-hand chatter of some Freudian quack?"

"Oh, Jay, please!" Her eyes were full of tears, and he marked, with his first astonished realization that he was going to succeed, that she neither looked about her to see who was watching, nor came to the defense of her doctor. "Give me time, dear. I'm such an odd mixture."

But Jay knew enough immediately to press his advantage. "I should think even a second-rate witch doctor would have made it possible for you to have a lover by now. Or is he saving you for himself?"

"Don't be revolting. Doctor Silverman? What an idea!"

"You think they never take advantage of their patients? Listening to all that sexy talk? Of course, I'm jealous of the guy! You lie on his couch and tell him the most intimate things you can imagine, and if I so much as hint that we translate our present talky-talk relationship into something we *both* want, you squeal like a Victorian virgin who's just seen her father in his shirt-sleeves. Come off it, Elly!"

All the time that he was talking he kept his eyes intently fixed on her. Oh, she took it all *far* better than he could have hoped, so much better that he was already cursing himself for not having spoken sooner.

"How long will you give me to decide?" she asked. She seemed to have entirely recovered from her initial shock. But how could she have been so shocked if it was over so quickly?

"How long do you need?"

"Days, anyway."

"Days!" Jay could not help the explosion of his exultant laugh now. "Oh, all the time in the world, so long as you tell me there's hope!"

"Of course there's hope. If a woman will even *talk* about that kind of thing, she'll do it. Everyone knows that. But it can't be here."

"Here?" He glanced about.

"In this country. I'd have to be away, somewhere. Some new place. Some romantic place."

"Morocco maybe?"

"Maybe Spain. Yes, I think, Spain. There now. Talk about something else. Tell me some gossip. Please, Jay. *Gossip!*"

7

Sophie was not finding her engagement to Hilary an easy period. She regretted, to begin with, her decision not to announce it in the newspapers. She had been embarrassed by her age, in an era of progressively younger marriages, and she had always shrunk from public commitments. Now she and Hilary seemed to exist in an odd social limbo where he continued to be invited out without her, and, far worse, where he continued to accept. Then she was bothered by the sense of emotional anticlimax that had followed their postponement of the ceremony until spring. What could she do with the interlude? If Hilary was socially too busy, partly on the excuse of building up patronage for his magazine, certainly she was far too idle. Yet there still was not time enough to take a job. And, finally, she was exasperated by Hilary's enthusiastic cultivation of his new friendship with Jay.

At the very least she found this indelicate. For what else could it seem to Jay but an apology on the part of her fiancé for her strange conduct in tearing up the model at the Shallcross Manor party, even a hint that she might not be quite a responsible person? And as for the magazine, what was that but downright disloyalty? Had she not herself for years tried to persuade Hilary to start just such a periodical and offered to help him to raise the money by composing and typing the necessary appeals to his rich friends? She tried now in every way, without directly quoting Martin, whose opinion she knew he would discount as cynical, to persuade Hilary of Jay's mercenary motivation.

One night, after an acrimonious dinner at an expensive restaurant (there was always an added row about this, she preferring the small quiet places, and he loving the smarter spots where he could wave to his friends), he accompanied her back to the Shallcrosses' new apartment to thrash this issue out. The discussion became heated, and she had to keep hushing him, for her parents had gone to bed.

"What it all boils down to is that you think Jay is smarter than I am because you think he's less scrupulous," he protested indignantly. "I'm not at all sure that in some illogical female fashion you don't find unscrupulousness rather virile! You take it so absolutely for granted that, even with me as feature editor, Jay will be running the whole show. Thank you very much!"

"But, darling, you're not equipped to deal with someone like that. It's not your fault, and it has nothing to do with virility. It's simply a question of training."

"May I remind you who it was that opened *your* eyes to what he was doing to Shallcross Manor?"

"You were."

"And having assessed his influence in one operation, must I necessarily be blinded to it in another?"

"No. I suppose not."

"Your trouble, sweetheart, is that you were so shocked by the revelation of Jay's bad taste that you tried to construct it into something malevolent."

Sophie at this began to reassemble her scattered offensive. "I was so anxious to save Shallcross Manor that I was willing to overlook certain faults in Jay . . ."

"I'll say you were! You were willing to marry him!"

"Oh, Hilary, don't be ridiculous. I would never have married him. But for a while I tried to shut my eyes to his shady side . . ."

"Shady? How is it shady?"

"Hilary, listen, will you? I had an excuse for dealing with Jay. I was trying to save something good and fine. At least I thought so. But you're going into business with him. That's much worse."

"*If* he's shady. But I repeat: how is he shady?"

"Oh, everyone knows he is."

"What sort of an answer is that, Sophie?"

"Ssh. You'll wake Daddy, and then there will be trouble. What about his blockbusting?" She was grateful to see him concede her random accusation with a wince. So she was right! He had been a blockbuster!

"Of course, I admit that's a dirty way of doing business. But is it actually dishonest? Anyway, Jay's given all that up."

"Oh, Hilary!" she hooted.

"You and I, my dear, were brought up in a world where we never had to think of such things. I wonder if it's fair to judge Jay by the same standards. He came up the hard way."

"That's pure snobbishness. Come, you can do better than that!"

Hilary paused to control his exasperation. "Let me put it this way, then. Jay doesn't see that kind of thing as you and I see it. To him, it's a question of market, pure and simple. If he buys a hill with a view, he'll stick a bar on top of it. If he owns a field by a highway, he'll put up a signpost. If he can bring down the price of a lot by selling the house next door to a Negro family, he's going to do it. He probably sees nothing wrong, anyway, with making people pay for their prejudices. He may even look on it as a means of achieving integration."

"If it was *intended* that way."

"Ah, there you are, Sophie, intent. That's just the difference between people like Jay and people like us. He doesn't go in for intent. He goes in for facts."

"Suppose the facts were different. Suppose this were 1861 instead of 1961. Would Jay be in the slave trade?"

"I think this argument is becoming inane."

"Because you're losing it?"

A lover's victory is always Pyrrhic. Sophie's reward was a barely perfunctory good-night kiss. Lying awake afterwards she could not help wondering if *all* his kisses had not been perfunctory and if what she had noticed that night had not simply been what on other occasions he had taken more trouble to conceal.

For why else should he limit himself to kisses? Would a man who really wanted her not try for more? No matter how much he professed to respect the delicacy of her psychic readjustments? Were his precautions really for her benefit or for his own? She reminded herself tearfully, over and over, sitting up in bed and smashing her clenched fist into the crumpled pillow, that she had vowed never to be the kind of female who would nag a man for his love. She reminded herself that Hilary was good and kind and sensitive, that his neuroticism was part of his charm. She almost screamed aloud that even half a loaf was too good for her, miserable, complaining creature that she was!

After two hours of this she gave in at last to her insomnia. She got out of bed and sat by the window and made herself consider her engagement coolly. Was it not perfectly evident that there was an air of treaty, of composition, to it? Obviously, Hilary still enjoyed his bachelor's life; equally obviously, he was sacrificing a part of it deliberately in the interests of his engagement. Why? Because he preferred to be with her? Or because he dreaded the idea of turning into a lonely, childless, unmarried old man? God in heaven, was that all the institution of marriage meant? She remembered now with terror what that powdered old hag, Mrs. Lydig, had told her.

"My dear, it's easy to see you don't like people. In fact, I suspect that, like most shy persons, you're actually rather proud of it. You think, deep down, there's something noble and romantic about the lone swallow that eschews the chattering flock. But don't delude yourself. You're marrying the most gregarious of mortals. Getting between Hilary and his parties would be like getting between the hog and the barn door!"

The next morning, haggard but calm, she decided to put into effect a new resolution. She would not be so demanding in the future. She would not meddle any more with Hilary's social engagements. She would sit home, like an Eastern lady, a *femme d'intérieure,* and wait for her master to return from his wars or his dinners. She would try to regard her smothered but eruptive disapproval as irrelevant, her own purer standards as unrealistic. She would remind herself hourly that she was not going to marry a man of her devising but a live man, not the imaginary, sympathetic, always-in-line companion conjured up by Dr. Damon's fantasies of marriage, but another wobbly graduate of the school of the couch. Who was *she,* after all, to expect a paragon?

At his first telephone call that morning, her resolution was fractured. He wanted to go that night to the monthly members' dinner at his club. Somebody, it seemed, had made up an amusing table. Sophie told him peevishly to do what he wanted and hung up. In another ten minutes she called him back to apologize and was frenzied to find his line busy. When it finally rang, there was no answer; he had gone out. Utterly dejected, she now bleakly acknowledged the falseness of her resolution. The last thing that she was going to give him was his social freedom.

That evening, when her father came home, she went to see him in the library. She told him that Jay was planning to finance Hilary's literary project and asked if he would not like to undertake the job instead. The Judge tapped his fingertips together.

"Do you anticipate that the venture will be profitable?"

"Oh, I don't suppose so. But it's so degrading to have Hilary backed by a man of Livingston's reputation. And he's put an editor over Hilary who's changing the original idea into the cheapest kind of 'chic' reporting."

"Let me see if I understand you, my dear." Her father was now at his chilliest. "You are suggesting that I scoop Mr. Livingston's money out of the East River where he is gaily flinging it and substitute my *own?*"

Sophie nodded her head gloomily. "I thought it might be a question of honor."

"Honor! To fleece your old father and save the realtor's pelt! Spare me such honor. But I'm glad of one thing. Hilary goes up several pegs in my estimate. If he can get money out of the likes of Livingston, he's got a stronger head for business than I ever credited him with!"

"I suppose you mean that as a compliment."

"You're darned right it's a compliment! You have to get up early in the morning, my girl, to put one over on your ex-beau. They were telling me at the Knickerbocker the other night about the coup he pulled on the management of Manley's."

"What is Manley's?"

"I should think even you, Sophie, would have heard of that old furniture store. It seems it had been running downhill for years under a sleepy family mismanagement. Well, your friend Jay kept a quiet eye on it until the price of the stock had dipped below the value of the inventory. Then, bang, he pounced! In the quickest proxy raid of the last ten years he seized control, shut up the shop and sold out the assets at a spanking profit. Oh, he's a daisy, your Mr. Livingston! If you've got him on your magazine, you'd be a fool to let him go. Who knows? He might even make money out of belles lettres!"

Sophie noted with disgust the admiration in her father's tone. He actually approved of such tactics! "I'm not sure I understand what he did to that store," she retorted, "but do I gather that the business was closed down and the employees all fired?"

"Ah, well, these days they'll find other jobs. Not like in the thirties, my girl."

On Saturday night, when Hilary drove her up to Bronxville to have supper with the Graus, she was once again in a repentant mood. She thoroughly liked the Graus. She enjoyed the friendly disorganization of their household and applauded their contempt for the social world. She hugged to her heart the reassuring conviction that Hilary could not have so long held the devotion of this highly critical couple without being worthy of it. But her mood hardly survived the discovery, at supper, that John Grau was actually representing Jay Livingston.

"After all Hilary's told me about your high ideals in the practice of law!" she burst out at him.

"Now, Sophie," Hilary warned her.

"I'm sorry, Hilary, but it's important for me to know how a man as honorable as your friend here can reconcile himself to Jay's way of doing business."

"She's a stuck whistle on this subject, John!"

"Let her talk, Hilary," John insisted. "I'm perfectly willing to answer her question. What do you mean, Sophie, by his 'way of doing business'?"

"Well, closing down that furniture store, for example!"

"Manley's? Is it a lawyer's job to look out for old, mismanaged stores?"

"Are you your brother's keeper?"

"No! No lawyer is. I doubt if he even should be. The Manley's deal was perfectly straight. Legally straight, that is."

"*Legally* straight?" Addie now joined forces vociferously with Sophie. "Is *that* all you care about, John Grau?"

"The subject is not an easy one." Here John made the surprising concession of shaking his head. "I won't conceal from you girls that I've done a lot of thinking about it. And, frankly, I was very reluctant to take Jay on as a client at first. But the guy has a funny fascination. He's a kind of belated pioneer, in a world where the frontier has vanished, gazing about for new gold or new lands or maybe just new adventure."

"That's what I keep telling her, John!" Hilary exclaimed. "Jay is fundamentally an idealist."

"An idealist!" Sophie echoed.

"Hilary's right," John insisted. "There's a naïve, little-boy quality in Jay. He looks around him and sees heaps of beautiful things. He falls in love with them and wants to possess them. His faith has to be that the process of acquisition will be somehow beneficial to the thing acquired. That the best of all possible worlds will materialize if only Jay Livingston is left free to make his profit!"

Addie's lengthened countenance presented an incredulity that was only half humorous. "Sophie, I'll never again say that lawyers are cynics!"

"Oh, I didn't say I believed it," John rebutted her. "Or even that Jay did. Oh, no, he sees clearly enough that the world he conquers is an inferior place to the one he assails. He sees his shoddy houses, his tinsel motels, his soulless stores. He understands that he is a kind of glorified junk dealer. But hope keeps bubbling. Somewhere, somehow, he has to believe that the brightness and smartness of a good boy like Jay Livingston is going to produce something admirable, something permanent, some bit of merchandise that will not fall to pieces before one has got it from the shop into one's car."

"And that is this new company he's after?" Addie demanded.

"That, for the moment, is Atlantic. Jay does the best he can in our dull world. He's like an eagle in an aviary flapping his wings."

"And eating dead mice," Sophie finished with a shudder of distaste. "Your eagle has turned scavenger."

"All eagles do."

Hilary was furious with her in the car going home. "This business with Jay is becoming an obsession!" he protested. "I'm beginning to wonder if you're not still in love with him!"

"How can you say that?" she cried. "I was never in love with him. I detest him!"

"Well, I suggest you try to detest him less. It's embarrassing,

Sophie. You're getting like your father with the Supreme Court."

Things were always better when Hilary scolded her. That night when she had gone to bed, she was much less tense. If only he would go beyond his good-night kiss, all might yet be well! Dared she suggest it? But that was ridiculous; she was only begging the question. He would go beyond if he *wanted* to go beyond. The trouble was: did he want to? If she were the one to suggest it, would she not be responsible for any fiasco that ensued?

Breakfasting with her father in the morning, she reproached him for not having informed her that Jay was a client of his firm.

"I don't consider that he is," he retorted. "I consider him purely a client of John's. At least, I'm told he won't talk to anyone but John."

"Everywhere I look in my life, he seems to pop up!"

"You haven't heard the half of *that*."

"What do you mean?"

The Judge waited for the maid to leave the dining room. "Your mother revealed to me last night that your sister Elly and Mr. Livingston have become the greatest of pals. Apparently they lunch together, dine together, do God knows what together."

Sophie knew that he would want her to be shocked, so she was careful to keep her countenance collected. "What is God knows what?" she inquired.

"Well, I never know what young people are up to," the Judge replied with a shrug. "Your sister has always been the most unpredictable creature in the world."

"You don't suppose she intends to leave Thad and marry him?"

"God, don't even say it!" The Judge glanced angrily at the closed pantry door. "Don't even think it! I thought we were safe when *you* gave him up. But Elly!"

Sophie hurried to her mother's bedroom after breakfast. Marian confirmed that Elly was seeing Jay frequently, but refused to be led into further speculations. In fact, she was distinctly testy at the suggestion that any were in order.

"Your poor sister has a bad enough time with Thad without being answerable to us for her friends. Just because she's pretty and well dressed and has lovely taste doesn't mean that she's happy, poor darling. Far from it! You think if a person doesn't suffer from your dumps that she doesn't suffer. Well, it's very egotistical of you, Sophie!"

There was nobody else with whom Sophie could discuss the matter. Hilary had gone to Boston to try to persuade an old friend in a publishing house to join his magazine. But it so happened that Jay was also in Boston, on his proxy fight, and when Hilary telephoned her excitedly to impart the good news that his financial underwriter had "found the time" to take him and his editor friend out to dinner, she blew up.

"Do you know he's after Elly now?"

" 'After'?"

"He's obviously determined to get himself a Shallcross, one way or another!"

"Sophie, you *are* jealous!"

"Of whom?"

"Of me. Of Elly. Of anyone who has anything at all to do with Jay. You're a dog in the manger. Just because you gave him up, you don't want anyone else to have him!"

For Sophie two days of misery ensued. The word "jealous" provided the keynote of her suffering. For it began to seem to her that Hilary might have hit the essence of the matter at last. Was it not possible that she *was* jealous, and not of Elly, but of him? Was it not possible that she feared that *he* was attracted to Jay, more attracted to Jay than to herself?

There it was, anyway, out in the open, the unthinkable thought, and she might as well learn to live with it. After all, it was Hilary who had suggested that she might have found Jay more virile than himself, and would such an idea have occurred to him had Jay's virility not been very much on his brain? Did not Elly feel the same thing, and possibly even the newly sentimental John Grau? Did they not all, herself included, find virility in the mere existence of Jay's activity, febrile activity, destructive activity, immoral activity? Surely, it was indicative of the final decadence, the last slow, toppling shudder before the crash, when the very bricks and mortar made love to the termite!

But try as she would to ravel out the unwelcome picture of an effeminate Hilary from the tapestry of these frenzied generalizations, it kept reappearing. She was not going to be able to avoid, in her own dirty mind, the bleak consideration of Hilary as a homosexual. A latent homosexual, of course. A repressed, or, better still, a sublimated homosexual. She could hardly conceive, after all, that Hilary wanted to *do* those things (what were they?) with Jay. No, it would be rather that Jay with his mocking green stare, his directness, his fitful energy had excited the admiration of the bigger but lazier man. Or perhaps even that Hilary, in a Greek sort of way, was attracted by the boyish quality in Jay, by his wavy hair and alabaster skin, by his good spirits, by his tight, muscular build. Had she not noted that Hilary's gaze in restaurants sometimes alighted on younger men, on boys?

And then there was the old business of Shakespeare's sonnets. She had read much of what he had read while he was working on the book that he had later withdrawn from publication; she had followed, step by step, his conversion from the Southhampton to the Pembroke candidacy in the time-honored game of identifying "Mr. W. H." They had studied together photographs of the seventeen portraits of Southhampton, and she remembered his vehemence in denying that such a "foolish, effeminate creature" could ever have been the poet's "lovely boy." And had he not boldly affirmed that Shakespeare's pure, impassioned love for a beautiful youth had been the source of his finest poetry?

Ah, but what a bitchy revenge the woman in her now sprang up to take! She hated herself, as the questions succeeded each other in her seething mind. What was all such romantic theorizing on his part but the disguise of something that every foul-minded school boy would promptly recognize? The "Canal Zonite," Hilary's first wife, had she been really sluttish or simply female? His indecision, his aimlessness, his love of the arts, his perfectionism, his platonic friendships with women, his delight in social life, were they not all indicia of repressed homosexuality?

Repressed? Why did she have to assume that it had been repressed? Would a man as big and handsome as Hilary not be the constant target of homosexuals? Could they not smell him out? Would they not subject him to endless harassment and temptation? How would he not succumb? Did he not swim naked every afternoon in the pool of the Manhattan Athletic Club? Sophie's mind became a dark fantasy of showers and locker rooms.

Really, it was unendurable. She thought she would go back to Dr. Damon, and she made an appointment, but then she canceled it. She could not, at the last moment, face the gentle firmness with which he would attempt to excise her doubts. He would turn her attention from Hilary to herself. Why, he would softly inquire, did she think such things of her betrothed? *That* to him would be the rewarding field of exploration. To a psychiatrist the world outside the patient's distortions, the world, indeed, that the patient distorted, was of only minor interest. But Sophie found that she was clinging to the mud that she wanted to fling. Her distortions, if distortions they were, had become her only reality!

The day that Hilary came back from Boston, full of hope and

excitement with his project, was the worst of all. As usual, he had a drink with her parents before taking her out for dinner, but now the pleasure that they had in his company, of which she had formerly been so proud, simply irritated her. It struck her of a sudden that Hilary's eternal good will, the perverse way in which he drew out her eager old father on that last unspeakable opinion of the high court or in which he related to her glowingly grateful mother some absurd bit of flattery that he had heard from Mrs. Lydig about Elly, was designed merely to postpone the moment when he would be alone with his fiancée, unprotected by the chaperoning cackle of her progenitors.

"Well, I confess that in the old days I never used to care much for Evalina Lydig," Marian Shallcross was saying. "But there's never been any question about her shrewdness. And, of course, she's always been a true friend of Elly's."

"Let me tell you, Hilary, a little story I heard the other day about Hugo Black . . ."

"Yet it seems so funny to me the way, in Elly's world, all the ages are mixed up. Evalina must be a good five years older than me."

"Marian, I'm trying to tell Hilary a story. Please don't go on about that Lydig woman. There was a time, when she wasn't so rich or grand, that she'd have been glad enough to entertain a proposal from one E. Shallcross. Anyway, it seems that Hugo Black and Bill Douglas were both dining at the White House . . ."

Sophie, impatiently listening, redefined her family in terms of the relationship of each one with Hilary. Was he not the greatest common denominator between the five of them? He went fishing with her father; he lunched with her mother; he helped Elly with her dinner parties; he talked market with Martin; and he was going to marry her! Ah, there was the clue, of course. An only child, an orphan, Hilary obviously craved a family. Shallcross Manor, in Martin's bachelor years, with all the friends coming and going, had provided that. But now, with the family shrunk to an old couple and an old maid in a much smaller dwelling, if he wanted to go on with it, he would have to marry her!

She rose suddenly, right in the middle of a story that Hilary was telling about some Mrs. Lowell in Boston who was interested in buying a "piece" of his magazine (already he seemed to exult in using Jay's vulgarisms) and insisted that he take her to dinner.

"I'm starved," she said flatly when her mother protested.

At Ludovico's, just after they were seated, Mayor Wagner came in and paused for a moment at their table to ask Hilary about a mutual friend who was ill. It disgusted Sophie that this brief recognition by executive authority should so obviously elate him, however hard he attempted, after the Mayor had gone on to his table, by flattening his voice as he talked of other, of casual things, to conceal it. She became convinced, staring at his hand enfolding the base of his cocktail glass, that it was trembling with pleasure.

"Admit you're ecstatic."

"Sophie, what's *wrong* with you tonight? Aren't you glad to see me back?"

His good humor, fostered by his trip to Boston and intensified by the Mayor's notice, was unbreakable. Never had she been more sullen; never he more patient. When she decided that he was treating her as Dr. Damon used to, she became desperate.

"Hilary, I have a bit of capital of my own. Let me put it into your magazine. Let's you and I do it together, and to hell with Jay Livingston!"

"Honey, we can't afford to lose your capital."

"Then how can we take his?"

"Because he gets all kinds of tax losses. It won't cost him a cent."

"Please, Hilary!" she pleaded. "Please, please, please! Do this one thing for me!"

He became very grave now as he took in the full extent of her concern. Then he placed his hand firmly on hers. "Darling, I'm going to have to be hard with you. I'm sorry, but it's the only way. I do not believe that your feeling about Jay is quite rational. I'm sorry, but I don't. I'm afraid you'll have to talk it over with your doctor. And in the meantime you are going to have to face up to the plain fact that I have no intention whatever of rejecting Jay's offer."

Sophie, staring across the restaurant, wondered for a second if the lamps on the tables had not actually dimmed under their pink shades. With a clutch of terror in her heart she recognized, gathering about her, the undulating arms of her old darkness, like a gas escaping through some aperture in the floor and stealing up around their table to engulf her.

"Hilary, marry me!' she gasped. "Marry me now!"

"Tomorrow, darling," he answered promptly, and the room was lighted again.

He ordered a bottle of champagne, and they toasted each other, and she was assailed by a violent bumpy happiness that rumbled around inside her, making her feel that if she tried to stand up, she would fall right down again.

"You know how people are always saying that this girl's problems or that man's problems will be solved by matrimony?" she was asking him now. "You know what faith people have in those few little words mumbled at an altar? Well, they're right! They're absolutely right!"

And then they drank more champagne and had a long, inebriated conversation about plans. Of course, they could not be able actually to marry in the morning. There was a license to get, a blood test to take. Hilary's old aunt from Burlington had to be invited. Sophie's parents had to be given some notice. A week would be necessary. Yes, yes, she thought, a week, a month, anything so long as he wanted to marry her!

Only much later, alone in her room, trying to sleep, did it occur to her that he might have suggested driving to Maryland.

And why had he not asked for an early wedding in the first place? Why? She knew why! She had behaved that night like a shameless hussy and forced his hand, a hand still trembling with pleasure at the Mayor's greeting! Falling on her knees at the window and looking, agonized, up at the moon, she prayed for death. For how could anyone who made such a mess of providence possibly deserve to live?

8

ELLY, in Paris, ostensibly for her wardrobe, telephoned to none of her friends and dined alone for three nights in her room at the Meurice. In the mornings she shopped; in the afternoons, walking, she had delicious glimpses of an early spring. She slept well and long and enjoyed her aloneness. She had made no final commitment to meet Jay in Madrid, but she had told him that she *might* be in the Ritz there on Friday. It would be interesting to see if he would fly the Atlantic on such slender assurance.

Before leaving New York, she had given up her sessions with Dr. Silverman. She had found herself unable to talk to him further about dream men or men casually observed — movie stars or taxi drivers — when she was for the first time in her life summoning up the courage to turn dream into fact. She did not fear the good doctor's disapproval, for he seemed to smile benignantly on the prospect of any sexual outlet, but she was afraid that he would try to break down her infatuation into all the less attractive parts of which it was made: of Jay's being a Jew, a ruthless realtor, of his being socially maladroit, even of his being an inch shorter than she was. Silverman knew too much about her, and, like all psychiatrists, he would try to convert her infatuation into something he called "love." But in the process might she not lose the infatuation? And she was very sure that she did not want to do that.

Her need for Jay's body, so far concealed from him and from Silverman alike, had become her sustaining preoccupation. At first, like all her previous needs, she had relegated it to the strict rules of her fantasies, keeping it vivid only by her constant meetings with him. But now Jay had broken through all that, and she had had to face the choice of giving him up or giving in. She had debated it, over a long weekend when the girls were home from school. She had sat through endless movies with them and listened listlessly as they chatted of heroes and boys. She had let them wear her dresses, use her makeup, ask friends in and dance and scream until the neighbors complained. She had put them back on the plane, noisy and tired, and marveled that the time had passed so swiftly. Then she had made the decision to go to Paris and come home by Madrid. She had tried to persuade herself that this was all she had decided, but she was only too aware of how much her excitement belied it.

She had never had an affair, but she knew that it would have to be in a strange place. For even though her yearning for Jay was so great that, walking in the street, she sometimes had to pause, put her hand on a stoop, even close her eyes, she was still ashamed of him. At restaurants she was embarrassed by his ruby cuff links and his diamond ring, by his familiarity with waiters, by the frank way he stared at other women. At her own parties she was mortified both by his informality and his overformality. He bowed from the waist, for example, when he greeted Mrs. Lydig and then proceeded to call her by her first name.

"I don't like your young man," Evalina Lydig had snapped to her. "Mr. Livingston, or whatever he calls himself. He's not the thing at all. God knows, I have no objection to *arrivistes*, but I expect them to pause, for a few minutes at least, on each rung of their ladder. I certainly expect them to pause long enough to catch their breath on the rung where *I* happen to be perched!"

"But that's the very top, Evalina!"

"Darling, I'm serious. Livingston is the kind who's always looking over your shoulder when he shakes your hand to see if

there isn't somebody more important behind you. If he ever
gets to hell, he'll do it to the devil himself! Why, he thinks I
must be a déclassée dowager because I talk to him! Maybe he's
right, at that. Maybe any connection with him is degrading.
You'd better watch out."

"Oh, I'll be all right."

"*Will* you?" Evalina's stare was upsettingly searching. "I'm
not so sure."

This interchange was very upsetting to Elly, for Evalina
Lydig was the court of last appeal in her little group, and however much she had learned to question its contribution to her
happiness, she was still timid at the prospect of cutting that
bridge. What else, after all, did she have? No man could be
expected to make up for everything else in life, particularly
when he combed his hair with a small gold comb in public. Jay
was not only unthinkable as a husband to Evalina's crowd; he
would hardly do as a lover.

In New York, that was. In Madrid, away from the friends, it
would not matter so much if a man said "Pleased to meecha" or
called curtains "drapes." He could be judged by simpler standards. It might even be that together she and Jay would find
something so much more important that she would be no longer
afraid to face her old set with him at her side. Oh, she did not
rule this possibility out! For Elly knew perfectly well that the
small rules of her world were important only *in* that world. Left
to herself she rather liked Jay's diamond ring. Left to herself,
she had her own vulgar streak.

Things happened now very fast. She arrived on a Thursday
in Madrid. All the next day she spent in her room at the Ritz,
smoking and reading magazines, and at seven he called.

"Oh, hello!" she exclaimed lightly. "Are you here already? I
didn't expect you for days."

"I came here straight from the airport."

"Here? Where is here?"

"Two doors down from you."

Her laugh was not quick enough to disguise her gasp. "Why, how cozy! Can we have a drink later on? I'm not sure about dinner. There's a buffet thing at the embassy that I should drop in on. But how about meeting in the bar at nine? Or aren't you used to Spanish hours?"

"You're darned right, I'm not. And I haven't flown four thousand miles for any drink in any bar."

"What have you flown them for?"

"Don't you know, Elly?"

"I can't imagine."

"Then let me come and tell you."

"Now?"

"Immediately."

This time she did not try to conceal the sharp intake of her breath. "Give me fifteen minutes," she said, and hung up.

When she opened the door to his ring after precisely that period of time had expired, they stared at each other, without smiling, and she knew that there was no point in further quibbling.

*

IT WAS a shimmering union of flesh and fantasy. Or *was* it love? Was that, possibly, what love was? It appalled her to think that she might have missed it, that she might have swept giddily into her fatuous forties in the same old foolish life without ever knowing that week of tumultuous nights in the quiet gray bedroom of the Ritz. They would drink champagne until they were perfectly uninhibited (it did not take many drinks), and then they would go about their principal business with the serious good faith of children at play. Jay had an energy that contrasted wonderfully with the heavy, snoring slumber into which Thad had used to lapse after a brief, selfish performance. All the erotic memories of her girlhood were evoked under her lover's expert manipulations. Her mind became a brilliant series of colored slides from the romantic history texts of her school days. One moment she was a haughty alabaster nude, some great lady captured by Tripoli pirates and stripped for the auction block; in another, she was a Sabine lady fleeing a would-be ravisher, her loose garments snatched, one by one, from behind. Then she was Bathsheba, spied on in her bath; then Helen with Paris, on the ship to Troy. The tour of myths and legends made actual Madrid seem as dull as a town in a Sinclair Lewis novel.

Not so for Jay. He loved the sight-seeing too. They drove out of Madrid on day-long excursions to the Escorial, to Toledo, to Segovia; they dined splendidly; they went to a bull fight and even to church. She gave hardly a thought to those two distant girls at the Foxcroft School or to Thad at the bar of the Racquet Club, and she was utterly indifferent already to being seen with Jay. What she and he had become to each other seemed so natural, so common, so indicated, that she could hardly take seriously, could hardly even believe in, people who might think it was wrong. And, to be entirely serious, *were* there any such?

"I never thought you'd throw it off so fast," Jay told her one night, as she nodded to a couple leaving the restaurant. They were cousins of Evalina Lydig!

"My past? But you see I never really believed in it. Perhaps faith is hard to shed. I wouldn't know. But fear . . . well, darling, once fear is gone, it's gone. What could be left?"

"You don't think Thad might kick up a row? Madrid was your idea, you know. I was perfectly willing to go to a quieter place."

"But I like doing things openly with you, Jay. What can Thad do? Divorce me? Let him try! With all I've got on *him!*"

"Wouldn't it be all right to let him? So you could marry me?"

Ah, there it was, she thought, with her first frown. It had

been bound to come, sooner or later. "But, darling, I thought you had a wife."

"Would you, if I didn't?"

"I suppose I'd have to think about it."

"Why don't we make them both divorce us, Elly? Why don't we send them compromising pictures?" Then he paused, and his smile disappeared. "But, of course, there are your daughters."

"Yes. I have to think of them."

"Wouldn't they like me?"

"As a stepfather? I couldn't possibly tell."

"Oh, please, Elly, say you'll marry me someday!"

"You want to coop me up, just as I'm enjoying the first real fling of my life!"

"Damn right I do!"

She was now even able to contemplate that she might not be in love with him. She could actually visualize a return to her old life, even a resumption of her sporadic sexual relations with Thad. She felt ready, indeed, for anything. But none of this seemed to affect, seemed even to be relevant to the wonderful quality of the moment. What filled her heart at the sight of Jay concentrating as he ordered from the menu, or of Jay, suddenly intent, staring up at a cathedral tower, or of Jay in his scarlet bathrobe, slipping into her room, was gratitude, a pulsating, boundless gratitude. God, what she owed that man! What but her very life? When she felt his deft fingers moving over her back and thighs, she would remember how hideously she had treated him, how blandly she had relegated him to the status of "pal," how dreadfully she must have bored him with all her psychiatric chatter.

Perhaps she *would* marry him in the end; perhaps she owed it to him. After all, was he not the only man who had ever really wanted her? And he was full of pleasant surprises. She had never anticipated, for example, that he would be so ardent a sightseer. He had started by knowing less of Spanish history and art than she did, which was little enough, but, unlike her, he had read all the guidebooks and retained what he read. He had the kind of mind that could absorb every last detail of a Baedeker, from the amount of an expected tip to the dates of Philip II. He seemed particularly to enjoy the Prado, near the Ritz, which they visited several times.

"They had style," he said of Velásquez' little sad-eyed hoop-skirted infantas. "Incredible style."

"I find I can never disassociate people in history from the terrible things they used to do to other people," she replied. "I see the royal family sitting up there on a dais watching an auto-da-fé. Ugh! Can you imagine? People writhing and screaming in the flames and turning all black? Perhaps that's why they look so sad and grave."

"They didn't watch. The heretics were paraded before the King, but they were 'relaxed,' as the term was, to the public executioner in another place."

"Still, everyone knew." She turned away from the Infanta Maria Theresa whose grave demeanor she could only see now through imagined smoke.

"People have always done terrible things. They always will. It's the same way back home."

"Yes," she conceded unwillingly, "I know that. I remember telling Daddy, when we were reading about the religious wars in school, that at least in New York people had never been burnt alive. He took the greatest glee in telling me about a Shallcross slave in the eighteenth century who had been roasted over a slow fire on Bowling Green for starting a riot. It took eight hours before he died! And my own ancestors did that. What a world!" Jay uttered a peal of laughter. "How can you laugh at such things? Would you like to be tortured like that?"

"I'm laughing at you, dearest. You get yourself so worked up over something that took place hundreds of years ago. To me history is a picture gallery. I pick and choose what I like. And I happen to like infantas."

"If my parents could hear you!"

"They'd be so surprised? Why?"

She turned away, faintly embarrassed, and paused before "The Surrender of Breda." "Well, darling, there's always been such an atmosphere of your *not* caring."

"About what?"

"Oh, beautiful things. Old things."

"Was *I* the one who sold Shallcross Manor?"

"Oh, lover, no, of course not!" she exclaimed, slipping her arm quickly under his as she saw the glint of anger in his eyes. "And I think you have greatest style yourself. More so then any old Velásquez."

"He whirled about and seized both her hands. "Elly, I love you! Promise you'll marry me?"

That afternoon they drove out to the Valley of the Fallen and walked through the huge tapestried tunnel to the crypt, their eardrums throbbing to the crash of the organ. Elly shivered in the damp air and at the realization that behind those rocky walls lay the bones of sixty thousand men, young men who had died in combat while she had been going to subscription dances in New York. But when she put her arm under Jay's and walked close to him, she felt the snooty little thrill of the living in the presence of so many dead. And then, as she was scolding herself for such presumptuousness, reminding herself how soon she would be as they, a passionate thought interrupted her reverie to announce to her whole consciousness: "But whatever comes, at least I've had this! I've had these days in Spain!"

There were more, too. After their week in Madrid they drove south to Granada where they stayed in the Alhambra Palace Hotel in rooms that looked out over the plain to the blue glory of the Sierra Nevada. Jay could not seem to have enough of the Alhambra itself. He wandered for hours through the formal

gardens and the great empty chambers of the palace, staring up
in fascination at the stalactite ceilings, gazing out of the high,
arched windows, musing before limpid pools and trickling fountains. He seemed dazzled by this last great monument of Moorish splendor.

"I feel as if my ancestors might have lived here," he told her.
"You may say it's an odd way for a Jew to talk about an Arab
stronghold, but wasn't it Disraeli who said an Arab was nothing
but a Jew on horseback?"

"You'll be putting me in a veil next."

"And then in my harem!"

They laughed, but Elly was very conscious of his serious note.
The Spanish experience and the enfranchisement of love was
already working differently in each of them. She began to
understand that while she was eagerly shedding the parapherna-
lia of the past: the Shallcross decorum, her mother's injunctions,
the whole wretched business of being a lady and (horror of horrors!) a "charming" one, Jay was finding his liberty in a nostal-
gic rendezvous with ancient disciplines that had very little to do
with his unrestrained present. If Iberia to her was a glittering
beach down which, at long last, she dared to walk, naked and
proud, to him it was a wardrobe of costumes to fling over his
bare twentieth-century pelt. She found herself wondering at
times what Dr. Silverman would have to say about it.

On their last day in Granada, before going home, they paid a
final visit to the Alhambra. By the main gate, huddled near the
tourist shop, was a shabby studio where couples could be photo-
graphed, against a painted backdrop of the Court of the Lions,
in Moorish costume. Jay suggested that they be done. Elly protested.

"Darling, it's the tourist trap to *end* all tourist traps!"

"It's not at all. It's become venerable. People in the eighties
had it done. It's a grand old tradition. Please, Elly! As a memento of all that's been."

"I'll feel such a fool."

"Do it for me."

It was part already of their brief relationship that they had tacitly agreed not to quarrel. For all their closeness there were territories that they chose not to explore or perhaps did not dare to. She agreed to the picture, and they donned the dirty robes of sultan and sultana and were seated before the crude painting of the glorious courtyard. When the picture was developed, Elly blushed. Reclining self-consciously on the divan, playing a lute to her lord, she looked as Arabian as a Junior Leaguer in a benefit performance of *The Sheik*. But Jay, in a burnoose, one hand imperially on the jeweled dagger at his hip, his eye haughty and disdainful, was magnificent. He might have been a hero out of Washington Irving. He fitted at last into the illustrations from her schoolgirl texts.

Part III

1

To THAD KAY the bitterness of Elly's defection was much more than the simple humiliation of being a cuckold. It lit up every dusky corner of his twilight existence and dazed him with the revelation of failure. Could one be a failure already at forty-two? But of course one could, and what was more, by any fair count, he had been a failure since twenty-eight. Fourteen years of self-delusion, while his world had slipped away as ineluctably as Rip Van Winkle's! And now, in this horrid awakening, he took in at last the full gap between himself and his old prep school crowd of the "annus mirabilis" at St. Jude's which had produced a United States senator, two ambassadors and a cabinet officer, all before forty! He had not even the ancient excuse of over-privilege. In modern America it paid to be born high. And what had he accomplished but, as a fleshening stockbroker (200 pounds) to have increased (and only slightly) the family fortune, to have bored his wife and daughters and bored (more fatally) his girl friends. The only thing he now did really well was to play squash, and he was getting heavy for that.

And nothing, moreover, not even the daily half-dozen Martinis, could haze the brightness of this terrible new vision. He began to see that part of his catastrophe was that from his earliest years, he had always seemed to offer the world more than he could deliver. Had he been able to deliver nothing, or little, the fraud would have been soon detected and nobody (at least not himself) so hurt. But in his boyhood, in the darkling moneyed world of the nineteen thirties, on a disillusioned and frightened Long Island, the young Thaddeus Kay, who had won all the cups and all the medals, had been deemed an angel child with a divine mission to redeem the wanderers in the financial wilderness.

Oh, yes, he had fooled every person but the one he had tried to fool: his charming, lazy, aristocratic father, the sportsman and womanizer, the almsgiver and spendthrift, the easily imposed-upon but never resentful, the gentleman builder whose taste had put together the Georgian showplace of the north shore of the island where he had lived in easy splendor, neighbored by the two smaller estates, copies of his own, of his generously endowed but forever jealous ex-wives. Thad as a boy might have had golden looks and the highest grades, as well as all the ribbons, but he had shivered at the touch of that long tweeded arm, placed around his shoulders by way of congratulation, knowing that its possessor, for all his easily showered apparent love, for all his gracefully delivered encomiums, did not really believe that his only male child had any style. And, surely, if any of the others, the shrilly possessive mother, the gushing stepmothers, the reluctantly admiring half-sisters, even the silly Kay aunts, had taken the trouble to study the glossy, fashionable portrait of the heir and pride of the family that stripped the mother's Adam mantel of its distinction, they would have seen that the sitter had not been a Shelley or even a Swinburne but a very regular, very straight, very conscientious Yankee lad. But no, people were too blinded by the slightest good looks that went with money. Make Croesus Hermes, and all the ladies fluttered around him on the green lawn parties of "Harborside," Edwardians in American mid-depression, well-wishers in fancy dress. How could Thad please them all, preserve the fortune and become a liberal, be old and modern, give away the dollars and accumulate them?

Thad was thorough and literal. If he started something, he

always finished it. He could dissect and analyze, take apart and put together again. He was constructive, considerate, a natural leader of other boys. At Harvard he was not "cliquey," like the others from St. Jude's; he played football, which gentlemen didn't, and made a point of seeing how many of his class he could address by their first names. He was Phi Beta Kappa, Crimson, Fly. He was adored by girls for his broad shoulders and blond brawn and the gleam of his gold, and his coming of age party at "Harborside" challenged the greatest debuts of that era. When war followed, it seemed to strike just the right note — revelry before Waterloo — and Thad was even vaguely to wonder, when his destroyer was hit at Guadalcanal, in the unbelievable moment on the bridge when he saw the bow come out of the water, if he had not selected the perfect moment to die.

Certainly, in retrospect, it would have been. It was the climax, the moment, usually in the third act, for which Shakespearean critics are on the watch. The long succession of anticlimaxes: the rescue, the injury in the water, the bronze star, the desk job in Washington, the marriage to Elly Shallcross, prettiest debutante of her year, the death of his father after V-J Day and the discovery of his heavy investments in unprofitable mines, all came in the order of a master dramatist. The dreams of establishing a liberal newspaper, of founding a publishing firm, of going into politics, of working for world peace had all to be set aside while Thad took over Thaddeus Kay & Son, and worked to salvage what could be salvaged of the family fortune.

He had done it well. Indeed, he was to wonder, in the years that followed, if it was not the one good job of a lifetime. The Kays, when he had finished, were no longer conspicuously wealthy, but they were as wealthy as anyone needed to be. Anyone, that is, but his wife. Sexually he and Elly had never achieved mutual satisfaction, and she had made him pay for the infidelities to which her reticences had driven him by buying eighteenth-century furniture. Elly, of course, had always maintained that he used this as his great excuse in life, that he blamed the fiction of her extravagance for his failure to leave the brokerage business when he was free at last to pick his dreams of a liberal future out of the dust bin to which they had been consigned on his father's death. In one of their bitterer fights she had even retorted that his career had gone with his looks, that his liberal aspirations had been no more than an attribute of his former beauty. Could it be true that he was simply the victim of an illusion created in others?

No wonder he had chosen to blame (not her extravagance, for which he had basically cared little) but his own guilt at having been too crude to arouse her. No wonder he had preferred to charge his appetites, and not his mind, with the alteration of the boy in the glossy portrait by the meretricious artist to the heavy, ruddy fellow who tried every afternoon to overcome the noon Martinis by smashing those black rubber balls harder and lower down the whitewashed wall of the squash court. Was it to justify his father's ironically smiling spirit that he had turned from a wife who never seemed ready for love to women who always were, or made a point of seeming so? If he had been born ugly, would he have accomplished more?

Time was bored by such as he. It gathered up its robes and fled from him. The fifteen years after V-J Day had been shorter than a single one of wartime. And then, long after he had decided that nothing was ever going to happen, that he and Elly would finish out the scenario as two porcelain figures on either end of a wide shelf, he, a grinning Toby jar and she a shepherdess in biscuit de Sèvres, giving each other, as vice and virtue, or virtue and vice, at least the consolation of teamship, of a kind of silent vaudeville act, what should she do but seize both roles for herself? It was unbearable that *Elly* should be the one to find passion!

He had not been even suspicious when she had gone to Europe alone. She had done that annually, anyway, for clothes.

He had hardly pricked up his ears when he had heard that she had been seen lunching with Livingston in Madrid. Was he not one of her regular luncheon pals? But when, in the steam room at his club, on a weekday morning after a particularly hard night, he heard from his best friend that Elly and Jay were generally talked about, he awoke at last to his asininity.

"They say she's absolutely mad about the little kike," Charlie Bradley told him. "It must be one of those things that happen to women her age. Now's your time, Thad, if you want to shed her cheap."

Even in his stupefaction Thad was able to react with further surprise (and some relief) to the fact that Charlie assumed that his news was good. All his friends, evidently, took for granted that Elly held him against his will. Thad now muttered something about going to see his lawyer and hurried off to dress and to have three strong, solitary drinks at the bar.

He found it difficult to focus either his mind or his emotions. He would try to picture Elly and Livingston engaged in the physical act, and then, just as he was beginning to tremble with ire, incredulity would cool him again. *Elly?* Elly who would glare and complain if a waiter's elbow so much as grazed her shoulder by mistake? Elly, who made him dress and undress in a separate room and come to bed in the dark? And then curiosity would flood his mind to succeed disbelief. What had Livingston *done* to change her? Had she been ready all along? Had a wink, a pinch, been sufficient? Had he simply mounted her, with a grunt?

Thad left the club and went home. He did so because there seemed nothing else to do. In the dark front hall he paused and listened to the sound of the vacuum cleaner from the dining room. Down the long bedroom corridor he could hear Elly's voice telephoning. She was still in bed. He tiptoed toward her room until he could make out her words.

"I'll have to ask Thad. Oh, I know he loves the Kernans, it's not that. I'm sure he'd adore to come. But I have a horrid little memory that he may have his Harvard Club dinner that night. And you know, my dear, we wives hardly count beside *that*. I'll let you know."

And then she said "Good-byee" in her particular way, dropping her voice to a stage whisper for the last two syllables. But today it did not irritate him. He was suddenly overcome by the idea that she should still be concerned with his welfare, that, despite her lover, she should still be sitting at home, keeping up her brave pretense that all was well, making gay little references to her husband's "club dinners" or other male habits, seeking for the right note to quell the suspicions of the gloating creatures at the other end of the line. Ah, if she could try so hard to maintain the appearance of *this* home, what might she not have done for a real one?

He shivered in pain at the first throb of one of his terrible headaches and raised his arms toward the ceiling as he felt the tears clog his eyeballs. What was the old saw about the bluebird? The bluebird was at home? He half staggered into the bedroom and fell on his knees by Elly's bed. She screamed as she pulled up her covers.

"Thad, what are you doing here? Are you sick? Oh, Thad, you're drunk!"

"Elly, couldn't you and I work things out again? Not just work them out the way they've been going, but *really* work them out — go back to our beginning? Do you suppose all this time you with your silly social life and I with my sluts have really been looking for each other? Could that be it? That we're just two self-deluded mortals who've all the time had everything we really want right here at home? Damn it all, why not? You're as much a woman as any of the ones I've been with, and I must be worth at least half a dozen of your cocktail parties. I know all about Livingston, and I'm not going to blame you. God knows, I've given you cause. But what can he give you that

I can't? Weren't we all right in the beginning? The very beginning? Why not let me get into bed with you, honey, right now, and see if we can't capture it or recapture it, whatever it was, *if* it was. Oh, Elly, don't look at me that way. Can't you try? Just once?"

He reached his arms toward her, but she sprang out of bed and tied the tassels of her bathrobe together with a vigor that hardly suggested the response he was seeking.

"How dare you burst in on me this way in the middle of the morning?" she cried. "Have you just been turned away by the last of your sluts, as you call them? Well, don't come pawing me. Go to your own room. Sleep it off!"

Because he was suddenly sick with fear at what might happen to him if he was rejected now, he continued, cravenly, to plead.

"For God's sake, Elly, have a bit of mercy, will you? Can't you see the state I'm in?"

"Only too well. And it's no state for eleven o'clock in the morning. Now get out! *Mother,* will you tell him I mean it?"

Thad spun around to find Mrs. Shallcross, very white and grave, in the doorway. He had the feeling that she had been tiptoeing up behind him, perhaps to bash him over the head with fire tongs. But this, of course, was ridiculous. She was just a scared old lady who had no lethal instrument and would not have dared use one if she had. Since she and the Judge had moved into the same building, she called on her daughter each morning.

"Good morning, Ma'am," he said gruffly and walked to the door. Mrs. Shallcross stood aside to let him pass, but she then followed him down the corridor to the hall.

"Thaddeus," she said in a low tone when he put his hand on the front door knob. "Thaddeus, listen to me a minute."

He turned to look in surprise at that round face, usually so bland, now thinner, almost haggard with maternal emotion.

"Why don't you let her go?" she still whispered.

"Her?" he asked dumbly. He could recall only the first name of his last girl friend.

"Elly! Haven't you made her wretched enough? Haven't you sufficiently wrecked her life?"

As Thad stared at those blazing old eyes that he had never seen even sparkle before, he felt again the throb of his headache. "Is that what she wants? Did she tell you so?"

"No! I'm speaking for myself. What have you ever done for her but sneer at her parties and diversions, scorned all her efforts to put a brave front on your monstrous adulteries? I know mothers aren't supposed to horn in. They're supposed to sit dry-eyed, like Roman ladies in an arena, while their darlings are picked apart, piece by piece. But I can't take it any more. Now she's found a man who's ready to offer his love and help and consolation, and what do *you* offer? I challenge you, Thaddeus Kay! What do you offer?"

He stared in shocked surprise. "I had no idea you hated me so much, Mrs. Shallcross."

"Of course you hadn't! You were hardly aware of my existence. Women to you mean just one thing. Without that, they're blotted out of your mind. But I'm not asking you to be aware of my existence. I'm not even asking you to be aware of your wife's existence. I'm just asking you to get out and leave us alone!"

"Leave you to Jay Livingston, you mean," he sneered. "Some catch! I congratulate you, Mrs. Shallcross, on your eligible new lover-in-law!"

"He's more of a man than you are, Thaddeus! More of a man any day in the week!"

He slammed the front door in the elevator vestibule and found himself actually wondering if the obscene old witch were not solemnly, perhaps even effectively, cursing him from behind it at that very moment!

*

In his office he sat alone and took four aspirins. He had told his secretary that he would see nobody, take no calls, but he was helpless against the intrusions of his partners, and at noon Martin, visiting from his new office at Atlantic Corporation, came in to suggest lunch. Martin had developed an irritatingly sleek look since Jay's victory in the proxy fight. But he changed his suggestion when he saw Thad's pallor and the circles beneath his eyes.

"Say! You'd better go home."

"I've *been* home. Got any other ideas?"

"What's wrong, old man?"

"Life is wrong. Your sister's wrong. Your mother's wrong. I daresay *you're* wrong. What do you want?"

Martin had never been one to push his way into private fields, particularly when he already knew what was going on there. "I wonder if you might not consider picking up some more Atlantic stock. There's a batch that's just come on the market. It's at one-ninety-eight, but it may be worth it. Jay says he has control, but Jay's an optimist."

"Buy more! I *will!* I'll buy every share I can get my hot little hands on and vote it for the old management!"

Martin's face became very calm as it was apt to do in a major crisis. "You know we have to have your stock for control. Have you and Jay had a row?"

"A row!" Thad almost shouted. "Don't you know what that bastard is doing to me?"

"I think I should know it better than anyone. After all, I've had *two* sisters involved with him. But what has that to do with Atlantic?"

Thad looked curiously now at the sullen features of his suddenly inscrutable brother-in-law. "Is business everything to you, Martin? Is honor nothing? Or even if honor's nothing, can't you understand plain, ordinary jealousy? Can't you take in that a man can *hate?*"

"I know a bit about hatred, Thad. Someday, if you ask me, I'll tell you about it. But right now we're engaged in developing Atlantic. If Jay succeeds, we'll be rich."

"And that's all you care about?"

"Listen to me, my friend." Martin came swiftly over to his desk now, and his voice rattled with his sudden, intense emotion. "Just listen to me for sixty seconds, will you? You and Jay both cheat on your wives. I don't cheat on mine. What I am suggesting is very simple. I am not asking either of you to be virtuous. I know you are both quite incapable of that. I am simply suggesting that you make yourself rich cheaters instead of poor ones." Here Martin's voice rose still more sharply. "Is that asking an intolerable sacrifice of you? It's all I can do for Elly!"

Thad rose from his desk to get away from him. Never would he have believed that he could feel such contempt as he now felt for Martin. "I think I've taken about all I can take from your family in one day. May I suggest that you leave now, before this dialogue becomes thoroughly uncivilized? You can't understand a man who would ruin himself to ruin a man he hated. Very well. There's no point arguing the point. But I give you fair warning that I intend to join up with Jay's opponents and fire him the hell out of Atlantic. No matter what it costs me!"

Martin had turned very white. Then slowly, and with unexpected theatricality, he raised his clasped hands to his brother-in-law. "You owe my family something, Thad. We're all in this thing together. For God's sake, don't do this to us, Thad!"

Thad, at the window, looked down on Wall Street, ten stories below, and wondered if he would ever reach his nadir. The quest was becoming almost interesting.

2

JAY LISTENED intently as Martin talked. Then he walked to a large chart on a wall of his office, drew a line through the circle marked "TK" and added a circle of the same size to the row representing the old, but now obviously resurgent, management. As he did so, he paused to consider, with a wry little smile, his own mental picture of Thad in football clothes, the pigskin clutched under one arm, the other stretched out stiffly, puffing down the field for a tremendous gain.

"Well, at least we've got Kay out in the open," he said. "We know where he stands. I wonder if I don't prefer it that way. I trust you don't mind my saying this. I've always despised your brother-in-law."

"Can you afford to despise him?"

"We have to deal with facts." Jay studied the board for two more minutes. He tried to consider the old principle that, so long as one played one's hand for the greatest advantage, it should be as interesting to lose as to win. It was little use, but at least he had altered the image from the football field to the card table. Thad's physical bulk would not do him much good in a proxy fight. Or had Thad won it already, as he had once won Elly? Jay closed his eyes as he felt the rising of jealousy under his heart, like hot bubbling liquid in a tube. No, that would never do. He had to be clear. When he turned back to Martin, he was still smiling.

"What do you advise?"

"Duck out," Martin said promptly. "Atlantic's at one-ninety-eight. We'll make a killing if we get out in time."

"That'll take some doing. We can't just dump, you know."

"It's our only chance."

"You think it's impossible for us to win?"

"Oh, impossible, I don't know about that. I think it's unlikely. Who else can we borrow from?"

"I think I might bring Linotex into our pool," Jay speculated. "That would give us twenty-eight percent."

"It still won't do it, Jay. You've got to have thirty."

Jay studied Martin's doleful countenance as he considered how best to try out a new line of thinking. He was still working on Thad Kay's image. Already he had reduced it to a puppet in a nickelodeon football game. "We have one untapped source."

"What's that?"

"Atlantic itself."

Martin stared. "What do you mean?"

"Simply that I as president and you as secretary have power to draw checks. And if we have power to draw checks, we have power to buy stock. And if we have power to buy stock, what's to prevent us from buying Atlantic stock and voting it for the present management?"

Martin studied his smile, trying vainly to read a joke into it.

"You want to plunder Atlantic for your own benefit? Surely that's some kind of crime?"

"Who's plundering? And where's the crime? It's not stealing, for Atlantic has title to the stock. It's not embezzlement, for Atlantic has possession of the stock. And it's not wasting corporate assets, for I shall damn well see that the stock goes up!"

"But it's wrong! It must be wrong!"

"It's in excess of our authority, without question. And we should be liable for any loss, without question. But there won't be any loss if we win. And we *will* win if we buy the stock. So there you are, Martin! If you don't take every opportunity that's offered you in this kind of row, you get left behind very quickly. It's a matter of constantly recalculating the odds and always playing your best chance. That's all there is to it, but you have to do that all."

"Shall we ask John Grau?"

"Are you crazy? He'd rail like a fishwife. You can't expect executive vision from counsel. This is a man's job."

"Breaking the law?"

"Oh, breaking the law, my ass. Grow up, Martin, will you? Every time you breathe, you break a law. You're on your own in this crazy century. You have to decide what taxes you're going to pay, what wars you're going to fight, what speed you're going to drive at, what sort of sex you want. If you don't, you become a Milquetoast with your nose always in the statute books. Everyone has to make his own compromises!"

Martin looked hard at the floor for a long still minute. "Could we go to jail?"

"It's hard to say what you could go to jail for today. I'm sure, for example, that I could find an indictable crime in most peoples' income tax returns, given all the true facts and figures. We can always take the position that we were acting in what we deemed Atlantic's best interest. And it'll be true! Probably the worst that could happen would be a stockholders' suit."

"All right, Jay, *if* that's the case."

"You'll go along?"

"I'll go along."

"Well, don't look so sick about it!"

"I *feel* sick about it. Like Macbeth, I'm still young in crime. But I suppose I'll get used to it. I want to be rich, and I'm a realist."

Jay laughed mockingly as he walked over to clap Martin on the shoulder. "It's just what you're not, my boy! Only a romantic wants to be rich today. Everyone else wants to be like his neighbor. But that's your secret. You're an old-fashioned dreamer. Wasn't that true about Alverta? Weren't you a romantic in love?"

"*You* seem to be the great romantic in that area."

"Oh, I admit it! Tell me, Martin, do you think Elly will ever marry me?"

"It seems to me she'll have to. With Thad on the warpath."

"You bastard! Would that be her only reason?"

Martin rose now and smiled his small smile. "No doubt she will recalculate the odds and play her best chance."

"Oh, go to hell. Or rather go and figure out how many shares we can buy."

"Isn't it perhaps the same thing?"

Jay ignored this. "We have to start cautiously. I'll work out a schedule when you give me the cash figure." Martin had turned away to the door. "And Martin?"

"Yes?"

"Try not to be so dreary."

Martin's drawn face was suddenly broken into sharp little lines of resentment. "I bet you'd just laugh if this whole thing blew up in our faces!"

"What else could I do?"

For just a few minutes, after Martin had left, Jay allowed himself to consider what he might be getting his melancholy associate into. If Martin lacked the stamina for success, how much more did he lack the guts for failure! But was he not in this thing of his own free will? And would he ever be able to satisfy that big wife of his without a pot of money? No, there was too much to worry about without worrying about Martin Shallcross.

First and foremost there was Elly, to whose apartment he now proceeded. The doorman, who knew him, let him up without calling, and the startled maid told him that Mrs. Kay was with her mother in the living room. He found Elly standing before the empty grate, looking oddly gaunt in the pale morning light. Mrs. Shallcross was sitting, or rather huddled, in the center of the white divan, her hat still on, holding her bag in her lap like an old woman in the subway.

"Jay!" Elly exclaimed harshly. "What are *you* doing here? Don't you know Thad may be having this place watched?"

"What's all this about?"

"He's going to sue me for divorce, that's what it's about! Right here in New York, that's what it's about! On you-know-what grounds! Go away, please! Please, Jay. Now!"

"Elly, don't get hysterical." Jay walked over to her and tried to put his hands on her elbows, but she pulled away from him roughly. She was actually shivering with fright. "All right. Tell me what's happened, and then I'll go. The doorman will know I haven't stayed more than fifteen minutes, and your mother will have been in the room all the time. Now calm down. You say Thad is going to divorce you. What evidence does he have?"

"Well, he may not have any, that's just it!" Elly cried. "That's what Mr. Bry says. That's why you mustn't come here any more."

"Bry? Don't tell me you're going to that shyster?"

"All my friends say he's the best divorce lawyer in New York!"

Jay realized that he had never seen her in a panic before. The hold that he had obtained over her was, after all, a fragile one. He remembered suddenly how she had shuddered in the Prado at the thought of burning flesh.

"All right," he said in a placating tone. "I'll go. But tell me this. Is Thad's threat unconditional?" She stared, not taking this in. "I mean, does he offer an alternative?"

"Oh. Well, no, not really. Only on the most humiliating terms."

"What are they?"

"They're not acceptable, Jay!"

"But what *are* they?"

"Why don't you tell him, Elly?" It was Mrs. Shallcross' first remark, and Jay felt immediately the force of her unexpected alliance.

"Very well, if you insist. If I agree to get out of this apartment, leaving everything behind but my clothes and jewels — and, by the way, jewels do not include the Kay diamonds which his mother *gave* me — and if I agree to divide custody of the girls on a fifty-fifty basis, and *if* — listen to this one! — I agree to a beggarly settlement of ten thousand a year — well, then His Gracious Majesty, King Thaddeus, will allow me to creep quietly down to Mexico and get my divorce without scandal. Did you ever hear the like?"

"I have only one objection," Jay replied calmly.

"And what is that, pray?"

"I suggest you refuse the alimony."

"Are you mad? Do you think for one solitary second . . ."

"Listen, Elly," he interrupted firmly. "Be quiet for just one minute. The part about the girls is fine. They've reached an age, anyway, where they're going to stay with the parent they want to stay with. And what do you need money for? You can have all of mine. I'll make any settlement on you you want. Go ahead. Get the divorce in Mexico. It's the best way out."

"Listen to him, Elly!"

Elly stared from her mother to her lover with a small, frozen smile of incredulity. "I believe you have both departed from this globe on which the rest of us have to live," she said cuttingly. "Do you really believe that a woman of my position can accept a settlement from a man who's not her husband?" Suddenly she seemed furious. "My God, what do you think I am?"

"But I'll *be* your husband, Elly!"

"Are you free?"

"No, but I will be."

"Has Hulda agreed?"

"Not yet. But I'll go to Mexico, anyway."

"And get an invalid divorce so you can offer me a bigamous marriage? No, thank you, very much. I prefer Mr. Bry. He offers better counsel. And I think I can promise you that Mr. Thaddeus Kay will find he has bitten off a considerably larger slice than he can possibly chew. By the time I'm through with him, he will rue the day he ever walked into his lawyer's office!"

"Can't you see what Bry's doing to you?" Jay demanded. "Can't you see he wants the biggest, dirtiest fight so he can get the biggest, dirtiest fee?"

"Well, he's going to *earn* this one! And Thad's the one who's going to pay it!"

The maid appeared to say that Mr. Bry was on the telephone, and Elly hurried into the library. Through the open doorway Jay and her mother could hear her eager monosyllables in response to what was evidently a progress report. She seemed to have already forgotten the listening pair in the next room. It occurred to Jay, looking at the white-faced, crumpled old lady before him, that as the Elly who had seemed so liberated in Spain was now binding herself back into her old world of fear and hate, round and round, with a thin hard wire of nervous resolution, so was her poor mother, sustained so long by the little conventional make-believes of her family background — that mothers always loved, that children were always grateful, that "nice" people were actually nice — seemed as suddenly unwound as her daughter was winding, seemed indeed to have collapsed into a heap of soft, fat, quivering female fragments. And Jay felt an odd and not altogether welcome affinity between her and him, sensing for the first time the common denominator of their humanity. To her he was no longer just a pushing Jew; to him she had ceased to be a banal nonentity. He felt sorry for her, but he wished at the same time that she was elsewhere. There was a kind of death in any union with Marian Shallcross.

Elly came back in now, with the same set look of reassurance that he remembered from the days when they used to lunch following her appointment with Dr. Silverman.

"He says you're to go right now," she told him. "He says you're not to come here again."

"You mean I can't see you at all."

"We can meet occasionally in public places if Mother's present."

Jay stared incredulously into those hostile blue eyes. "But Elly . . ." he began, and then he remembered Mrs. Shallcross. "Come out in the hall with me, anyway. Even a litigant should be able to see a caller to the elevator."

She followed him to the foyer and seemed to relax once he had actually opened the front door. "It won't be forever, you know," she said.

"But, darling, I can't get on without you now. Can you without me? Really? Can you turn yourself on and off like a spigot? I thought we'd learned more about ourselves in Spain. Maybe just I did."

"Jay, what else can I *do?*"

"I've told you."

"But you won't understand. You won't *see.*" She seemed distraught at his unreasonableness. "And I was so counting on your help and sympathy!"

He looked at her in total perplexity. How could he have ever thought that he was in control of such a woman? He had simply pitted himself against her whole past. But his failure in no way diminished his desire. "We could meet, honey, in ways that would baffle any detective. You've no idea what resources I have in this city. If you'll just leave it to me . . ."

"No, Jay! I won't risk it! We'll meet my way or not at all."

"If I get my divorce, will you listen to me?"

She hesitated. "A valid divorce?"

"A valid divorce. If I get a valid divorce and come back prepared to make a settlement on you larger than any Bry can extort out of Thad, will you consider going to Mexico, as I've suggested?"

"You make me sound so mercenary," she protested, stamping her foot. "It's not fair. You know it's not fair!"

"But would you?" he repeated.

"I shouldn't consider any settlement while I was married to Thad, no. How could I? I don't want your money, Jay."

"I'd much rather have you want mine than his."

"But he *owes* it to me!" she cried passionately.

"And I don't?"

At last she looked at him, if only for a moment, as she had looked at him in Spain. "Oh, you poor boy, you owe me nothing. There it's all the other way round."

Jay was dimly aware, in that dark little vestibule that seemed actually to be tightening around his heart, that he had forgiven her everything for those words. "Meaning I was just a toy?" he said gruffly, trying to smother the elation in his tone. "Just for weekends?"

"Well, what's wrong with toys and weekends?" she asked, with her first smile.

"Elly, if I get a proper divorce, will you discuss marriage with me?"

"When I'm divorced and you're divorced, Jay, when *and* if, I'll discuss it."

At this point the elevator doors opened behind him, and the operator reached out to place the mail on the little marble-topped table in the foyer. "Wait," Elly called to him, "this gentleman is just going down. Good-bye, Jay. Remember to call me for lunch!"

*

At MacManus & Shallcross Jay was too familiar a client to be announced by the receptionist. She simply smiled in answer to the kiss he blew to her on his way to John Grau's office. The latter was telephoning. As usual, he did not interrupt his conversation by so much as a nod or a wink, and Jay listened fretfully, roaming the office, with a vague, unreasonable jealousy that his lawyer should give the same attention to other clients that he gave to him. But when John had finished, he came straight to Jay's point, as if he had guessed the purpose of this unscheduled visit.

"Bad news," he said. "Hulda wants cash. Her price is still a million."

"But she'll have it!" Jay exclaimed indignantly. "She'll have it and more if she'll only wait. Can't she take a commitment?"

John shook his head as decisively as if it had been his decision and not Hulda's. "No go. Her lawyer says cash now, and I'm sure he means it."

"Why are you sure?"

"Because he knows it's perfectly ridiculous. Because he knows, as you and I do, that she'll do better by waiting. 'Mr. Grau, we're not dealing with a rational human being,' he keeps whining. 'We're dealing with a woman scorned'!"

"I never scorned Hulda as she scorned me!"

"That may be. But this is her inning. Of course, she knows everything you've got is tied up in the proxy fight. She's like Thad Kay. She's not out for money. She's out for your skin! Now, listen to me, Jay. When you're dealing with this kind of hysteria, the only thing to do is to mark time. Drop this whole divorce business until you've won the battle of the Atlantic. What's the hurry, anyway? You've put it off more than ten years already."

"The hurry is that I've got to get Elly out of this mud-slinging contest she's getting into with Kay. She won't listen to me until I'm free. Well, then, I've got to be free! There must be a way, and it's up to my lawyer to find it. If I can't get a divorce in New York, I'll leave New York!"

"And this new proxy fight?"

"I can run that anywhere. Look, man, we're living in the 1960s. The age of the jet and the telephone. I can fight from Timbuctoo!"

John sighed as he filled his pipe with tobacco from the pouch on his desk. "Look," he argued in a reasoning tone, "please don't think me too out-of-line, but I can't help knowing what you and Elly were up to in Europe. That's all right. That's your business. But, after all, you're both sophisticated people. If she spends a little time litigating with her husband while you finish up your proxy fight, is that so terrible? I've known her, if you'll pardon me, a good bit longer than you have, and I think you'll find she's tougher than you think."

"But that's just the point! I want to keep Elly out of all that. I don't want her to get any tougher than she is. Not *that* way, anyway. Elly and I discovered something about ourselves in Spain, and now it's about to go down the drain. She's panicked, and she's fighting like a beast. All her old bogies are at her again. She sees herself stripped of her dough and her reputation with nothing left but a Jew lover whom everyone sneers at."

"Then how will it help that Jew lover to get a divorce?"

"It's my one chance. If I can offer her marriage and money when everything else is gone, won't she have to jump at it?"

John puffed at his pipe intently as he held a lighted match over it. "Forgive me, Jay, if I ask this question, but I guess I have to. Can such a woman be worth it?"

"That's my risk."

"I suppose it is." John nodded now as he gave in, and Jay knew that when he gave in, it was final. "Tell me, then. What have you got that Hulda's lawyer can attach if you leave the state?"

"Practically nothing. My securities are all in New Jersey— the few I haven't hocked. I'm ready to move to any state in the union. Just tell me which it shall be."

John scratched his ears. "Nevada, then. You'll have to make

it a real residence, though. None of this six weeks' business. Not if Hulda won't consent. You may have to live there a year."

"Can you arrange for the best divorce lawyer in Reno to see me tomorrow?"

"I guess so. I'm getting pretty good at arranging things for you."

"Then I'm on my way. I'll leave you and Martin as my lieutenants. There's no objection, I suppose, if I hop back here every couple of days?"

"Jay, you'll kill yourself!"

"Oh, I think you'll find it'll take more than Elly and Thad to do that." Jay took up his hat now and went to the door, but before leaving he could not resist, recalling John's old reluctance to represent him, one last retort. "I note that when a Shallcross wants a tough lawyer she doesn't go to MacManus and Shallcross. She leaves those 'softies' to the unclean Jew!"

3

ELLY FOUND that the business of litigating a divorce could very comfortably fill a day. She rose late, breakfasted leisurely and telephoned Mr. Bry at half past ten. He always had some bit of news for her. If it happened to be good — and it usually was — he made it seem a great victory, for which she, quite as much as he, was responsible. If, on the other hand, it was bad, he always brushed it off as an insignificant casualty, the kind of thing to be expected in a long campaign. Frequently he took her out to lunch at a good restaurant, or stopped by the apartment for a drink. It was notoriously part of his magic to be able to make each of his clients imagine that he had only one.

He was a round, soft, bald, blinking man, with an infinite capacity for listening and no apparent temper at all. He could reduce some thundering lawyer, who had made the mistake of emotionally identifying himself with the estranged husband of a Bry client, to near irrationality by listening patiently to an impassioned rebuttal and then calmly reiterating his demand for prohibitive alimony without a single concession. Yet he was just as exacting when he represented a husband against a wife. He was absolutely sexless in such matters. The Bry client had always to be in the right. Jay Livingston, for example, was never mentioned in his talks with Elly except by implication. He became simply one of the "single gentlemen," with whom, because of the world's slanderous tongue, it was wisest not to be seen alone.

Elly began to learn now that a woman with a good lawyer and a dash of boldness had little to fear, either from the courts of justice or from the judgment of her peers. What Thad was trying to do to her, in his action for a judicial separation (he was too vindictive even to let her get a divorce out of it) was simply what she had always, deep in her heart, suspected that society was trying to do to her: annihilate her. And now she was fighting back! Silverman had done his best to reason away as absurd her old fear that people considered her coldness only the mask of a yearning for promiscuity. But Silverman had now been proved wrong. Thad, bloated, beefy bull that he was, might well be acting as society's surrogate in his lewd and filthy suit! And the glorious thing about Bry was that, instead of eternally asking her to understand herself, he simply taught her the art of self-defense.

She learned quickly. She refused Thad access to the apartment, even to get his clothes. She scattered the Kay diamonds over the second-hand market so that, even if Thad tried to reassemble them, it would prove a hopeless task. She sent for her daughters and swore that Jay was simply an understanding friend while revealing to them every detail of their father's sex history, including his bizarre behavior on the wedding night. The girls, horrified and vociferously partisan, protested they would never see him again. Elly then counterclaimed for a divorce, naming every one of Thad's girl friends whose name she could remember, a list extending back fifteen years and including two famous society matrons. The evening papers obliged their old friend Bry by printing every word of her petition, right down to the supporting affidavits. And finally Bry obtained an allowance, *pendente lite,* of five hundred dollars a week, exclusive of the support of the girls. It was pleasant to imagine Thad Kay howling in pain and cursing his lawyers for ever allowing him to get into such a mess!

Elly was astonished by her new fearlessness. It seemed to her, when friends called to protest the appalling publicity, when the Kay sisters-in-law came to her in tears, when her own mother begged for moderation, that she was living in a popping fairy-land where one paper dragon after another was going up in smoke. And by dint of denying Jay, even he began to seem deniable; the gray bedroom in the Ritz of Madrid retreated into the back of her mind like a remembered stage set of some favorite old play. *That* had seemed reality at the time; it had seemed the first, maybe the ultimate reality. But now she was like a soldier in his first battle to whom the whole of his military indoctrination seems a children's tale.

It was a good deal harder, however, to deny Jay when he was in New York than when he was in Reno. He was exhausted from his cross-country shuttle, and very tense, so she dared not put him off altogether. She met him once for lunch, once for tea at the Plaza, once at an art gallery. It was in the gallery, where she had insisted on sitting on a bench in the window, so that they could both be plainly seen, like two paintings of backs, from Madison Avenue, that they had their most serious talk. Before them, on an easel, was a Martin Heade of two humming-birds, hovering above an enormous spray orchid.

"I think it's beautiful," he commented. "I mean, I feel I really get it."

She was about to make a joke about the monstrous quality of the flower and its spooky background, but something in his tone made her hesitate. "What is it you get?"

"It's hard to say. But I've been trying so long to see what you see in paintings, that now I'm beginning to see what I see."

"I suppose it might be a good investment. They say American art is going up."

"Oh, yes," he answered, as though there had been no hint of mockery in her tone. "One has to think of that, too. But I can't buy anything now. I'll have to wait till I'm sure of Atlantic."

"How is it coming?"

"Oh, we're going to win, of course."

"You're so sure?"

"So sure. And you. What about yours?"

"I'm going to win, too."

"And then?"

She was about to say something brusque, but the circles beneath his eyes were too dark. "And then we'll see, Jay."

"Elly, I wish you'd give it up," he pleaded. "I wish you'd give it up and take Thad's original offer."

"Oh, it's too late for that now!"

"It's terrible what you're doing to yourself. You ought to be concentrating on the future, not raking over the past. Why can't you and Thad call it quits? God knows I've been engaged in some dirty fights in my life, but they've always had a kind of dirty common sense to them. But this! This spectacle of wrangling for dollars and children and furniture in the wreck of a sacrament that none of you believe in any more — why, it's degrading!"

"He started it!"

"But you want his money!"

"I'm *entitled* to it, Jay!"

"All right. But if this mess ever clears up, and if you ever marry me, you're going to have to settle every penny you extort from Thad on those kids of yours. If I take you at all, I'll take you naked as a jaybird!"

Elly turned in horror to see if they were being overheard, but, of course, they weren't. Jay never spoke without knowing exactly what he was saying and who was hearing it. Then she stood up and turned away from him so that he should not see the sudden tears in her eyes. For her heart was torn with the suspicion that he might, after all, be right, and she had her first untrammeled glimpse of what it was that he might be offering her. He was more, no matter how much she tried to minimize him, than an adroit lover, than an oddly congenial friend, than a clever Jew who excited her by the clean sweep that he made of things that she had once taken for granted. He was a man, in short, and how many of them had she known? Very possibly the only notable thing that Elly Shallcross had accomplished in her trumpery life was to engage his affection. Affection? She turned, now indignant at herself, away from the window as she spurned the word. His *love*. Did he not love her? Was not that the point?

"Things may work out," she murmured. "Who knows?"

The salesman was returning with the Helleu sketch that she had purchased, wrapped up to take away.

"Would you care to step over to the desk, Mrs. Kay?"

"What for?"

"I thought you'd be more comfortable there writing the check."

"But I'm not writing a check. You can charge it."

"Pardon me, Ma'am." The young man was obviously wretched. "But do you wish to open an account?"

Elly gave him her coolest glance. "I have an account. I've had one for years."

"I'm afraid that was in Mr. Kay's name. He's canceled it."

Elly turned away to stride rapidly toward the door. "Keep the picture." She flung the words crisply back over her shoulder. "It will be a little memento of my last dealing with your gallery."

In the street she silenced Jay's incipient protest.

"Now do you see what I'm up against?" she hissed. "Goodbye!"

Later that evening, when she recalled the scene, she remembered that there had been anger as well as frustration in his parting stare — anger and something dangerously close to contempt. Was it not inevitable — had it not been inevitable from the beginning — that his uniqueness would prove an illusion, that he would end up with all the others who had sneered at her? Had there really ever been hope of anything else? Was that not the pre-Silverman truth? And the truth?

4

JAY, spending twenty-four hours a week in the sky between
Reno and New York, had more time for philosophy than he had
had ever before in his life. The proxy fight was going badly, and
it was beginning to look as if he would lose. Elly was more and
more hysterically preoccupied with her suit, and he had at times
to close his eyes and desperately rub his eyeballs in the effort to
recall the glorious days in Spain. Then he would gaze out at the
sky and clouds and idly question how much he really wanted his
corporate victory and how much he really wanted Elly. That
was the trouble with detachment — it was synonymous with
doubt. Away from Atlantic and its properties, stretched out
along the border of Queens and Nassau, so obviously, so even
tritely dwarfed in his aerial view, away from Elly and her spite-
ful litigation, was it not bound to appear that he was breaking
his heart for a miserable strip of city-rotten earth and a selfish
bitch? Yet what goal could not be made to seem undesirable if
one kept shifting the point of view from which one regarded it?
If Napoleon's world vision could be reduced to a handful of
frozen fingers in Moscow, could not the philanthropist's be
shriveled to a few stomachs filled in a world that was threatened
with a fatal excess of them? No, the mystic had the only answer,
by placing his faith in another dimension, but if one could not
believe in such a dimension, why, then, one was simply back in
the plane from Reno, or *to* Reno, making the best of it.

Cousin Florence was more in his thoughts than she had been

in years. She seemed peculiarly present to him in the air, as if her remembered being had been transcendentalized into the heavens, so that the gray streaked clouds had become her hair and the patches of cerulean blue her brooding eyes. Her great soul embraced him and embraced his little whizzing plane; it made mock, no doubt, of his activity, but of whose activity did it not? He thought he could make out now what Cousin Florence's basic error in her own self-assessment had been: she had believed that her values had been ethical, whereas they had been purely aesthetic. Cousin Florence had had nothing to do, really, with the nonsensical values of her world. She had simply responded to beauty and had seen it everywhere that it could be seen. That had been the *thing* about her, the element that had made her different, and some of her seeds had sprouted even in his unlikely soil. For who but Cousin Florence had caused him to sense the mystery in the dark background of the Martin Heade hummingbirds; who but she had made him aware of the "style" of the Velásquez infantas, who else had opened his eyes to the extraordinary beauty in Elly, a beauty that was almost concealed by its very obviousness, a subtle beauty under the blond glare of her radiance of which even Elly herself was unaware? Yes, Cousin Florence had bequeathed to him, in addition to ten thousand dollars, a curious doctrinal legacy for a businessman!

It was questionable if she would have understood this. Certainly she would have despised his proxy fight, and almost as certainly she would have despised poor Elly. Sometimes, speeding in his car to Idlewild, feeling so tired that he wondered if he could wait for his plane before falling asleep, he would have a blurred sense of the motor crash that had ended her life, and he could still weep for her.

But regrets? Did he, he kept asking himself, have any real regrets? It was still unimaginable to him to be anything but a free individual. The world in which he had had to live had largely substituted rules for individual aspirations: soldiers, for example, were drafted, charities supported by tax deductions, social work transferred to professionals. It was no longer the fashion to do anything one was not compelled to do or very well remunerated for doing. Mankind seemed dominated by a new sense of economic inevitability. Who but he, after all, had tried to save Shallcross Manor? The old families, for all their pious pronouncements, sacrificed their landmarks to personal profit as automatically as they sacrificed their old doormen to self-service elevators. They would have been considered odd to do otherwise.

All that he had really done was to refuse lip service to defunct rules that had been designed to govern a defunct society. But people still clung to the idea that they were altruistic, that they were self-sacrificing, that they were religious, that they were monogamous, or that they even tried to be any of these things, long after the state had lifted such responsibilities and the need of such responsibilities from their not-so-weary shoulders. Now, so long as they paid their taxes and filled out their forms they could live for themselves. If they wanted to. Well, he *did* pay his taxes (every one that the smartest accountant in New York couldn't get him out of) and he did fill out his forms (as many as the bureaucrats could invent) and he was still determined to be free!

No, for all his ruminating, he did not see what else he should be doing. If he lost Atlantic, he would still have a fortune in Atlantic's stock. If he lost Elly, he would have the memory of her, as he had the memory of Cousin Florence. He would become a bigger owner of things, and he would, from time to time, enjoy being a bigger owner of things. As the things became tiresome, he would acquire others. The people employed in these things would be treated quite as well by him as by any other owner, for no owner would do more than he had to do, and here again were the laws. And if it all went to pieces, it would be no more than if the great motors of the plane suddenly stopped, and he dropped from the sky to a planet for a tiny piece of which he had been perhaps too greedy.

*

Victory continued to elude him, and he now tried desperate measures. He barged in on Thad Kay at his office to suggest a compromise and was hit in the chest by a hurled inkwell. He made a point of walking out through the stenographers' room so that all the Kay employees could see his stained shirt, and that night in a radio interview he stated that Thad was temporarily deranged, but it was not good publicity. He went out to Queens to call on Hulda and to beg her to see reason, but this interview was equally unsuccessful. Hulda was simply glad of the chance to humiliate him. She did not throw ink, but she spat.

And then, suddenly, one of his basic defenses shuddered. Martin was waiting in his office late one night when he arrived from the airport, and Jay saw at once that he was in for it.

"You told me you were going to buy Atlantic stock for Atlantic!" Martin cried in an anguished tone. "You didn't tell me you were going to buy it for yourself!"

"That's only a technicality," Jay replied with a shrug. "I *did* buy a thousand shares for Atlantic, but one of Kay's people brought a stockholders' suit to enjoin Atlantic from voting its own stock. They smelled us out. So, to be on the safe side, I had the next five hundred shares I bought registered in my own name."

"That may be a technicality but it's one that'll send us to jail!"

Jay surveyed Martin's darkening countenance calmly. He remembered being stuck once in an elevator with a fat old man who had started screaming. There had been no danger, no discomfort, only tedium. Yet the man had panicked, and his panic had filled Jay with icy contempt.

"Not you," he said at last. "The responsibility is entirely mine."

"But if what you've done ever gets out, Atlantic will drop to nothing. We'll lose our shirts, even if we win this damn proxy fight!"

"Why should word get out?"

"How should I know? We're watched, aren't we? And what about the new stock in the name of Tallard and Company? Isn't that one of your nominees?"

"It is."

"How'd you dig up the money for *that?* You didn't get it from Atlantic. I know, because I checked!"

"I got it from World Inc."

"From World!" Martin's voice rose to something like a scream. "Jesus, man, you *will* go to jail!"

"It's perfectly possible, I grant, if everything goes wrong — as you rather hysterically presume — that I may have to face some disagreeable consequences. I'm quite prepared for that, but I don't choose to worry about it until it occurs, and I don't expect it to occur. What I do expect is that *all* my companies shall work for me in this crisis. It will certainly be to all their benefits if I pull it off. As president of World Inc., I consider myself not only qualified but entitled to make investments of its cash in such a way as to ensure a profit. For Atlantic *and* for World!"

"Unfortunately there happen to be some rather nasty laws that might put your action in a very different light."

"I can't help that. I've got a proxy fight to win, and one that has been quite unnecessarily aggravated by your lout of a brother-in-law."

"At least the stock the lout votes is his own!"

"Oh, dry up, will you, Martin!" Jay snapped in a sudden eruption of anger, slapping his hand on the blotter. "I take all the risk, and you get the profit. What's wrong with that for a deal?"

"If there *is* a profit. I've half a mind to dump what I've got and scuttle."

"Why don't you?"

"I suppose because I'm too damn much of a gentleman! That's always been in my way."

"And for one other, a very simple little reason," Jay pointed out wearily as he rose, for he felt he could not endure for another minute the sight of Martin's fear. "You still think I'm going to win. I know I can count on you all the way, my friend, while *that's* still so!"

5

SOPHIE WAS BEGINNING to resign herself to the advance symptoms of one of her old depressions. She would awaken to a state of inertia and passivity that would last for several moments before she could even recall what season of the year it was. Then she would think she was back in Shallcross Manor, until the discomfort behind this thought revealed itself in a sudden picture of a heap of rubble. When she had finally fixed herself in time and space, she would feel an insurmountable reluctance to get up, and she would sometimes lie for as much as an hour in bed, in one position, her eyes closed or staring at the same object. At meals she was moody and silent, and in the mornings she preferred walking to reading and roamed up and down the Mall in Central Park with her mother's poodles or sat disconsolately on benches. For she seemed always now to be tired.

Her parents treated her gingerly, but she sensed more exasperation than sympathy in their attitude. How *could* she do this to them, their exchanged glances over the dining room table seemed to communicate, after all the money and fuss of the past and with a wedding to be planned? Her mother suggested that she make an appointment with Dr. Damon, but Sophie simply burst into tears. She could not face the prospect of all that weary talk and all those weary reassurances. What she was, she was. She was going to have to learn to live with Sophie Shallcross.

She had not been clear enough in her mind to do anything

about her engagement. That Hilary did not ask her to affirm it or break it, that he never referred now to wedding dates or wedding plans, indicated that he recognized (probably after many nervous conferences with her parents) that no pressures should be placed on her. But perhaps, too, he enjoyed the amorphous state of being engaged without a wedding commitment. Perhaps he liked being able to continue his social life and at the same time to persuade himself that he had done all a man reasonably could be expected to do about his marital future. He took her out to dinner twice a week, on nights of his choosing, for she was always free now, and when their evening was over he planted his parting kiss chastely on her cheek. Oh, yes, it was a situation that could go on forever!

Sometimes she found herself wishing that she had been born in a less prosperous society. Why could she not have been a Christian under Commodus, a Moor under Philip II, a Jew under Hitler? Why did her misery have to be wasted? Why could it not be inscribed in the roll of martyrs? Shivering in the arena as a starved beast paced snarling around her, lashed to a stake amid the rising flames, standing in a stinking naked line of humans by the door of an oven, she might have had the bleak consolation of knowing that her misery at least fitted her facts.

And then one night Martin, haggard and restless-eyed, for the first time in her memory of him almost suggesting the unkempt, ended her immunity from the outside world. He had been living in the family's apartment and working late hours, but as Sophie never went to bed before one, she was apt to be up when he came in. On that night, he looked particularly exhausted, and he doubled his usual dose of whiskey. Then the whole story about Jay and the World Inc. shares came gushing out. What brought Sophie up most sharply against the horror of the situation, as she strove to take in the unfamiliar facts and terms, was that he, Martin, the businessman of the family, the ever-cool, the ever-competent, was asking *her* advice!

It had an immediate curative effect. There was an obvious shock value in being jostled from her habitual self-contemplation. At first she rejected with a shudder of disgust the idea of any connection between Jay's action and herself. But in the long day that followed, in the Mall and in the Rambles, feeding pigeons and sparrows, watching the boaters from the bridge, gazing at the weather-beaten statues, indulging in the useless melancholy that comes with viewing a skyline from a bench, she began to wonder if Martin's revelation might not be the most important thing that had ever happened to her. *Or to the Shallcrosses.* For was it not possible that Martin had revealed at last the secret that she had all along suspected, and that everybody else had all along suspected (no matter how hard they tried to hide it) that the entire foundation of their lives rested on crime: plain, simple, common, ordinary, indictable crime?

That night she waited impatiently for Hilary's arrival. He came early, for he was taking her to the theater, and she watched his back almost gloatingly as he mixed his drink at the bar table.

"I had a rather curious talk with Martin last night," she said, as he turned.

"Oh? How is the old proxy battle going?"

Sophie bridled at the casualness of his tone. "He had some pretty bad news about Jay."

"Is he in trouble?"

"No. But he may be. And we *are.* I say 'we,' as opposed to 'he,' because I don't suppose Jay would regard it as trouble unless he was actually found out."

"What on earth are you talking about?"

"I'm afraid it's a classic case of the hand in the till."

Hilary flushed slowly as he took in her accusing stare. "I wish you'd stop playing with me and explain what the devil you're driving at."

"Apparently Jay has been using money that didn't belong to him to buy stock in Atlantic." In the considerable pause that followed this, it struck her that Hilary's reaction seemed to consist largely in his awareness that some reaction was expected.

"How?"

"Does it matter how?"

"Of course it matters how. Modern business is highly complicated. You know nothing about it, Sophie. Neither do I, for that matter, but I don't presume to judge people. The same thing may be legal or illegal, depending on how it's done."

"Well, Martin said he could go to jail!"

Hilary was plainly making a great effort now to control his impatience. "Why then is Martin broadcasting it?"

"He's not broadcasting it. On the contrary, he's sitting on it as tight as he can. He came to me for help. He says that now the proxy fight's got to be won immediately, before this thing gets out, and that Jay's got to be here all the time to win it. Obviously, he can't be here if he's in Reno."

"And what are you supposed to do about *that?*"

"Martin wants me to go to Jay's wife. He wants me to try to talk her into consenting to a divorce."

Hilary's attention was thoroughly engaged now. "He must be out of his mind. Why would Mrs. Livingston listen to *you?*"

"Because I have no axe to grind. Because I might have married Jay and didn't. Martin thinks she'd be flattered if a member of the family went to see her and pointed out that we're all in the same boat."

Hilary frowned and rubbed his chin. "I suppose you could try it. After all, what could you lose?"

"Try it!" Sophie's hands flew to her lips. "You mean you think I *should?*"

"Well, why else on earth are we discussing it?"

"Because I wanted to discuss with you what I *ought* to do, not what Martin *wants* me to do! Oh, Hilary, have you no moral sense left? Would you be happy to sit back and cover this up so you could get Jay's money for your magazine?"

Hilary looked as if bewilderment were beginning to prevail over anger. "What do you want me to do? Go to the police?"

"No, no, no. Of course not. But I thought at least you'd realize that you couldn't run a magazine on tainted money. I hoped you might suggest that we use this information in some way to free us once and for all from Jay Livingston and his crooked schemes! And free Elly and Martin and John Grau, too! Let Jay win his stupid proxy battle. I couldn't care less. Let him win a hundred of them! But let's you and I get off his filthy bandwagon once and for all!"

"Don't be hysterical."

"That's what you always say when I'm being honest. I reject your attitude totally, Hilary! I'm afraid I can't go on seeing you unless you promise to give up all association with Jay."

"Darling, pull yourself together."

"I mean it!"

"Let's go out to dinner."

"No, I don't want to. I'm going to stay home tonight, thank you. I couldn't sit at the same table with you after this!"

"Sophie! Does this mean you're breaking our engagement?"

"I don't know what it means yet. I have to do a lot of thinking about that. Please go now."

Hilary rose, tight-lipped with exasperation, and strode to the door where he met Judge Shallcross.

"Ah, my dear fellow, how are you? Are you just taking Sophie out? She'll have to cook a good many meals to make up for all the money you're spending on her in restaurants. Oh, no, you're not? Well, that's right, too. Take advantage of the few bachelor evenings you have left. Things will never be the same, I assure you, my boy . . ."

"Please, Daddy! Let Hilary *go!*"

The Judge looked from one to the other with a splendid show of astonishment. "What's this, my dear. A lovers' quarrel? Well, don't take it too seriously. I . . ."

"Daddy! *Please!*"

In the awkward pause that followed her cry Hilary made his escape. The Judge now stared reprovingly at his youngest child.

"I had hoped, Sophie, that your engagement would give you greater stability. If you continue to show Hilary your moods, you may lose him altogether. The women of your generation are sadly lacking in subtlety. Why it should be considered commendably 'honest' to flaunt the emotional side of one's nature least apt to attract the opposite sex is beyond me. Happily for you, the men of your generation seem built to take greater punishment than those of mine. But I wouldn't push Hilary too far if I were you. Even he may have his limits."

"Even he?"

"I simply meant that he has always struck me as a very patient man."

"Do you think him an honorable one?"

"Honorable?" The Judge's eyebrows were two Gothic arches. "Has he given you occasion to doubt it?"

"He has. Of course, he thinks I'm super-sensitive. Perhaps I am. You always told us so much about honor when we were little. I remember those wonderful Roman stories you used to read to us. Brutus and his conscience. Marius going back to his death in Carthage because he had given his word. All that is quite dead today, I suppose?"

Eben Shallcross moved to the bar table and proceeded to the ritual of his cocktail, making it as he had made it for forty years, with grenadine, sugar, rum, Angostura Bitters and cognac. It took him a full five minutes of total concentration to get his concoction exactly right.

"If we're going to talk about honor, my dear," he said, turning at last and raising the silver tumbler slowly to his lips, "you must allow me to fortify myself first."

6

At ten o'clock that same night Eben Shallcross entered the paneled bar of the New Orange Club. It had once been the dining room, darkly and heavily *dix-huitième*, at least as decorators of the 1890s had conceived that century in France, of the great Jewish banker who had built the house. Now its ceiling was dimly lit up by hidden bulbs, and a television set, unwatched, made a pale showing of Western violence. The club was political; the atmosphere elderly, distinguished, close. At any of the square, cafeteria tables one might meet a forgotten mayor, an ex-governor.

Eben stood at the bar and chatted amiably with Patrick, the bartender of thirty years' tenure. He did not wish to join a group, as he was waiting for a friend.

"Murder, Patrick, even murder people will put up with now. Rape, of course, has long been socially accepted. Arson may still be frowned at, but theft goes for nothing at all. Go to your local police station and tell them your apartment's been robbed and watch them stifle their yawns! And why shouldn't they? What chance have they of nabbing your thief? Who will help them? A woman was held up yesterday in broad daylight, in Times Square, and not a soul made a move to help her!"

"Things have sure gone to hell, Judge."

"You may say that again, my dear Patrick. You may assuredly say it again!"

Eben was unusually benign that night as he sniffed and

quaffed his rare old Scotch, kept especially for him in a decanter with a silver label. *One* man, anyway, would be brought to justice! And what was that man but the very symbol of corruption in a corrupt world? With his red cars and bright suits, his cigars and his smiles, his tax evasions and his adulteries!

"I tell you, Patrick, it all started with FDR's stamp collection. Imagine the President of the United States building up his own estate by gifts of rare issues from kings and dictators! What a cynic that man was. What a sublime cynic! Why, he tore down the whole moral fabric of America by forging his unholy alliance between capital and labor and passing the bill on to the middle class. And now what have we left, Patrick? Millionaire wheeler-dealers with tax exemptions and labor racketeers with crooked tax returns, laughing their heads off over us honest earners who pay for their so-called 'revolution' !"

He reached his tumbler forward for another splash of the delicious whiskey. He deserved more than his usual dose tonight, for his task was worth celebrating. To fell the odious man who paraded jauntily through an inane society enjoying the success that rightly belonged to such men as Eben Shallcross! What a fool the ghost of the laughing FDR, the fiddle-playing emperor, would look when the *real* beneficiary of his jumbled laws, his maze of tax dodges, marched off to the penitentiary! Ah, an old Roman senator, an Eben Shallcross, despite the latter-day tyrants, had still his bite! Watch out for his venerable fangs!

"You know about the young people today, Patrick? They don't object to crime because they don't believe in criminals. Truly! When they read of some old bum, dead drunk on a park bench, who's had his feet burnt off by a fiend with a kerosene can, they say, 'How awful it must be to *feel* that way.' And they mean the fiend's feelings, not the bum's! They blame society, never the individual. Well, there are still individuals, Patrick, whom you and I can blame. And still individuals whom you and I can catch! And *punish,* Patrick! Thank God for that!"

Eben frowned at his own reflection in the mirror behind the bartender as he thought of his son. Martin, of course, would be ruined. Every stockholder of Atlantic would be ruined! But might it not be the best way? Might it not redeem Martin from his bull-headed materialism and provide a clean break from his willful association with such a man as Livingston? And, after all, could not Martin's father stake him to another start? What was Martin's chance of wealth compared to the chance of Elly's degrading marriage? Oh, she had to be saved from *that*, at all cost!

"We have lost our liberties, Patrick. We have lost our liberties as surely as if we were crouching under the shadow of the Kremlin! The late FDR was shrewd enough to create a supreme court whose role is to persuade us that we are still free. You can strut up and down the sidewalks at noontime and disrupt the luncheon crowds, shrieking for a twenty-hour week. You can refuse to fight, or refuse to pray, or refuse to take an oath in court! But that's only to distract your attention from the things you can't do, the *real* liberties, liberty to hire and fire, to choose your associates, to run your business . . ."

"Judge, Mr. Dennis is over there now."

And Eben turned, at once smiling, yet still grave, to meet his old friend, the former District Attorney. It would hardly have done to speak to the acting one. After all, the wretched Livingston *was* a client. But the beauty of politics was that there was always a tactful way to do everything.

"Jim!" Eben called. "Jim, I want to talk to you. Let us go into the library, my dear fellow, where we can be agreeably private. Patrick, send in my decanter!"

7

MARTIN SHALLCROSS stood with John Grau, their backs to the big window in the file room of World Inc., and watched the two detectives on their knees going through a drawer at floor level. At the door stood a policeman drinking coffee. Beyond, in the big passageway, secretaries and clerks walked rapidly to and fro on artificial errands, casting rapid, furtive looks within.

Martin remembered how he had felt before a hernia operation the year before. After the preliminary shot, on the way to the surgeon, there had been a suspension of all apprehension. He had been able to contemplate the operating room and attendants with a total detachment, physically aware only of a funny hollow sensation in the top of his head.

"You mean that's *all* Jay told you?" John asked.

"That's all. He called last night. His tone was so matter-of-fact that at first I couldn't believe he was saying what he *was* saying. He said Hilary had warned him that Sophie was out of control. That she might tell her father or even the police. He said he was getting out of town for a couple of weeks. Going to Lisbon. Well, he was just in time!"

"But how did Sophie know?"

"I told her."

"You told her!"

"I wanted her to go to Hulda and persuade her to give Jay his divorce so he could come home and straighten things out." There was an abrupt end now to Martin's numbness. As much to his own surprise as to John's, he suddenly sobbed. "The sanctimonious bitch!" he cried. "She couldn't wait to turn him in! What a bloody ass I was to forget what it was hell hath no fury like!"

"But how did she do it?" John pursued, frowning. "I can't see Sophie going to the police. What did Jay mean about her father? You don't suppose she told *him?*"

"What does it matter who she told? She *told.*"

But very clearly it mattered to John. "Your father would never have betrayed a client." He shook his head, as if to shut the possibility out of his mind. "No, professional ethics would have required him to go first to Jay and tell him what he knew. And even then, it seems to me, he couldn't have revealed what he'd learned in the scope of our retainer."

Martin almost laughed. He found a little nook in his empty, reverberating heart in which he could actually feel sorry for John. It was so obvious to him what had happened, but he saw no reason to add to anyone's misery. If John wanted to believe in his father, well, let him do so. "Sophie's revenge must be everything her mean little soul could have craved," he speculated bitterly. "Jay bust. Me bust. Hilary's magazine on the blink. It's pretty total, you must admit!"

"What's all this bust talk. You and Jay still have your Atlantic stock, haven't you?"

"Yea. What'll you give me for *that* today?"

"Well, intrinsically, it must have value."

"Intrinsically!" Martin's laugh was shrill. "There's no such word on the money market. Atlantic's down to zero. Do you think the news isn't all over the Street? Hell's bells, man, the D.A. got here at ten, and it's now three!"

"Okay, so there's a panic. But hang on. Things will come back."

"How do I hang on, John? You've got to have capital to do that. Yesterday's purchases alone would put me in the red. I tell you, I'm cleaned out. Bankrupt. I've lost everything I've made in sixteen years. If I died right now, Alverta would have nothing but my insurance."

"You can come back. Like Jay."

"Not Shallcrosses. Only . . . Livingstons."

"Your father will give you a new start."

"You don't know him! Spare me the boy scout talk."

But John could be very aggressive in his consolation. He seemed to wax almost angry at Martin. "Money isn't everything," he lectured him. "As a matter of fact, *I* don't have any. Addie and I and Uncle Sam pretty well dispose of my income."

Martin shook his head stubbornly. "You won't see it, John. To a money man money is everything. Your capital is your professional ability. Mine is cash. Or *was* cash."

One of the girls came over to them. "I'm sorry, Mr. Shallcross, I know you said you wouldn't take any calls, but Mrs. Kay says she *must* speak to you."

Martin nodded and went over to the desk to which she pointed. He picked up the receiver. "Yes, Elly?"

"Is it true?"

"I don't know what you've heard, but, yes, it's true."

"Jay's gone? He's ducked out?"

"He's gone."

"And he's a criminal? Is *that* true? He's stolen money?"

Martin felt his first brief twinge of sympathy for his absconded partner. "No more than Ma did, when she gave you Aunt Elly Chalmers' diamond ring before the estate appraiser had seen it."

"What are you talking about?" His sister's voice soared giddily with startled outrage. "Aunt Elly *gave* me that ring in her lifetime!"

"Maybe. But she was still wearing it when she died, which means it was subject to estate tax. You and Ma stole that tax money!"

"Oh, Martin, how can you be so ridiculous? Everyone does things like that. This business of Jay's is utterly different. Jay could go to *jail*. And he *will* go to jail if they catch him! How could he *do* it?"

"How? He did it for you."

"For *me*! How in God's name could it help me?"

"He wanted to be free to marry you." Martin laughed drily. "He wanted to lay the world at your feet."

"Did I ask for that?"

"Oh, Elly."

"Well, *did* I?"

"No, you asked him nothing, and you gave him nothing. You wouldn't take the teeniest little risk."

"I had my girls to think of!"

"Oh, your girls." Martin snorted. "A fat lot you think about them. If you had the decency you were born with, you'd get off your ass and fly over to Lisbon to give some comfort and consolation to the one man who's ever cared about you."

"Martin!" Elly's voice had shrunk to a hollow gasp. "How can you talk to me that way? This terrible thing must have driven you out of your mind! Suppose I'd got my divorce the way Jay suggested? A fine pickle I'd be in now, with him off in Lisbon and Thad off the hook! You don't understand that a girl's got to look after herself. How can I depend on men who steal, like Jay, or men who publish outrageous libels, like Thad? I tell you, Martin, I'm alone in this world!"

"You have Ma," he said bitterly.

"Oh, Ma. What can *she* do? My only hope is that Thad won't be able to use this scandal against me in his lawsuit."

"He won't."

"How do you know that?"

"Because Thad isn't going to be able to pay a lawyer after the Atlantic market breaks," Martin said coolly. "He's in this thing up to his ears, and he'll be just as broke as the rest of us!"

"Oh, no!" Elly's groan might have affected her brother had he been still capable of being affected. "Do you mean that even if Mr. Bry *wins*, we won't be paid?"

"Nor Mr. Bry either. That will really be a cause for tears."

"Martin! What will I *do*?"

"Ma can look after you," he said wearily. *"She* isn't in Atlantic. Nor the old man. He was far too coony. And don't your girls have their own trusts? You'll be all right. I've got to hang up now."

"Martin . . ."

But he placed the receiver back in its cradle and started out of the room. John Grau caught up with him.

"Is that Elly? Is she going to Lisbon?"

Martin paused to stare at him and then laughed again. "Dream on, my friend. Dream on."

"I had hoped better things of her."

"Oh, John! Stop hoping things of us, will you? I tell you, I'm through. We're all through."

"Be a good loser, then."

Martin left him finally at this. He went to the washroom and out by the back door. He had answered enough questions for one day. The police had the files; they could rampage at will. He had to get away from the telephone, from his mother's lamentations, from his father's "I told you so," from Alverta's terrible courage. Alverta, poor soul, had been the worst of all. When he had told her about it, after Jay's call, she had sat up in bed with a pad and pencil, brisk, non-recriminating, the Betsy Ross of disaster, the heroine of *his* errors.

"I've been poor before, and I can be poor again. You'll find, my dear, that it's nothing we can't cope with. I think I can persuade Mrs. Anthon to cancel the lease on this house. She's a very nice woman. Then we can move in with your parents until you get on your feet again. I assume they'll show the right spirit? It won't be exactly fun for any of us, but then we can't expect fun, can we? And if worse comes to worst, and you don't get started again, *I* can always go back to work, after Baby comes. If it's a boy I'm sure your father will put him through college. He'll do that, won't he? For his only male grandchild?"

Oh, yes, yes. Yes, of course. Like everything Alverta did, it had to be better done than by anyone else. It had to demonstrate a greater resolution, a more banal common sense. Life, he could see, was going to be remorselessly remedial. Nobody could face the fact that there was no cure.

In the two hours that elapsed before his train for Greenwich he stopped at several bars, yet his vision grew clearer and clearer. He saw that his own career, like his father's, had been lost to chance. There was no point in blaming himself or in cursing out the impersonal laws of the universe. One either succeeded or one did not succeed — there was no more to it than that. Of course, he had been to blame in telling Sophie — that *had* been stupid — but events had already reached such a sorry pass that it had probably made no difference. No, he had simply lost. He might, with another shuffle of the cards, have made a fortune and developed cancer at the same time. Or he might have got the cancer without the fortune.

And yet he had had something more than nothing. He still had it. He began to see this, as the passage of the minutes seemed to accelerate in the dark blue smoky submarine atmosphere of his bars, the "easeful death" that accompanied modern failure or fear of failure. Did the successful, the happy, not drink in sunlight, on porches? No doubt! The something that he had, or rather that he seemed to be clutching to his chest for fear of dropping it, the hard, cold, slithery something that he pressed against his heart like a large dead fish, was simply the remarkable fact that, unlike the fools around him, he *knew* that there wasn't anything more in life than a chance of winning and a chance of losing and then a winning or a losing. And once one knew that, once one really knew it, once one took it into one's bloodstream and bones, then did it really so much matter *which* one had? When all was said and done, what had he really missed in life? What was there to miss? When he walked down the platform to board the 5:21 he was still fairly steady.

The bar car, as usual, was full, but Martin managed to find a space for himself. Unfortunately, the man next to him, whose name he could never remember, was the type he least wanted to see, the flashy, falsely hearty young broker who, with a scant two years' experience on the Street and knowing of naught but good times, gave all the credit for the astounding little pile that luck had already netted him to his own perspicacity.

"I've been meaning to call you, Shallcross. Time we got together for lunch. Lunch is like the weather. Everybody talks about it, but nobody *does* anything about it." Here the young man threw his head back and gave vent to a horrid bray. "But some of the boys in my shop would love to meet some of the boys in yours. We might arrange a cross-fertilization of ideas. Particularly with your Jay Livingston. We'd all love to meet *him!*"

"I'm afraid you'll have to go to Lisbon for that."

"Oh, is he abroad? Well, when he's back. Say, old man, you look as if you'd had a hard day." At this he took in for the first time just how badly Martin *did* look. "Hell, you look as if you'd had a *really* hard day!"

"I think perhaps I have. I've just discovered that my principal associate is a crook."

"Christ, man! Really?"

"Really. And that I myself am broke."

The man laughed again his braying laugh, until, taking in again his companion's unchanged countenance, he decided that what he had heard might not have been intended to be funny. He finished his drink in one swallow, nodded and moved hastily away.

When Martin left the bar car, he paused in the vestibule before entering the coach. The outside door was open, as it usually was, and looking down over the four steel steps, he watched the gravel roadbed of the track rush past. The racket of the creaking train and the thunder of its wheels seemed to increase to a deafening roar as he stared, hypnotized, at the speeding ground. His fingers clenched the handrail; he was safe. But supposing he took his hand away and allowed himself to balance on that top step? Supposing he put himself at the disposition of a railway car and the next bend in the tracks? It would be perfectly safe, so long as the train did not lurch. And now he did so, and his heart missed a beat as he stood there, poised. A moment afterwards, when he had regrasped the rail, the train did lurch and violently, and he almost screamed at the idea of what he had missed. But the terror and relief lasted only for seconds. It seemed so 'fraidy-cat to do it only once. He would try it once more, just once more. If it worked, it would prove . . . well, something. If it didn't, it would prove . . . well, that there was nothing. Surely it could not matter now whether such a thing happened or failed to happen. It could only be interesting. And then he felt suddenly curious, passionately curious. He *had* to know. And, having to know, he again released his hold.

8

JAY IN LISBON, for the first few days, felt as if he had died and were visiting purgatory. New York and bankruptcy and an Elly lost seemed too far away from this ancient capital to be even on the earth. The feeling, of course, was intensified by his necessity. He *had* to be separated from them all, and from Martin's horrible death, by more than just an ocean. Sometimes, walking in the crowded, colorful streets, a pang would seem almost to split his heart when he remembered the rapture of the first days of his affair with Elly. But then he would remind himself sternly how hopelessly she had failed to rise to the challenge that he had offered. No, it had been made so sordidly, so brutally clear that Elly was not the woman for him or even he the man for her, that only an irrational mind could fail in the end to overcome the grief of their mutual failure. That old Lydig woman had, after all, been right.

His was not a morbid mind, yet he also carried with him about Lisbon the picture of Martin's broken body by the track. He had never cared for Martin, and he blamed the whole disaster of Atlantic on Martin's indiscretion, yet there was no escaping his own role in that long road of causation, nor was it agreeable to consider that one whole family would forever regard him as the murderer of the heir of the Shallcrosses.

Yet there were so many "ifs"! If Hulda had been less greedy, if Elly had been braver, if Thad had been more rational, if Martin had been more secretive, if Sophie had been less venomous . . .

really, what a crazy group they were! The only sane person in the picture had been himself, and had *he* been really sane not to take into greater account their insanity?

But he could not, even in disaster, remain long purposeless. He bought a guidebook and sought out the monuments of old Lisbon with some of that same thoroughness that he had cultivated in Madrid. That he enjoyed himself less was not only the result of his change of circumstance. It was also because he did not take to Portugal.

Where Spain had style, he found its smaller neighbor merely fussy. Queluz was a beautiful palace, but he found it a doll's house. The people who had lived in it had been children dressed up as kings and queens. It had none of the awesome splendor of the Escorial. It was all dead, and pompously dead. The monuments seemed to cry out, in squeaky voices, their disapproval of all but their silly selves. In the shopwindow of the antique store near the small hotel where he was staying there was a wooden madonna, with tiny hands petulantly clasped to her bosom, whose round white painted face expressed her rancor against her fellow men. She reminded him of Sophie Shallcross.

Indeed, by the end of his second week Lisbon seemed to him a parody of the Shallcrosses' New York. What were its pale, implacable virgins, its bleeding Jesuses, its damp, incense-heavy churches, its absurd baroque but the hatred of any real innovation? What better outlet could that ancient Iberian capital have found than burning Jews?

When John Grau flew over to see him, Jay surprised him by suggesting that they meet at the Ritz. The time had come already to get on with things, and for this he needed the sumptuousness of a new hotel.

"I think it's rotten luck about Elly," John said with feeling, as soon as the waiter had departed with their order. "She should be right over here with you. But that's the way with that spoiled-brat type of New York girl. You could put her in a book of adages to illustrate the fair-weather friend."

Jay shrugged. He appreciated John's old-fashioned ideas of loyalty, but what could one do with them? "I wouldn't have wanted her if she had come," he replied. "A girl like Elly has nothing to do with bankruptcies and indictments. She'd be wretched here, and she'd make me wretched. No, John, it's better to break things off clean when they don't work."

John stared, a surprised disapproval in his suddenly hardened gray eyes. "I thought you loved her!"

"I loved her when I was a millionaire. To court Elly in poverty would be like taking a diamond necklace on a safari. All you could do would be to lose it."

"I have a somewhat higher view of what a woman can mean to a man. Addie has stood by me through thick and thin!"

"Why not? Your life has been right for her. Both thick *and* thin. My life at the moment is right for nobody. Least of all for me. I've got to be alone, John. There's no other way."

And, watching his lawyer as he said this, Jay saw that John might, after all, understand. There was no need of consolation. What had happened was desolating, but it was not unbearable. When things became unbearable, one died.

"What have you decided to do?" John asked.

"What does counsel advise?"

"That you go home and give yourself up." John might have been the sentencing judge and not the defendant's lawyer. When the bartender put down their drinks, he glared at the interruption, and the man hurried off. "Plead guilty, and I'll throw everything I've got into a plea for leniency."

"How much will I get?"

"Maybe a year. Maybe even, with a bit of luck, a suspended sentence."

Jay considered this silently for a moment. It was a good deal better than he had hoped. He lifted his Martini and took a long sip.

"You know, John, even in the Ritz they don't make these dry enough." He plucked out the olive and swallowed it. "When I was a schoolboy, I did something wrong, and an older cousin of mine, Florence Schoenberg, to whom I was very devoted, told me what you have just told me. She said there was only one way to remedy a shabby deed."

"And did you?"

"No. But that's another story. Now I probably shall."

"Oh, Jay, I'm glad!"

Jay held up a warning hand. "But not for the reasons you think. If I go back, it's because there's no place else I can go, unless it's behind the Iron Curtain, and what would a capitalist like me be doing there? No, an American today is a sort of *civis Romanus*. He can be reached, one way or another, almost anywhere. And if he wants to do business again, he has to be able to go home."

"You mean, you're not sorry?"

"Oh, John, come off it!"

"You don't think what you did was wrong?"

Jay sighed, not so much at his friend's density, as at the prospect of all the similar densities that he would have to face in the future. "It was wrong," he explained, "the way it's wrong to go through a stop sign on a country road when there's no one in sight. If there happens to be a cop behind the haystack, okay, you get a ticket. But no one thinks the worse of you. That's how the world of business is today. You play it by the law of chances, which is what your government expects. It's cops and robbers. Life has become too complicated to be played any other way."

"Then there are no morals any more?"

"Oh, I don't suppose one should torture a little child or beat up an old woman, if that's what you mean. I'm not concerned with those things."

"And Martin?"

Jay met John's accusing stare without blinking. He was not going to give anyone, not even John, the smallest satisfaction in this respect. Not ever! "What about Martin?"

"You don't feel you were responsible for what happened to him?"

"Why should I? He lost his head. He was a fool, and a weak one. Of course, I was a fool, too, to leave him in charge. But he still didn't have to jump off that train. He had as much to live for as I do. Can you deny it?"

John could not. "What do you expect out of life, Jay? After all this is over? Will you go for another fortune?"

"I can try, though the odds will be against me. I've used up a lot of luck, and luck is capital. But it may interest you to know that I've already had an offer of a new backer."

How John stared now! "May I ask who?"

"Hulda."

"Hulda! My God, man, I thought she was after your neck!"

"But now she's got it, she's more merciful. Her letter was in that little bag of mail you forwarded to me. She's been saving and investing through the years, and she's got enough to stake me to a new start. A modest start, I grant, but you and I can agree that even a modest start is more than I could have reasonably looked for."

"Jay, you're prodigious! What is it that makes you tick? Obviously, it's not religion or love or ambition. You may laugh, but I don't think you even care much about money. Here you've lost it all, and you're gay as a cricket!"

"Not quite. But none of those things ever keep a man going. They're given a lot of false credit. The only thing that keeps a man going is energy. And what is energy but liking life?"

"You mean it's all a vaudeville show?"

"Ah, there you go again with your eternal labels."

They turned, with the arrival of their first course, to a technical discussion of the wreck of Atlantic and the question of possible salvage. When John had left for his plane, Jay took a bus out to Estoril. He had had enough of the old squares and churches of the quiet capital. In Estoril, by a glittering sea, along a coast that might have been Miami, he visited a develop-

ment of motels and pondered on the triumph of the civilization
of that once distant new world recoiling eastward to overwhelm
the land of Henry the Navigator. When he returned to Lisbon
he paused by the shopwindow in which he had seen the wooden
madonna that had reminded him of Sophie. But there was another madonna now in its place that struck him with instant
astonishment and near awe. It was a painting, very old, vaguely
in the manner of El Greco, showing the Virgin with a long melancholy face and upturned eyes, the same sad blue eyes that he
had not seen since Cousin Florence's death. There was no point
even asking the price, for he had no money, but he jotted down
the address against the day when he might.

9

HILARY AND SOPHIE sat in two armchairs at the conservatory end of the long, empty saloon. It was a late October Saturday afternoon, and the other inmates were walking outside or watching football or television. Beyond the glass doors lay a graveled walk between two little regular flower beds stretching across the strip of lawn to a tumbled stone wall. Beyond this patch of faintly tawdry human order loomed the red and yellow wonder of the Connecticut woods. Sophie's color was good, but her eyes distressed him. They moved to and fro with a sullen furtiveness.

"You're going to see them off?" she asked.

"Oh, yes. I'll go straight from here to the dock. I'll pick up Johnny Grau in Bronxville on the way."

"It's nice of you to do it."

"Nonsense. Of course, I would. But I still don't think they should go away while you're here."

"But, Hilary, I may be here for *months*. No, it's much better this way. Elly's still half hysterical, and Mummie mustn't just sit home and brood about Martin. A cruise is exactly what they both need. And Daddy loves the Caribbean. Of course, he's indestructible. He'll be the one who actually enjoys it!"

"And Elly's daughters?"

"They'll be with Thad's mother. Hilary, don't be such a fussy old maid. It's only for two months!" Her tone was dry and petulant, and he reached over to touch her hand, which she at once withdrew. "You underestimate the healing powers of the human mind," she continued bitterly. "Alverta is staying on in Greenwich. The baby's not due till after Christmas, and the doctor says she's absolutely fine. She's got some old aunt coming to stay with her. Is there anyone else you want to know about?"

"Only you, dear."

"Well, I'm perfectly safe here, thank you. You needn't worry about my doing what Martin did. They watch me much too carefully. I know them of old. Besides, I'm not the suicidal type. I drive people to it. I don't do it myself."

"Sophie, *please!*"

Suddenly she pursed her lips very tightly, closed her eyes and leaned her head forward as if she were suffering from a terrible spasm of pain. This time she did not withdraw her hand from his, and he squeezed it as tightly as he could. With her free hand she dabbed her eyes with a handkerchief and breathed heavily.

"Thank you," she said at last, in a milder tone. "That's better now. I'm learning to live with ghosts. It isn't easy."

"Have you heard from Jay? Speaking of ghosts?"

"No, but John Grau's been to see him."

"In Lisbon?"

"Yes, he flew over Monday. He'll tell you all about it tonight. Jay's coming back."

"To give himself up?"

"Exactly."

"I shall have plenty of time to visit him in jail," Hilary said, a bit sourly. "Of course, the magazine is folding too, you know. Oh, he did quite a job!"

"That magazine's folding up is the one silver lining to the whole cloud!" Sophie exclaimed with something of her old ardor. "At least you're free now to get a decent job. Or write that novel you've always been talking about. And I tell you something else. I, too, shall visit Jay in jail. If he'll see me, which is problematical. I'm afraid he's taken enough from me and my family. Not to speak of our friends."

"Has he taken any more from us than we've taken from him? I won't pound poor Jay now that he's down, but he certainly left a mess behind him! Do you think we still owe him anything?"

"Yes," she insisted, and her voice was peevish and petulant again. "He was the only one of us who had the guts to live. We all sensed that and fed off him, like vampires. Oh, not like vampires, excuse the hamminess. This place encourages it. Like mosquitoes! What did Thad do, at least before he became jealous, with all his hope and inheritance? Or Martin, with all his brains and ambition? What could they think of but hitch their wagons to Jay's star? And what did John Grau do, with all his sacred legal principles, but oil the machinery of Jay's deals? What did *you* do, Hilary, but take the first wretched scribbling job he offered you? Why, you all ran to him like a mouse to cheese!"

"It's true. It's true."

Sophie relented with his concession. This time it was she who touched him, placing her hand for a moment on his arm. "And look who's talking!" she exclaimed derisively. "What did *I* do, with all my solitary integrity, but try to marry him? Oh, sure, he was the candle and I was the moth, but a jealous, vicious moth. I was trying to put him out!"

"Sophie, Sophie."

"You know it's true. I had done nothing all my life but sneer at the wicked world. I yearned to be a saint, a martyr. As a child I used to imagine myself Ann Hutchinson, unafraid, exiled to the wilderness for my opinions, clasping my children to me under a rain of tomahawks. But it was all resentment, never true contempt. When I had my first good look at life, in Jay, I hated it. I struck at it, as if it had been a snake. I didn't mean Daddy to turn him in, but I might have foreseen it. All I could do was wreck, wreck, wreck!" Again her lips puckered, and her face was that of a little girl trying not to cry. "The first time in my whole life I ever *did* anything, the very first time I ever came out of my sloth to *act,* look what I did! But of course! It's arrogant to act. It takes years and years of practice to act. And I, poor, blind, petulant, selfish idot that I was, took it upon myself to save the world. Small wonder I smashed it! Do you know who I'm like, Hilary? I'm just like Daddy! After all!"

The tears came now, at last, followed by sobs, and Sophie seemed to crumple up into a little heap. Hilary put his arms around her and tried to comfort her, but she would not come out of herself, would not acknowledge him, and in the end he had to ring for the nurse.

*

Hilary felt calmer and happier than he had in many months as he drove into Bronxville to pick up John Grau. He had talked at length with Dr. Damon who had been very gloomy about Sophie's case, but who had ended by seeming to take on some of Hilary's own hope.

"Don't you think it possible, Doctor," Hilary had asked him, "that if I come to see Sophie every day, or at least every day that you allow me, in the next months or years — however long it takes — and try my very best to convince her that I shall always love and cherish her and want her to be my wife — no matter what her condition — that she might one day come out of this? *Might,* is all I'm asking?"

Dr. Damon had grown quite grave at this. "Oh, my dear fellow, who am I to play God? Who am I to say that Sophie will not recover and be able to marry and raise a family? I could never be so presumptuous. Let me say at once *yes,* yes, indeed, she might respond to such devotion as that."

"That's all I need, then."

"But, Mr. Knowles, she also may not. You have yourself to consider. How can you come out here every day? Don't you work?"

"Oh, I do free-lance things. I'll have the time. Don't worry."

"But you have your own life to think of and your own future!"

"Sophie is everything to me, Doctor. I need her every bit as much as she needs me. More, even."

"God bless you, then. We'll both do our best."

The commitment now offered, Hilary had not the least temptation to withdraw it. Fighting for Sophie would give his life point and direction. He did not even mind the tears that he felt welling up in his eyes at the beauty of his own sacrifice and devotion. How could he expect the habit of self-dramatization of forty years to drop off overnight? No, he had to learn to accept himself as he was, sentimental, self-pitying, full of fantasies and daydreams. There was no use saying Hilary Knowles was absurd. Hilary Knowles was what he was. But what he was he did not have to be always.

Nor did it matter any more that he was consciously working to develop his love for Sophie. Nothing mattered any more but that he should bring her back to health. For whatever motive he did it, for his good, for her good, for their good, the simple fact remained that it was a good thing to do. And good things, in the long run, had to be counted on to dignify their own motives.

John Grau, as they drove down the West Side Highway to the pier from which the *Samaria* was sailing, told him about the trip to Lisbon.

"It seems a funny place for Jay to end up, that quiet, dignified, decadent little Iberian capital. And yet there's a new spirit in Lisbon, a pushing, modern, building spirit. Perhaps it's more his climate than I had thought. At any rate, he was nicer than I have ever known him. Quiet, resigned, perfectly cheerful, not in the least bitter. We had a long lunch at the Ritz, and he seemed to enjoy it. I had a funny feeling that he had more respect for the world now that it's caught him out. There's always

been the naughty schoolboy aspect of Jay. The kid who will
burn the place down unless he's stopped. But once he meets a
headmaster who can't be bamboozled, he's more respectful. He
may even like it!"

"Will you continue to represent him? In criminal court?"

"Oh, yes. It's not exactly my line, but if he pleads guilty, the
only thing I'll have to do is beg for leniency."

"You lawyers do better than undertakers. You make money
out of the end as well as the beginning."

"Oh, this isn't the end for Jay. Not by a long shot!"

On board the white cruise ship they made their way to the
Judge's cabin. Elly answered their knock. Behind her the room
was dark, illuminated only by the porthole.

"Daddy's in two-o-three," she whispered. "I'm sitting with
Mummie. She has a ghastly headache."

"Say good-bye for me, will you?"

"Is that Hilary?" came Mrs. Shallcross' weak voice from the
bunk. "Come in, Hilary. How nice of you to see us off."

As John moved tactfully off to the other cabin, being the less
intimate, Hilary stepped in to say farewell to Mrs. Shallcross.
She was lying on her back in her dark traveling suit, her shoes
off, her head propped stiffly up on a little pillow. She looked as
she had ever since Martin's death: exhausted, baffled, resentful.

"Good-bye, dear Mrs. Shallcross," Hilary said in a low voice as
he stepped over to her. "I won't say bon voyage because it won't
be. But try to get some rest. And I'll keep an eye on Sophie.
Don't worry. I'll call every day."

"Oh, thank you, my dear! You're a good boy. Martin always
said you were."

He leaned down to kiss her on the cheek, but he succeeded
only in startling her. Mrs. Shallcross was not the kissing sort.
Deploring his clumsiness, he silently pressed her hand and escaped.

Elly was waiting for him outside her mother's cabin. Her eyes had a hard, desperate, darting look. For the first time in all the years of their acquaintance he saw a resemblance to Sophie.

"I suppose you think I should have gone to Lisbon, too," she began accusingly, when the cabin door was closed. "I suppose you think I let him down!"

"Me? Not in the least."

"What a crew you all are!" she exclaimed, sweeping this aside. "What a bunch of movie-struck sentimentalists! Why, I think even Daddy would enjoy the spectacle of love conquering all, love among the ruins! Who but me cares about the future of my children? And do I get any credit for it? Oh, no! That's just part of my old coldness, isn't it? Who doesn't know about Elly Kay's coldness?"

"I don't."

"And if I *had* gone to Lisbon, do you think he'd have cared? Far from it! John Grau told Daddy he looks on the whole thing as just another slam bid he didn't make. Just a few tricks down, that's all! Doubled and vulnerable! Well, back here we take these things a bit more seriously. We don't exactly relish having a brother driven to suicide. We're not particularly amused at being bust. Even *I* mind being dependent again on my mean old Daddy. Oh, yes, cold as I am, unromantic as I am, I still have *some* feeling!"

Hilary had been looking down at the deck during this harangue. When she had finished, he tried to take a firmer tone. "Elly, stop orating and listen to me a minute. I'm *not* criticizing you. Aren't we graduates of the same couch? Didn't we get our degrees from Silverman? Don't you think I learned anything in all those sessions?"

"Well, I didn't! I see now that my original view of the world was the correct one. The one thing I've learned since is that all the people who called me a cold fish are colder fish themselves! Particularly Mr. Jay Livingston!"

Hilary, watching her lips pucker, smiled quickly to fend off the sob. "I never saw such a gloomy bunch in my life. I'm glad I'm not going on this cruise! Try to forget him, can't you? You were a crazy pair from the beginning."

"All he had to do was be straight, and everything would have worked out. What difference did his silly proxy fight make? I could have supported him on the money I got from Thad. But, oh no, he had to do it *his* way. He had to make his God damn fortune. And smash the whole apple cart in the process!"

"I grant you all that."

"Yet I'm the one everyone calls mercenary! I'm the icy, designing bitch!"

Hilary saw it was hopeless and leaned forward to kiss her on the cheek. "Good-bye, Elly. Forget him. He's not worth all this. Nobody is."

In 203 the Judge in his shirt-sleeves was sitting on the bunk, his feet on the deck, drinking whiskey straight, out of the washstand glass. John was pouring himself a drink in a paper cup from the bottle on the bureau.

"Tank up, Hilary," the old man said when he appeared in the doorway. "I can't abide these seeing-offs. When they ring the 'all ashore' bell, the attractive people disembark and leave you with the frights. How could it be otherwise? Nobody goes by sea now unless they're looking for a mate. This vessel is nothing but a Catskill summer hotel that has lost its moorings!"

Hilary took a paper cup and poured himself a generous dose of whiskey. Sophie had been right. The incorrigible old monster was actually going to enjoy the cruise!

"John and I will hold the fort, sir," he observed.

"Such as it is, my dear fellow, such as it is. It's a sorry sort of fort I'm leaving, isn't it?" He shook his head rapidly half a dozen times. "And not a much better one that I'm taking with me. I'll tell you something, gentlemen. Something very frank. I wouldn't belong to your generation, even to have your life expectancy. I wouldn't! My generation had a chance, anyway, whatever misuse we may have made of it. And Martin's baby may have one. But Martin never did. None of you did."

"Why did we have no chance?" John demanded gruffly.

"Because you're a bankrupt generation," the Judge replied cheerfully. "No offense, I trust. It's not *your* fault. We can discuss these things impersonally, can't we? We're not a bunch of old women, after all."

"Go ahead, Eben," John enjoined him. "Anything you can dish out I can take."

"Well, personally, I find it all rather interesting. One might as well get something out of one's own bad luck, if it's only the satisfaction of truth. What I mean is simply this: Your generation came into its prime just as the twentieth century knocked the stuffing out of its two big causes: capitalism and communism. America went left and Russia went right, and, though it's still heresy to say it, there's very little left to choose between them. Oh, true, we still have a handful of liberties, the ones our Supreme Court is so faithful to protect, like the liberty of the criminal syndicate that sells dope to minors from interference by police wire-tapping. But nobody here believes any longer in real capitalism, any more than anyone in Russia believes in real communism. Everybody agrees, in Washington or in Moscow, that you need a dictatorial government to see that the masses get their cars and their TV sets. Political liberalism has gone the way of religion and gets the same public lip service that religion gets. You boys were the last to be brought up to believe in an ideal. Your children are better off. They'll learn to do without."

"But my children *do* care about ideals!" John exclaimed. "More than I ever did! They care about social justice."

"Ah, yes, they protest. They're *looking* for an ideal. They make the most of what injustice they still can find. And when that's gone, they'll be better off than you. Because looking for something and believing in something are two different things."

John simply laughed at this and crumpled his empty paper cup. "If the lecture's over, Professor, I'll go and reserve your deck chairs and see that you have a table in the dining room."

"Thanks, dear boy." The Judge smiled patronizingly after his departed partner. "He's a great fellow," he continued to Hilary, "but he's never had any philosophy. He sees every tree but never a forest. Never the forest he's lost in, anyway. He doesn't see, for example, that all his meticulous skill with words and phrases — in the office we call him the magician of small print — is merely his form of dope."

"Dope? Against what?"

The Judge flung his arms up. "Against despair!"

Hilary felt suddenly weary and deflated. He had no more energy to bandy words with the old charlatan. "My generation wasn't too bankrupt to fight a war," he pointed out sullenly. "Even if I spent it at a desk."

"Oh, physical courage." The Judge shrugged his shoulders contemptuously. "That's the last thing young men lose."

"And for all your superiority, sir, your generation didn't accomplish such great things!"

"But, my dear fellow, my generation made the mess of messes! There's no difference, really, between generations. No question of merit, anyway. It's all pure luck and chronology."

"I wish I could persuade Sophie of that."

"Ah, Sophie. Poor Sophie. I wanted to talk about her. Let us do so, before John comes back. Hilary, listen to me and mark my words." To Hilary's astonishment the older man now rose and came over to lay a hand on his shoulder. "You and I know that everything I've said tonight is a lot of crap. There's only one real truth, and that is that we're individuals. There are no generations or tendencies or inheritances or curses or blessings. For you there's only *you*, Hilary Knowles, and maybe there's Sophie, too, if you're lucky and if she's lucky. Don't give her up, my boy. Love her until her bruises are healed. They *will* heal, too. She's got more of her old man in her than she knows. There isn't any reason that you two stupid kids shouldn't pick up the pieces and put together a decent life. And look who's telling you!"

"Judge, I . . ."

"Shut up! I don't want to discuss the matter any further. It's entirely too personal and embarrassing. Let's go up on deck now and find John. I'm quite capable of picking my own deck chairs. And you two fellows have done more than your duty by us old folks. You can go home!"

Hilary followed the Judge down the passageway and up the stairs to the main deck. It was a cool evening, and across the Hudson an enormous, red sun was setting over the black hulk of New Jersey and turning the dirty water to a golden gray. The city behind him seemed gaunt and grim and somehow spent, yet at the same time sullen, defiant, as if the warehouses and towers, like the huge billboards along the river drive, were proclaiming, under that darkening sky, that they existed, quite as importantly — however little that was — as all the more ancient and beautiful places to which the murky waters around them might ultimately flow. He left the Judge, who was looking for John, and walked to the stern of the ship to take in, over the water, the full glory of the twilight. His heart was very full, but a part of that weight was hope. They were going away, all of them, and leaving Sophie to him.

90735